HAMMERHEAD

A Nick Bradshaw Series Novel

JASON GARBO

Amazon Publishing

Copyright © 2023 Jason Garbo

All rights reserved

The characters and events portrayed in this book are fictitious. Any similarity to real persons, living or dead, is coincidental and not intended by the author.

No part of this book may be reproduced, or stored in a retrieval system, or transmitted in any form or by any means, electronic, mechanical, photocopying, recording, or otherwise, without express written permission of the publisher.

ISBN: 9798393220839

Cover design by: Desygner Book Covers
Printed in the United States of America

*For my wife and children, who put up with
months of long nights and weekends of typing*

On January 10, 49 B.C. General Julius Caesar and his 3,500 men Legio XIII crossed the Rubicon River in Northern Italy. Caesar knew it was a risky move, and once he and his army were over the river, he knew there was no turning back. The gamble paid off, and after five years of brutal warfare unlike the Romans had ever seen before, Julius Caesar won and ruled the Empire.

CONTENTS

Title Page

Copyright

Dedication

Epigraph

HAMMERHEAD 1

Acknowledgment 2

PROLOGUE 3

Chapter 1 14

Chapter 2 32

Chapter 3 66

Chapter 4 87

Chapter 5 107

Chapter 6 128

Chapter 7 138

Chapter 8 168

Chapter 9 182

Chapter 10 190

Chapter 11	203
Chapter 12	214
Chapter 13	285
EPILOGUE	288
About The Author	291

HAMMERHEAD

**BY
JASON GARBO**

ACKNOWLEDGMENT

My Mother and father for having a love for books and introducing me to reading

Ronnie G for giving it a read and a helpful eye

The many men and women that I served with that gave inspiration to the novel

PROLOGUE

The weather in Northern Mexico in the spring is tolerable. The mornings and evenings are cool, with a dry desert climate during the day. The arid landscape is broken up by dry seasonal creek beds choked with brush, having once been green from the water that now seldom flows through them. The mostly flat terrain of the state of Coahuila is interrupted by slight hills and knolls in the northern region, with the central region being more mountainous. In the remote areas of Coahuila, small stores and gas stations sit remotely along dusty backroads, scattered here and there across the sparsely populated region.

A slight breeze kicked up a small bit of dust whirling around the sage-type brush near one of these old stores. This particular store had been the only gas station north of Federal Highway 30 linking the municipalities of Lamadrid and Cuatrocienegas, Mexico. The store sits on the edge of a dirt road with a front island that was once a gas pump, long since run dry from a lack of customers. A fuel truck had not stopped to top the tanks off at the store for a few years. The only part of the gas pump area that still worked was the pressure tube that rang a bell when a car would pull up to pump gas. The store had been painted white with a blue, single wide stripe many years ago. The white had now faded to a dust-colored beige, and the blue stripe was hardly visible beneath the flaking paint and sun-faded outer walls. The roof of the old store creaked and moaned with every gust of wind as it bent back and fluttered old pieces of tin that had become unfastened over time.

Several old dilapidated stools and chairs littered the front parking area of the store, with one chair, a wicker one, leaning back against the left corner of the structure near a large plate glass window. An old Mexican man had sat in the wicker chair in this same spot at the old store many times over the last several weeks watching this particular stretch of road. He leaned back in the chair, hat pulled down, wearing old blue jeans tattered at the legs, with several holes, exposing sections of his weathered skin. His brown jacket was not in much better shape, but it kept him warm on the cool spring mornings.

The Drug Enforcement Administration, better known as the DEA, had developed the old Mexican as a confidential source several years previously when he had been caught muling a load of heroin into the United States. It had been the eleventh and final trip the old Mexican would take into the United States. Always claiming to be hauling fruit, the old Mexican thought he could get away with it one last time. After all, he was only trying to provide for his family back in Lamadrid. The DEA had done their homework, and after catching the old Mexican driving a load of drugs on Interstate 10, just outside of New Orleans, DEA agents found that his cell phone registers and call log numbers ultimately could be traced back to the head of the Golfo Norte Cartel.

For several years, the Golfo Norte Cartel had been the most prevalent drug cartel in north-central Mexico. The state of Coahuila, Mexico, was prime cartel territory, with its northern border inching up to the United States. Like most real estate, one looks for certain attractive aspects. The Golfo Norte Cartel found many attractions in Coahuila. The United States border to the North, direct access to the Gulf of Mexico to the East, and the remote towns and villages provided plenty of young Soldatos, Sicarios or soldiers, and assassins. The drug war was as violent as one could imagine, especially among the rival Cartels. Always fighting for territory and more ports of entry into the United States and fighting with the few Mexican Government police and military that thought they could make a difference.

The Old Mexican had made the old desolate storefront his daily routine for drinking and multiple siestas, all on the DEA's dime. The store's owner, Juanita, who turned 78 years old in January, had been unable to keep up with the maintenance needed for a working store since her husband had been killed three years ago. Her only customers were a few stragglers, some locals, and the old Mexican. She lived in the back of the old store. The two rooms her deceased husband had partitioned off twenty-plus years ago had been large enough for them to raise a small family. The children were now grown. There were two children, one boy, now 24 and living in Mexico City, and a daughter who was 22, and it was unknown to Juanita what had happened to her daughter. The daughter left for school when she was 18, and after several months she was not heard from again. It pained Juanita to think of her daughter, which had aged her beyond her years. Old now, with many sun-dried wrinkles, her jet-black hair had now been interlaced with thousands of silver strands.

Juanita had tolerated the old Mexican sitting in front of her store almost every day for the last several weeks so she could have someone to talk to occasionally and to let the random passerby see that the dilapidated store was still in business. The old Mexican was several years younger than her, at 72, and Juanita was a bit smitten with him. Thinking he was hanging around her store to flirt with her, Juanita would put on her best dress and take a second look in the mirror when she knew the Old Mexican was outside her store. Unbeknownst to Juanita, there was a more important reason the old Mexican hung around.

In the far distance, a dust cloud could be seen for what seemed like miles emanating from a speeding caravan of armored SUVs and trucks carrying precious cargo. The old Mexican, leaning back in the wicker chair, slowly and carefully looked up from his slumber as the caravan approached and passed. The wide-brimmed straw hat that sat upon the old Mexican's head was pulled down to block the sunlight from his eyes during his afternoon nap. He only raised his head just enough to see below the brim to not draw attention to himself gawking at the caravan. The lead black SUV had tinted windows, but the old Mexican knew what lurked inside. There were several Cartel soldiers that the Hispanic culture referred to as Sicarios, with automatic weapons at the ready, more than willing to protect their cargo. As the fifth dark SUV sped past, the old Mexican could hardly contain himself. His weeks of sitting had finally paid off. The wicker chair fell over as the old Mexican slowly stood. As the caravan disappeared into its dust cloud a safe distance away, the old Mexican wandered to the back side of the store, and from inside his well-worn canvas jacket, he pulled out a satellite phone that had been provided to him by the DEA. His old weathered fingers dialed the international number that had been provided—

"The Beast has arrived" were the only words that the old Mexican muttered in broken English into the phone as the person on the other end answered—

"Hello?"

The conversation ended as quickly as it had begun, and the answering DEA Agent on the other end darted from his cubicle across a short span of office space and past the group secretary's desk to his supervisor's office and excitedly informed him that the confidential source had eyes on the target.

Two months prior, the United States President sat at the Hayes desk in the oval office of the White House, mulling over the intel that had just been provided to him minutes before. It was late in the evening, his blue dress shirt sleeves rolled up to just below the elbows, his collar unbuttoned by one button, and he had pulled his half Windsor loose by one tug, studying the documents laid out over the aged, oak top of the remnants of the H.M.S. Resolute. The documents being toiled over consisted of intelligence on the Mexican Cartels and the increase, over the past several years, of the delivery of heroin and fentanyl into the United States that he had taken an oath to serve. The Golfo Norte Cartel was at the top of the list. His Presidential election had been won by a large majority of constituents that saw the southern border of the United States as being invaded. Not necessarily invaded by Mexican immigrants but by narcos and Sicarios that went along with them. Narcos and Sicarios were flooding the American streets with heroin, fentanyl, and murder at Mexican cartels' hands.

The President took the glasses from his face, rubbed his eyes, and then ran both hands through his hair in obvious deep thought. He glanced up from the paperwork, and his eyes focused on the painting he had chosen to be straight ahead of his desk on the oval-shaped wall. Each new President chooses the artwork for the oval office for the duration of their presidency, and a nostalgic piece had been chosen for this term.

George Washington stared back at the President. He was wearing his Continental Army Generals uniform, brass buttons, long blue-tailed jacket, and tan trousers. His left arm rested on a canon peeking out of a redoubt with the Boston harbor in the distance. It was as if General Washington was speaking to him. The men and women who had sacrificed, the country built on the back of heroes and visionaries with no tolerance for dictators and bullies, and the Cartels embody most of these things Washington fought to suppress and end. The President knew what he had to do. The President thought that no matter the cost or repercussions, it must be done to protect his people.

Over the next several days, the President convened his cabinet and other high-ranking Agency and Military heads. The President told his cabinet—

"We will never turn the tide in the drug war until we send special operations forces south of the border to deal with the Cartels."

The President received a mixed reaction to his plan but ultimately prevailed. At the end of the day, he was the boss. The negative media and the outpouring of concern from the American people for the narcotics problem in the United States had kept the President up at night. Over the days and months preceding the first meeting, Operation Hammerhead had been set in motion. This would be the first strong message sent south across the border to all of the Cartels that the United States was serious about ending the flood of illegal narcotics into the country since the DEA's participation in taking down Pablo Escobar. The Golfo Norte Cartel was the target.

The Mexican government had always turned a blind eye or did not care that the Cartels were flooding the United States with "killer" narcotics. They had their problems with corruption and instability, and narcotics trafficking to the United States was the least of their concern. The United States President wanted to send the message that —

"If you are the head of a cartel organization that gloats at sending tons of heroin and fentanyl into this country and think you are untouchable because of an imaginary line...YOU ARE WRONG! This is our river Rubicon, gentlemen!"

The President hoped that this proactive operation against the Golfo Norte Cartel would make the other Cartels think twice about how comfortable they had become in supplying illegal narcotics to the United States.

During the initial meetings and planning phase of Operation Hammerhead, the President contemplated using Department of Defense operators or Department of Justice operators, more commonly referred to as the DOD and DOJ. The President's cabinet warned against the DOD involvement with a foreign country as being seen as an act of war with Mexico. Frankly, the President had been upset enough about the problem not to care what Mexico thought, at least for now. The President considered the Cartels a threat to the Nation's defense of its people and wanted a full-court press to get an operation mounted. After deep consideration and convincing argument, the DOJ won the coin toss after the President felt that the Cartels should be dealt with by the very three letter Agency that had fought this war since 1973, not to mention the bolstering of the capabilities of the DEAs Special Operators by the Administrator of the DEA.

DEA Administrator Douglas Hedley was 52 years old. Hedley had served his country at the DEA in various field divisions and roles throughout his career. To look at Hedley, one would not think he carried a firearm daily or was involved in any sort of law enforcement role. Hedley was tall, at six feet-one inch. He had a thin build but kept in shape. Hedley wore thin wire glasses that accented his dark brown hair that had not yet grayed with age. It had initially been a nuisance to Hedley when he had to begin wearing glasses two years prior at 50. He had always been a pretty good shot on the range during qualifying, but his scores had declined the closer he approached 50. Hedley started his career in the DEA Chicago Field Office, where he cut his teeth on basic narcotic crimes. Hedley rose through the DEA ranks, finding favor with the Houston Division's Special Agent in Charge, known within the Agency as the SAC. After several years of making notable high-level narcotics cases, Hedley was named a Group Supervisor in the Houston Office, and the ladder went up from there.

Hedley lived just over the river in Virginia and commuted to DC. He would make the short commute when he was summoned or needed for a meeting. Other than that, he ran the Agency from his office in Quantico, Virginia. Hedley saw this as an opportunity, or a gamble, to put his name in the hat for more powerful political aspirations if Operation Hammerhead was successful. Hedley presented the President with facts and operational experience of the DEA FAST and SRT teams. Hedley explained that the FAST and SRT operators had operational experience almost daily and that most, if not all, of the DEA operators had trained with and alongside United States Special Forces. The President was also smart enough to realize that the DEA had been present in Mexico almost since the agency's inception. Using DEA assets to carry out the operation would not raise as many eyebrows in the Mexican government. The President further authorized the CIA to assist the DEA in the form of air assets and intelligence through the Special Activities Division. The President felt that including the CIA in the operation would provide just enough involvement from the DOD since the DEA would be carrying out the operation in a foreign country.

CHAPTER 1

The Operators

Spring storms are common in Virginia. The weather fluctuates from mild, warm days to sometimes cold fronts that pass through, carrying with them spring snowfalls. This spring day had begun at 05:00, or 5:00 A.M., when the alarm clock had sounded in the Bradshaw residence in a quiet suburban neighborhood on the northern outskirts of Fredericksburg, Virginia. The day began as usual, a quick jog, shower, and getting ready for work. The day was overcast, with the potential of one of those spring storms likely.

Nick Bradshaw poured the last bit of coffee from the pot into his mug as he hurried through the kitchen, kissing Mitsy, his wife, as he was on the way out of the door. Nick was late and almost made it to the door. Remembering his Sig Sauer P229 pistol, Nick turned around and childishly scooted past Mitsy, slapping her on the rear end---

"Forgot something," Nick said.

Seeing Nick return with his Sig Sauer in hand, Mitsy returned the slap and said—

"You might need that!" with a raise of her eyebrows.

Nick walked to the garage, opened the back passenger door to his FBI-issued Ford Explorer, and placed his folded suit jacket on the back seat. Nick tucked the paddle of his Sig Sauer pistol holster into the right side of his pants near where his FBI badge was affixed to his belt and got into the driver's seat, backed out, and drove the short sixteen-mile trek to the base.

Nick pulled up to the guard stationed at the gate of the Quantico Marine base from Onville Road, rolled his window down, and flashed his FBI credentials, as he had done every day for the last five months.

"Go ahead, Agent Bradshaw," the Marine guard said as Nick replied almost in unison,

"Have a good day."

Nick made his way through the base to the second guard shack, the one that allowed him into the FBI and DEA area of the base, and again flashed his credentials—

"Nasty weather today Agent Bradshaw," the guard stated as he squinted, looking at the credentials through a misting rain.

"Yeah, I heard it was supposed to slack up around noon, but who knows," Nick replied as he shrugged his shoulders and slowly rolled through the checkpoint.

Nick had been offered a position of instruction at the FBI Academy in Quantico to beef up the intelligence-gathering knowledge in FBI recruits. Nick had been on the front lines dealing with some of the nation's top crimes for years now; before that, he had served locally at the Sheriff's Office in his home County. However, Nick and Mitsy had wanted kids and to settle down at some point, and this was the perfect opportunity to attempt just that!

Mitsy Bradshaw had been born in Georgia and lived in many different places by the time she graduated high school in West Texas. Mitsy was a military brat. Her dad had been in the Air Force, and as promotions presented themselves, so did new duty stations. Mitsy was a blue-eyed, blonde-headed beauty Nick had fallen in love with when he was a senior at Notre Dame, and Mitsy was beginning her first year in law school at Notre Dame. Both had been from devout Catholic families, and Notre Dame just made sense. Mitsy had completed her undergraduate at Illinois State University. After graduating with exemplary grades and with some help from her now Lieutenant Colonel father, Mitsy was accepted into the Notre Dame School of Law. The years of marriage to an FBI Agent had begun to cause some midnight talks, and when Nick was offered the position to teach at the Quantico training center, she nudged Nick in that direction. Now pregnant with their first child Mitsy had settled into a new life in Virginia.

The last time Agent Nick Bradshaw had spent any length of time at Quantico was in 2007 when he had graduated from the FBI Academy as a Special Agent. After graduating, Nick took his first duty station in El Paso, Texas. Nick spent three years at the Bureaus office in El Paso before being promoted to a supervisory position in intelligence at the DEA's multi-agency El Paso Intelligence Center. At the Center, Nick had worked hand in hand with DEA and other local and Federal Agencies to thwart just about every type of crime imaginable, including terrorism. Nick did not see things as other Agents did, and he had a knack for knowing how to speak to people.

"You get more bees with honey than vinegar!" Nick would always say after a successful interrogation.

The promotion to the supervisory position over intelligence for the FBI section of the Center was great for Nick, and he thought that job would last a while. But, now, Nick had been promoted again. The latest promotion landed him at Quantico, Virginia, teaching at the FBI Academy.

Nick had been asked to teach a course at the academy's primary school for intelligence gathering and procuring and utilizing confidential informants. Nick had become somewhat of a legend in the El Paso law enforcement community for being able to flip suspects and gather intelligence. Everyone was always baffled at the way that Nick was able to conduct an interview with someone with such poise and what other Agents described as cool, calm, and collective.

The time was after midnight as the prop wash

from the rotors whirled dust and debris into the night air. The pitch black darkness was penetrated as the 19 million dollar hulk of black steel and weaponry descended to the ground. The Blackhawk helicopter hovered for less than 20 seconds, then left and faded away as quickly as it had arrived. The landing zone had been five kilometers from El Chupadero Canyon. The distant thump of rotors faded behind the two camouflage-clad men as they were on one knee, their faces painted black, brown, and green. Their M-4 rifles shouldered, pointed into the darkness at the ready. A sliver of green tint illuminated the outline around the edges of where their night vision goggles clung to their faces. Each man looked around the landing zone, or in military vernacular LZ, to ensure they were alone. Hand motions were the only language used as they looked at each other in the darkness, the goggles allowing each man to see everything in the dark in a green tint. Move-out was the motion given as the lead man made a knife hand motion forward in succession. Operation Hammerhead had begun.

The two-man reconnaissance team had made its way in the dark of night to the edge of one of the high canyon walls of El Chupadero Canyon. The canyon was as wide as it was long, with walls that varied in height from several hundred feet to points that were only seventy-five to one hundred feet high near the only opening to the canyon to the south. Sporadic limber pine trees and fragrant ash littered the canyon floor, some in clumps and hundreds of individual trees. The canyon floor was flat toward the mouth at the southern end, and more rock, boulders, and knolls rolled across the floor as the canyon expanded almost two miles north. Shorter spruce and limber pine trees, some in the shape of an elbow, clung to the canyon walls as they reached for sunlight.

The two men had silently crept up to the edge of the canyon's western wall and lay down prone. Both lay on the canyon's rim for about thirty minutes observing their surroundings and making sure no one had seen them approach. Once comfortable, they slowly and silently moved to just below the rim of the canyon, where they set up an observation post, or OP, just below the ridgeline. The OP hide site was just below the crest of the ridge and was amongst some outcroppings of rock that had been camouflaged by the two-man team with foliage from the immediate area. The limber pine and ash brush clung to the side walls and all around the edges of the canyon, giving the operators a concealable spot for observation. To the naked eye, the OP looked as though it had been a clump of brush and rock attached to the side of the canyon wall for a hundred years. Once comfortably inside the OP, each man took their packs off and spread the gear they might need immediately. They each did this slowly, with no quick movements to not draw attention to themselves. The OP shaded the men from the day's sun. It provided enough shadow inside to make it difficult for anyone from the outside to see inside the OP.

Each man wore tan Salomon boots, a Multicam uniform, and a matching boonie hat. They each had tucked their boonie hat into a pocket of their pants until they felt comfortable enough to take off their helmets. Their Peltor headsets consisted of two ear muffs, each containing a speaker and a boom mic that reached around from the left side toward the mouth. The Peltor headset fit over the top of their heads with a form-fitting mesh strap to be worn under their helmets and boonie hats. Both operators had a camouflaged pack with a ghillie suit strapped to the molle at the base by the pack straps. The operators had studied the terrain they would be operating in and had built their ghillie suits accordingly. They made their ghillie suits out of long green mesh jackets that had been spray-painted coyote tan. Each operator had tied hundreds of tan burlap strips to the mesh and interlaced them with a few green and dark brown burlap strips. Once donned, each man looked like a miniature wooly mammoth.

Special Agent Joseph "Joey" Keller and Task Force Officer James "Jim" Cado had multiple real-world ground operations reconnaissance missions under their belts. Joey stood just under six feet tall with dark hair and a matching beard that was not well groomed. Joey was four months into his thirty-seventh year on this earth, with almost half of that dedicated to DEA. Jim was only one month away from his thirty-fifth birthday.

Jim was taller than Joey at a little over six feet and picked at Joey about the height difference when the opportunity presented itself. Jim had lighter-colored, sandy brown hair and a short, neatly cropped beard. Both men possessed athletic physiques maintained for the daily riggers of the life of a DEA special operator.

The only difference between this reconnaissance operation and the others that Jim had been on was that this operation was outside the confines of the United States. On the other hand, Joey gained international experience when he was assigned to a DEA FAST team in Afghanistan and carried out operations with a narcotics nexus within the country. Joey had dedicated his career to the DEA and had met Jim when Jim was assigned to the Field Division as a Task Force Officer. The DEA SRT team leader noticed Jim's state agency SWAT team experience and asked Jim to try out for the DEA SRT team. After Jim passed the DEA SRT selection, he and Joey were chosen for advanced training in close reconnaissance. Jim and Joey had spent countless hours together on reconnaissance operations for DEA and for some local agencies in their field divisions' areas of operation. They had not been assigned to the same group at the DEA field division, but they had grown close, spending, sometimes days, in hide sites gathering intelligence.

Born into a very outdoors family, Jim had been raised in the woods of Central Mississippi, hunting and stalking game almost all of his life. Jim's father had taught him to hunt turkey by belly crawling as close to the flock as possible and using the terrain and structure to mask and camouflage his movement. As a kid growing up learning these skills, Jim had no idea those skills would prove to be manners of life or death as the flock of turkeys turned into narcotics traffickers.

Jim and Joey had advanced training in camouflage, concealment, and intelligence gathering. Before their real-world operations, both men had trained with the United States Army's 20th Special Forces Group. Each had proved themselves in the field alongside Green Berets and Rangers.

A few years prior, on a hot August day at Army Base Camp Shelby in central Mississippi, Jim found himself in a ghillie suit crawling across a field scattered with downed timber. The day was scorching for a summer Mississippi afternoon, with temperatures reaching the upper nineties. The training operation for the day had been to obtain the license plate from the back of a pickup truck parked at the other end of the field, which was several hundred yards long. The Rangers and Green Berets were riding in the back of a truck that made circuits around the field's perimeter. Each

Ranger and Green Beret had a pair of field glasses, and they would abruptly stop the truck and scan the field with the glasses. If a student were spotted, they would send a field spotter to your location and declare—

"Ground operator at your feet!"

If a ground operator were spotted and marked, that ground
operator would have to start the iteration of training over.

Jim was clad in a full ghillie suit with his face painted green, black, and brown. The school had taught the students to paint the shiny areas of their faces with dark colors and the creases and crevices of their faces with lighter colors. The only shade in the open field was sporadic, ten-foot-tall scrub trees. Jim had belly crawled halfway across the field when he heard the truck passing by then stop, and a voice yells to the field spotter. Jim froze and hugged the hot, dusty ground as tight as he could, hoping they had not spotted him. Jim heard the field spotters' steps approaching, passing by, and stopping about 20 yards away. The whole time hearing the voice from the truck yelling—

"Left, go to your left, alright, go about ten yards. Okay, look to the ground on your right. A

ground operator at your feet!"

Jim heard the field spotter conversing with a student, and then the student stood up. The student had been told he had been spotted and to restart the training iteration. The field spotter left the immediate area, and Jim could hear the truck pulling away. Jim began crawling again toward the objective. Jim crawled another 50 yards and could see the top of the truck's cab, which was the objective. Jim knew that he was close. Jim began to feel the effects of the hot day. Every breath Jim took was five inches from the dusty, hot ground, and the air going in and out of Jim's lungs was like air from a heater. The woodland camouflage uniform adorned with the ghillie suit was like a heavy winter coat. Jim knew it was only a matter of minutes before he passed out from heat exhaustion, or worse, heat stroke. Jim heard the truck approaching and slowly raised his head just enough to see the truck as it passed by without stopping. Jim knew he had about thirty to forty-five seconds before the truck made another round. Seeing the truck disappear, Jim jumped up and sprinted twenty yards and leapt to the ground onto his belly and pulled his field glasses up, and was just barely able to see and memorize the license plate—

"BPA219," Jim said under his breath multiple times to commit the tag to memory.

Jim turned around and began the egress out of the field when he began to black out. Jim was in and out of consciousness as two fellow students started yelling to the instructors—

"Index, index!" this was the universal code for training to stop because something had happened, usually something terrible!

The fellow students began stripping the clothes from Jim's limp body to let the heat out and cool him off as the Instructor's truck raced across the field to help. As the lead instructor was loading Jim into the truck to take him to the base medics, Jim was repeating—

"BPA219, BPA219...BPA219!"

The instructor was impressed and chuckled and told Jim—

"Good job, buddy, you got it. You're good. You don't need to keep repeating it!"

Jim woke up in the base medical facility half-naked with an IV in his arm and cold, wet rags draped around his neck and torso.

As daylight cracked on Mexico's eastern horizon, Jim peered through the rubber-armored binoculars at the Cartel ranch, which he had a clear view of over the tops of the limber pines several hundred yards across the canyon floor. Jim had customized the original solid green Steiner binoculars with tan spray paint in a waffle pattern. The waffle pattern was just enough color breakup to confuse the eye. The Spring morning was cool, and unlike the summertimes in Mississippi, Jim was glad to be wearing the heavy ghillie suit.

As the dark of night turned into the low light of dawn, Jim squinted and could see seven high-end SUVs and Toyota trucks.

"Joey, ...wake up, Joey, we've got movement!" Jim said, nudging Joey with his elbow while still peering through the binoculars.

"Son of a bitch, what time is it?" Joey asked, trying not to stretch from his nap and move too much.

"Early!"

"No shit, how long was I out?"

"Bout three hours."

"When's our next check-in?" Joey asked.

"Bout 20 minutes", Jim said in his Mississippi draw.

The two operators had each been issued an Isat 2 satellite phone that would be used to check in with the missions Operations Center or Op-Cen, located in Texas, every six hours. Their DEA-issued Motorola SRT radios would only work for ten to twelve miles pushing about five watts per key up at their line of sight. The plan had been to check in every six hours by sat phone, and once the balance of the team was on station, their Motorolas would communicate with the inbound teams. They had been tasked with relaying movement, personnel size, weaponry, and the most important thing, the target presence, back to the Op-Cen code-named Alamo. This valuable information was used to ensure the inbound team of DEA operators would not encounter too many surprises. Satellite imagery or high-altitude reconnaissance was not as accurate as boots on the ground. Jim and Joey had packed enough MREs and water for a three-day operation. They had each hoped it would not take long to spot the target and call in the balance of the operators.

"How many you see down there?" Joey asked as he rolled over onto his stomach and pulled out his pencil to jot down the stats to relay back and record on a small weatherproof tablet he had laid out next to him before he took his nap earlier that morning.

"I currently see three, but I saw two others with long guns about five minutes ago," Jim said, letting Joey know he had observed multiple subjects with rifles.

Joey jotted the numbers and details of the enemy personnel down as Jim called them out—

"One drinking coffee, one playing with some mangy dog, and one with a long gun leaning on one of the SUV's. That's all we got right now, boss," Jim said, still peering through the glasses.

"Well, that's not enough people for all those vehicles, that's for sure!" exclaimed Joey as he reached over to a nearby fragrant ash limb, plucked several fronds, and squished them between his fingers as he smelled the aromatic odor.

The Cartel weekend getaway home consisted of a large two-story residence with adobe-type walls and terracotta roof with several smaller outbuildings near the structure. A short adobe wall surrounded the primary residence but was not high enough to be a problem. Any average person would consider the home a mansion but to a Cartel leader, it was only a getaway house.

There were three large warehouse-type structures about three hundred yards from the ranch, but they appeared to be vacant. Joey had taken over the glasses mid-morning, and Jim was now cataloging the movement.

"It's about that time!" Jim exclaimed as he grabbed the satellite phone lying on the pile of gear to his left and flipped out the side antenna.

Jim punched the redial number on the phone, and a voice on the other end answered—

"This is Alamo. Go ahead", the voice on the other end said with a half-second delay as the transmission traveled to and from the satellite orbiting above the earth.

"Alamo, this is Lariat with sitrep," replied Jim as he thumbed over to the recently jotted-down intel page and prepared to give a situation report.

" Lariat, go with sitrep."

"Alamo, since last we've got nine adult males, multiple long guns observed, still seven total vehicles, no sign of the target, over."

"Roger, good copy. IC1 wants to know if you think the target is on-site", the voice said, referring to a question from the Incident Commander.

"Hard to tell at this time, but we don't think this kind of Sicario presence would be here if the target weren't here, over," Jim replied as he looked over at Joey, who had raccoon eyes from staring into the glasses so long.

Jim cupped the mic end of the phone to muffle it and said—

"What the hell, I better not have got dressed up for nothing!" Joey laughed as he turned and got back on the glasses.

"I'm almost positive we didn't," Jim said.

"See you in six Alamo, all good here, over," Jim told the voice, "see you in six, Alamo out," as the voice hung up.

Several hours had passed as the day lingered on. The sun had warmed up the rock and dirt around the hide site making small amounts of heat vapor rise from the ground, causing a slight distortion in the view of the binoculars.

"Bingo, I've got bingo, Jim! Target's on the second story, outside on the side porch, huh? Go figure," Joey laughed, "he's on his satellite phone!"

"Well, let's hope he isn't calling Alamo," Jim said, smirking as he looked down at the pad writing the time and location of the target.

"Target's a Hispanic male, cigar in hand, dark full head of hair. I see the tattoo on the side of his neck. This looks like our boy!"

Joey was straining his eyes to see every detail when he exclaimed to Jim, "What the hell's this?"

"What you got?"

"He's on the phone talking to someone and pointing out toward the opening of the canyon where the main road comes in, and now I see four more SUVs approaching," Joey said with slight dismay.

The opening to the canyon was roughly a mile away from the ranch. The ranch commanded the canyon floor by being built on a large knoll that could see anyone coming in or out. The four SUVs sped along the dirt road and pulled up to the front gate of the small adobe wall where the cartel boss had now walked out with an entourage of armed guards.

"I've got three adult males exiting the first SUV, two with long guns shouldered, two adult males exiting the second and fourth SUV, only two with long guns," Joey relayed to Jim.

"What about the third?"

"Nobody's getting out yet…wait, here we go, driver and front passenger doors just opened … exiting. Two more adult males, one with a long gun. Third SUV's back passenger door just opened, an adult male…doesn't look Hispanic" Joey pulled the glasses away and looked over at Jim and, with a puzzled look, said, "He looks Asian!"

"Asian! What the hell? Let me look. You've been on the glass too long, boss!" Jim said jokingly.

"Third SUV, right?"

"Mmmhm," Joey uttered as he peered through the glasses again.

"That's weird! He does look Asian", Jim exclaimed. "Now that I'm looking at them, a couple of the guards look Asian to me also," Jim said, as he also muttered "what the hell" under his breath.

Jim put the glasses down and went back to writing on the pad. Joey said—

"The Asian guy and a couple of the guys he came with are at the back of the third SUV. Wait!

Target's shaking hands with one of the Asian guys, and both are laughing. Hand me the camera!"Joey said sternly.

"Quick, they just pulled something from the back of the SUV" Joey grabbed the camera and took several photos with the digital camera—

"That doesn't look like a narcotics transaction!"

"What's that, some type of weapon system?" Jim asked.

"No idea but next check-in, we gotta send this photo in!"

Joey and Jim watched as the men unloaded several small bags and Pelican-type cases from the back of the SUV that the Asian males had arrived in. The guards milled around outside the adobe wall, and several guards followed the target and the Asian males as they all proceeded to go inside the residence.

CHAPTER 2

The Assault

The night air was cool 400 feet above the Mexican landscape on this dark April night. The prop wash from the UH-60 Blackhawk's 54 feet of rotors cast waves of cool air and a reverberating thump inside the cabin of the aircraft. The Blackhawk helicopter was staying just above the powerline level but low enough to avoid detection and cruising at 170 miles per hour. The sliding doors were closed on the Blackhawks, and the operators of the DEA SRT were quiet. Each operator is thinking about the task at hand. They each had a job to do. The operators wore Multicam uniforms adorned with plate carriers of similar camouflage. The plate carrier was a vest with a ten-inch by twelve-inch pocket on the front and back that held either steel or ceramic bullet-resistant plates. Steel plates were much heavier at around seven pounds per plate, with the ceramic plates coming in at about three pounds each. The DEA had paid extra and opted for their special operators to use the lighter ceramic plates for better speed and agility. Each operator's plate carrier was covered in Multicam fabric with multiple magazine pouches on the front, a radio pouch, and two pouches for flash-bang grenades. Some operators had their extra gear and ammo affixed to their plate carriers, and others preferred to wear combat belts bristling with tactical accouterments. Each operator carried at least six extra rifle magazines and six extra pistol magazines, along with a personal assortment of knives and other lethal and less lethal gear. Zip cuffs hung off the backside of several of the operator's vests along with flash-bang grenades and rolling distraction devices, and two of the operators carried 40-mm projectiles and launchers. Each operator wore a combat helmet of choice, either MICH or FAST, both helmets comparable to do the job. The look on each operator's face told the tale! Their team had been selected to carry out Operation Hammerhead with hopes that it would change the United States drug war in a way that had never been seen before. Most of these operators had either been on FAST teams or had been operators on SRT or SWAT teams for as long as they could remember. Given the tenure of each man, they had all been in some sort of gunfight in their careers. The operators' experience and advanced day-in-day-out training proved them fit for operation Hammerhead. Each man sat, harnessed into their seat, some calm as a cucumber, some tapping a foot or chewing gum.

The COVID-19 Pandemic dealt a blow to the world recently, but this night it proved to be on the operators' side. The SENMAR and SEDENA, Mexico's navy and army, had been in a joint venture producing the country's first air defense radar system. Tzinacan, *the bat god*, had been in production and scheduled to come online, but the Pandemic had halted the production and research, leaving the Mexican skies wide open.

Inside the Blackhawks, the only light emanating from within was the green anti-night vision glow from the cabin lights. Special Agent Greg Dean, the DEA SRT team leader, was the only one with his Peltor headset plugged into the onboard communications system, talking back and forth with the Blackhawk pilots and listening to the chatter between the aircraft. Greg was knocking on the door of fifty years old, but to look at him, you would not be able to tell. Greg was fit, worked out, and ran every chance he got. His lean face was only masked by his full bushy beard of dark and gray hair. Greg had been a DEA SRT team leader for several years and years before that as a breacher and stack operator. This meant that when a special operations team lined up one behind the other to enter a structure, Greg had been lined up in the stack. Greg had spent one year apart from his Field Division SRT team assigned to a FAST team in Afghanistan in 2013. During Greg's tour of duty in Afghanistan, he had flown by helicopter into combat more than once.

SA Matt Grayson, sitting to the left of Dean, had the window seat. Matt's seat was first on the row nearest to one of the two sliding side doors of the Blackhawk. Matt peered through the darkness out of the window on the door and saw the second operator-laden Blackhawk cruising off their port side, no lights on, silhouetted against the night sky. Matt was the assistant team leader. He was tough as nails and had been shot twice in his career. He had been shot once during a drug deal gone wrong as an undercover Agent, also known as a UC, and the second time during an SRT operation five years prior in Little Rock, Arkansas.

The UH-60 Blackhawks, a CIA predator drone, one medevac UH-60 helicopter, and an AWAC had taken off from Laughlin AFB approximately forty-five minutes prior. The round-trip mileage for the Blackhawks was 340 miles from Laughlin AFB. Each Blackhawk had been fitted with extra internal fuel tanks to boost its effective range to approximately 880 nautical miles. Laughlin AFB had been chosen as the jumping-off point because of its proximity to the area of operation or AO and the fact that the CIA's overt drone program had more accessible access to some of the assets needed for the operation.

The United States Air Force AWAC was an E3 airplane by designation. The aircraft looked a lot like a commercial airliner except for the color, which was gray, and the sizeable circular-shaped radar dome affixed to the top of the plane. The AWAC cruised at 40,000 feet and jammed any radar for about 245 miles. The AWAC was tasked with the operation out of an abundance of caution for Mexican interceptor F-5 jets that might be patrolling the area and to patch the UHF communications between the ground and air elements. As unlikely as this notion was, Murphy's Law was a legitimate concern. The AWAC also had the capability of relaying the radio frequency of the ground element as long as they were on station.

The DEA operator's objective was Rancho de la Bestia in Northern Mexico, the "vacation" home of Senior Sanchez Guirrillo, the head of the Golfo Norte Cartel. Guirrillo had orchestrated the cartel's heroin and methamphetamine shipments into the United States for years. Now, DEA intel had put him at Rancho De La Bestia along with 10 to 15 of his Soldatos and Sicarios on this very night. The mission had been deemed a capture and arrest mission by the powers that be, but that order came with a wink. Collateral damage and damage to the primary target could be overlooked if that type of scenario played out.

El Chupadero Canyon sits in the middle of the Mexican State of Coahuila, with an elevation of 3500 feet. The canyon has one passable main dirt road into the canyon and two other roads that are almost impossible to get over the mountain's canyon sides without a 4x4. West of Lamadrid, the dirt road leading to the canyon cuts off to the North and passes Juanita's store about a mile north of the intersection. Rancho de la Bestia sits in the Southeastern corner of the open canyon, surrounded by a wall of mountains. This was the perfect location for a narco Kingpin's getaway house.

It was close to midnight when the lead Blackhawk pilot radioed the Op-Cen and AWACS and told them they were dropping their passengers at the LZ. The crew chief in each operator-laden helicopter slid the side doors open, bent down on one knee, swiveled the FRIES, or Fast Rope Insertion Extraction System, into position, and dropped the repelling rope twenty-five feet to the ground below. After reaching out and tugging on the rope to check for its strength, the crew chief began calling out into his helmet mic —

"Ropes, ropes, ropes!
The first operator grabbed the thick rope with his gloved hands, then placed one foot on one side of the rope and the other foot on the other side and squeezed his feet together, forming a brake as such. The crew chief, commanding the situation through the view in his night vision goggles, seeing that the operator was set and ready, slapped the operator on the back of the helmet, giving him the signal to slide down the rope. Seconds later, the crew chief could see the first roper running to the perimeter away from the rope—

"First roper is on deck!" the crew chief exclaimed into the mic that was wired into the Blackhawk's onboard communications system.
The second operator slid into the same position as the first and waited for the slap on his helmet.

Seconds later—

"Second roper's on the deck!"

The crew chief commanded this situation six more times until all Ropers were on the deck.

"All out! Standby to make it safe!" the crew chief said, grunting as he, hand over hand, pulled in the heavy rope dangling to the ground out of the helicopter's side.

"Cleared for flight, cleared for flight!" came the anticipatory response from the crew chief as he hauled the last foot of rope into the helicopter's cabin.

"Rodeo 1 to Alamo, all black shoes are on the deck, we're outta here, over", the pilot said into the mic attached to his helmet as he looked over his left shoulder in the pitch black dark with his night vision goggles.

As each operator touched the ground, they ducked and sprinted to establish a security perimeter in a semi-circle below the hovering helicopter. Each operator faced away from the LZ with their backs to one another. Their night vision goggles flipped down in front of their eyes, allowing them to see the arid mountainous terrain. Each was scanning the horizon of the same spot Jim and Joey had deployed from. As the Blackhawk's rotor noise faded in the distance, the scene became deathly quiet. The grass that had been dancing to the tune of the rotor wash slowed to a halt. The ground elements of the operation had been code-named, Gunslinger. Greg reached up to his left front shoulder and depressed the rubberized button, and spoke into the boom mic on his Peltor headset —

"Thanks for the ride, boys!"

"Roger that, happy hunting!" came the reply from one of the pilots of Rodeo 1.

The intelligence planners of the operation had designated an uninhabited staging zone about two miles from the operation LZ, code-named Arena, for the helicopters to set down. The three Blackhawks that made up Rodeo touched down at Arena LZ and radioed the Op-Cen to let them know all was going as planned. The Blackhawks that made up the Rodeo element were each designated as Rodeo 1, 2, and 3, with Rodeo 3 being the Medevac. The AWACS, cruising at a high altitude several hundred miles to the north, and the CIA Predator Drone, prowling the skies high above the AO, provided security for the now vulnerable helicopters as they waited for the update from Gunslinger that they were about to execute the operation on the ranch.

Greg paused in the darkness for a quick moment to get his bearings and reference the map in the clear pocket on the wrist of his camouflage jacket. He removed a small penlight from a pouch on his plate carrier and pushed the ON button with his thumb. The green anti-night vision green light lit up the map.

In unison, the sixteen operators moved toward Greg as he whispered into his mic—

"We have five clicks, boys, keep your heads on a swivel, and let's move quickly!"

Greg keyed up the mic as the teams moved through the tight gorge again—

"Lariat, this is Gunslinger. Do you copy over?"

"Probably sleeping like babies cuddled up to one another," DEA Operator Jonathan Martin said into his mic with a smirk as he and the other members of Gunslinger moved across the ridgeline.

Chuckling into the mic, Greg responded, "High probability...a lot of terrain between them and us, or they haven't come on station yet, ... possibly conserving batteries."

The LZ had been five kilometers north of El Chupadero Canyon and, by all intel, not inhabited. To several of the ex-FAST guys, it reminded them of night operations in the middle east with the arid terrain and moving at night with their NVGs on.

Greg's team moved through the darkness, pausing every few hundred yards to acquire their bearings and then keep moving. After two hours of trekking in the dark, the team found themselves one kilometer from the canyon. The teams crossed a ridgeline, and Greg whispered into his mic—

"Lariat, this is Gunslinger. Do you copy?"

"We copy you, Gunslinger. What took yall so long" Joey exclaimed on the other end of the radio.

"Oh, you know, mountains, valleys, streams... and almost five kilometers! Lariat, are we still clear on the approach?" Greg asked.

"Gunslinger, you're still clear. We have eyes on three roving guards, and one dog has been moving around inside and outside the front gate. No one has come or gone since late yesterday afternoon, over"

"Roger that Lariat. We'll be on target in less than an hour. Anything changes, let us know. Gunslinger out", Greg said as he looked over through his NVGs and could see both of his teams staggered along the crest of the ridge, some squatting down and taking advantage of the quick break.

"Gunslinger, let's move. We're almost there," Greg whispered into the mic.

The time was now 03:30, and Jim was on the glasses calling out any changes to the environment around the ranch. Joey reached over, picked up his NVGs, and placed them up to his eyes to scan the opposite canyon rim to search for Gunslinger. Greg's most recent communication advised that Gunslinger was ten minutes out. Both Jim and Joey could feel the adrenaline begin to be released as they were both anticipating the rush of what they knew was about to happen. Jim, peering intently through the glasses, saw one guard smoking a cigarette and leaning on a corner of the adobe wall near the entrance gate. The dog was lying down and asleep just inside the yard of the residence between the adobe wall and the residence. Two other guards had come and gone on the opposite side of the structure and were unaccounted for at the time. A few low lights lit up the inside of the residence, and no movement could be seen passing by the windows.

"Most of the others must still be asleep," Jim told Joey.

Joey shrugged as he wrote the info on the tablet and replied—

"Probably playing bingo and watching the golden girls," chuckling as he wrote.

"Probably wearing those moo-moo nightgowns like on the show," both laughing as Jim stared through the glasses at the ranch below.

"Lariat, this is Gunslinger. Do you copy over?" came the voice through Jim and Joey's earphones.

"Roger, Gunslinger, we have a good copy"

"Lariat, give us a designation for a pos, over," Greg asked Lariat to show him their position.

Jim rolled over on his back and grabbed his Colt M-4 rifle, and pointed across the canyon at the same time while pushing the button on his infrared laser designator mounted on the side of the gun in a one-second burst.

Greg was able to see the infrared laser through his night vision goggles. The naked eye could not see the infrared laser.

"Right, where you should be, Lariat. Thanks for the pos. What do yall see down there, over?"

"We have one tango with a long gun at the front gate of the wall, the dog asleep just inside the gate, and two rovers that we haven't seen in the last few minutes, over "

"Lariat, no change on the target, over?"

"Correct, target and the plus one are still present. No vehicles have arrived or left since 15:30 yesterday. Any word on the plus one package?"

" Negative, Lariat, nothing that I was briefed on before ingress, over", Greg advised regarding the unidentified weapon the photos had been taken of. Greg keyed up the mic again, using a different vernacular this time. Knowing that the air element of the operation at the Arena LZ had been patched in by the AWACs to their frequency said—

"Rodeo, this is Gunslinger. Do you copy?", After a several-second delay—

"Gunslinger, this is Rodeo 1 we have a good copy, over." came the voice of one of the pilots who was still sitting in the cockpit of the aircraft after taking turns with the other pilot to stretch their legs and piss.

"Rodeo, we are about to descend on the target. Probably take us ten minutes before we start this party over.", Greg advised looking around at his operators in the green tint of his NVGs and making sure everyone was ready.

Bradshaw had already taught his afternoon iteration of training and settled into his small office at the academy to answer emails and look up subject matter for the upcoming class. His office at the Academy was only a fraction of the size of his office at the Intelligence Center. A desk, his high-back chair, and two guest chairs were about all that could fit into the small space. *Peacefulness, that's what it was. That's why I gave it up.* He thought as he squeezed between the wall and his desk to sit down. Bradshaw set his third cup of coffee for the day down on a black coaster bearing the FBI seal on it, letting out a sigh as he sat down and logged into his computer. As he went through his unopened email, Bradshaw saw an email titled Daily Intel Report. The Daily Intel Report email was an FBI daily report of active investigations and intelligence either gathered for dissemination or for other Agents to be aware of and provide any knowledge of if the information supported an inquiry. Bradshaw read the Daily Intel Reports daily to stay abreast of the threats and active significant investigations that might need an outside eye. Bradshaw opened the email, which read in the Alert Sensitivity Level field, *SECRET*, the date and time fields were blank, and the location of the incident field was empty, raising Bradshaws' eyebrows a little. Bradshaw reached with his right hand for the handle on his coffee mug, picked it up, and took a sip as he scrolled the email on his computer screen with his left index finger, reading as he scrolled. Most daily intel emails sent out by the FBI had a security level of *LAW ENFORCEMENT SENSITIVE*. The email read, *Attached are photos of an unknown device or weapon. If anyone has knowledge or experience with this type of device, please call..., El Paso Intelligence Center*, which got Bradshaw's attention.

Attached at the bottom, below the jargon, were two photos. The images were of a person near an SUV, whose face was blurred out, holding a large black in color device that almost looked like a weapon except for its blockiness.

"Damn, I think that's a thump gun!" Bradshaw exclaimed out loud, talking to himself and quickly placing the coffee mug back on its coaster.

Bradshaw scrolled and enlarged the photo on his screen.

"Man, I wonder who's looking into one of these things if that's what it is?" Bradshaw again spoke to himself under his breath.

Bradshaw picked up the handset to his secure desk phone and dialed the number in the email, which was to the FBI section head at the El Paso Intelligence Center. He had been gone a few months but still remembered the number by heart. The phone rang twice—

"Dan!" Bradshaw exclaimed as the voice on the other end of the phone answered.

"You got 'em! Who is this?", Special agent Dan Bryant questioned.

"This is Bradshaw. Been a while, Chief."

"How's life treating you with your new promotion?" Nick asked.

"Agent Bradshaw! That's a voice I haven't heard in a few years! The last time I remember hearing your voice was when we got drunk in El Paso about two weeks before you got moved to the Center.", Dan said jokingly, referring to the move Bradshaw had made from the Bureaus office in El Paso to the El Paso Intelligence center years before.

"Yes, sir, wild night in old Mexico! Still can't stomach guacamole since that night!" Bradshaw exclaimed, laughing into the phone.

"Good times, what can I do you for, old friend? It's a little hectic around here right now, and I've got someone in my office!" Dan hurriedly told Bradshaw in an obvious statement to get off the phone.

"No problem, I understand. I just wanted to offer my opinion on the daily Intel Report email I received" Bradshaw was cut off mid-sentence.

"You're talking about the photo we sent out?"

"Uhh..yeah, I had a case when I was down there in Texas that had a similar device involved. I mean, on paper, I never saw one in a photo or physically, but...." Bradshaw explained and again was cut off by Dan—

"Say no more! Are you still in Quantico?"

"Yep, sitting at my desk...." Bradshaw attempted again to finish a sentence and was cut off again by Dan—

"I'm making a call. Pack a bag, and take the next FBI bird out of Quantico!"

"You're serious? Umm, ok" Bradshaw realized the possible importance of whatever it was he was now involved with.

"Very serious! I'll call the flight line up there

and get the pilots on board to fly you straight here. Talk to you in a few hours when you land. Someone will be waiting to bring you here to the office."

"Yes sir, see you soon then."

The sixteen operators of Gunslinger slipped quietly from the rim of the canyon, crisscrossing an animal trail to the edge of the Northernmost wall of the compound. Each operator picked their way down the path, trying to see any rocks or limbs that might make unnecessary noise. The night vision goggles allowed the men to see each footstep they placed.

"Lariat, we're set! Any contacts or movements since last over?" Greg asked as he knelt near the front element of the team with his suppressed Colt M-4 at the high ready.

"Negative, Gunslinger, still the same, no changes, tango at the gate, and don't forget about the dog," Joey replied as he stared through the night vision glasses.

"Rodeo, you might want to fire those birds up if you haven't already because business is about to pick up over," Greg advised the Blackhawk pilots, who he knew were listening in on their chatter.

"Roger, good copy Gunslinger. We will be in the air in five, over."

Greg's team had run the operation on a mockup of the ranch thirty-plus times. Each operator knew their role down to the step. They had practiced the execution and extraction so many times that each operator could do their job in their sleep. The ranch had been broken down into four sections or four sides of a square that the operators referred to as alpha, bravo, charlie, and delta. The front or gate side was referred to as alpha, and each side name moved left or clockwise, with Bravo being the left side, Charlie being the back side, and Delta being the right side, or in a clockwise direction, Alpha, Bravo, Charlie, and Delta. Alpha was the front side of the square. Greg had assigned jobs to each operator and broken Gunslinger down into four smaller teams to execute the breach of the ranch. For radio communication during the breach of the ranch, each smaller team was to be called whichever side they were assigned to.

Greg huddled with the Alpha team at the Alpha Bravo corner of the adobe wall and waited for the other three groups to radio that they were set. The dry night air was cool, but the stress and hike had Greg sweating. Still waiting on the other teams to get set, Greg lifted his goggles and wiped the sweat trickling down from his forehead. He pulled the goggles back down to his face and peered around the corner. Greg could see the guard about 40 yards away, pacing back and forth over a few feet and smoking a cigarette. Each time the guard would draw a drag from the cigarette, the guard's face would glow bright white in Greg's goggles. Greg had done this type of operation in Afghanistan, and as he looked around the corner, he was assessing the ground between him and the guard, coming up with a plan in his head. *Soft ground, not many sticks, less than thirty seconds to creep down the wall,* all the things going through Greg's mind. The three teams reported to Greg over the radio in a whisper, one after the other, that they were set—

"Bravo set!"

"Charlie set!"

"Delta set!"

Greg looked around at his Alpha team. All were looking at him, waiting on his hand signal, his right thumb feeling the horizontal safety switch on the left side of his rifle, making sure the switch was on safe. Looking around at his men, he gave the walking man symbol with two fingers and then changed to a knife hand to move forward. Greg and the Alpha Operators crouched down and walked slowly and silently down the Alpha side of the adobe wall to within several feet of the guard. Greg quietly shifted his rifle to his back by the sling and poised to lunge at the guard. The guard had been quartering away from Greg but turned his feet to face away from him. Greg lunged and grabbed the guard with one hand over his mouth and the other around his chest and pulled the guard away from the gate's opening a short distance to the waiting team. One of the operators helped Greg unshoulder the guards' weapon and placed him face down, and zip-tied his hands behind his back. Greg's hand was still over the guard's mouth as Greg repeatedly whispered to the guard—

"no haggis ruido o te mataremos", which translates to *Do not make a sound, or we will kill you.*

As Greg took down the guard, the dog that had been asleep in the yard of the residence sprung its head up at the same time one of the operators had peeked around the corner of the gate to provide cover for Greg. The operator placed one shot into the dog with his suppressed rifle, silencing the potential threat.

"Dog's down," the operator muttered into his headset.

Still dealing with the guard and his team member, Greg exclaimed into his headset,

"Execute, execute, execute!"

Joey and Jim had front-row seats to the show as they peered through their night vision binoculars.

"Delta, we see one guard moving on the inside of the Delta wall, over ", Joey advised.

"Good copy Lariat. We're moving to the delta wall now", the operator said into his mic with a slight sound of being winded in his tone.

The Charlie team operator keyed up his mic just as the suppressed sound of a rifle and its reciprocating bolt could be heard through the earphones from the Charlie end of the mic—

"Tango down, he spotted us... we're over the wall."

The Alpha team moved through the gate into

the yard. The arid conditions of the landscape changed drastically once the operators entered through the gate. Thick green, manicured grass covered most of the yard inside the low wall except for the walkways that serpentined toward the front door. The pathways were lined with flower beds with seasonal flowers planted. A swimming pool was located on the left side of the yard near the residence that had a small pool house and lounge chairs scattered around it. The Operators moved slowly, crouched, placing their heels down first and then rolling to their toes as they moved through the front yard and using the shadows to make their way silently to the front door—

"Breacher up," Greg requested earnestly into the headset.

The breacher ran to the side of the front door, portable ram in hand, and reached slowly for the doorknob to check if it was unlocked.

"Doors unlocked, boss," the breacher exclaimed in a whisper as he moved to the side and waited for the signal from Greg to breach.

The Charlie team reached the back section of the residence and realized it had multiple points of egress—

"Charlie's at the rear entrance, but we've got multiple points of entry, standing by "

"Breach, breach, breach," Greg excitedly whispered into the mic.

The first operator in the stack of the Alpha team slowly and quietly opened the front door to the residence. The second operator in the stack had a flash-bang grenade in hand with his finger through the ring, ready to place if the team leader deemed they needed a distraction. The residence was dimly lit, with only one light down a long hallway. The light from the lamp cast off shadows down to the tile floor. There were two cowhide chairs, one on each side of the entrance hallway, a long credenza with Western-style ornaments scattered across the top, and a single lamp. The residence was eerily quiet as each operator of the Alpha team squeezed up and moved into the home's main hallway. As the team moved down the hallway, the second operator in the stack reached over and turned the single light off so that the operators could have superior visibility through their NVGs. The only sound in the house was the patter of multiple feet as the operators moved in unison. Two men of the Alpha team quietly moved past the hallway and across the open living room to the back glass door of the residence at the same time whispering—

"Blue, blue blue, at the back door," the whispering voice said as it relayed through each operator's headphones.

One of the operators of Alpha quietly opened the glass door to let in the other five operators of the Charlie team. The operators slowly moved down the hall to the first room, halted, and waited for the squeeze-up from the operator behind each one to the back of the thigh. As each operator squeezed up, the first operator in the stack moved into the room and saw a bed with an individual sound asleep. At the same time, moving past the three operators in the first room, the remaining operators moved down the hall to the next room.

While the operators on the ground were looking for work in and around the residence, the Blackhawks were airborne and orbiting two miles away to the North—

"Gunslinger. This is Rodeo 1. We're orbiting two clicks out."

The pilots listening for a response heard the key up on the open mic three times for acknowledgment from Greg.

"Roger that Gunslinger, we know you're working over," the pilot answered.

"Rodeo, this is Lariat. Gunslinger's a little busy right now. We have eyes on the AO, and all seems quiet at the moment, over", Joey advised.

The operators in the first room approached the bed with rifles ready. One operator yanked the sheet back with one hand, still shouldering his rifle with the other—

"Mue'strame tus manos," translated to *Show me your hands* the second operator spoke to the person in the bed.

Startled, the person sprung to life. Even though the room was dark and the operators saw everything in a green tint from the NVGs, they immediately noticed the person in the bed was an Asian male. The operator said in English—

"Do you understand? Show us your hands?"

"Yes, yes," in broken English came the startled reply.

At the same time, the other operator breached the second room. An Asian male also occupied it, and the same scenario took place. In the second room, the operators noticed an AK-47 rifle leaning up in the corner. Enough commotion was taking place in the residence now that lights began coming on in rooms down the hall. The operators holding the hallway flipped up their NVGs onto their helmets so they could operate in a brighter environment. A Hispanic male with a large tattoo on his neck and wearing a silk robe entered the hallway half asleep to check on the commotion and stopped dead in his tracks as he came face to face with the operators. The Hispanic male turned to run back into the room, but the operator lunged and tackled the robed subject. Bravo and Delta teams, who had stayed outside the residence to hold the perimeter, began seeing lights in the second-story windows.

"Alpha, not sure where yall are, but we got lights coming on and movement on the second floor, over," the operator of the Delta team advised.

"Not us, we're on the first floor, over," Greg exclaimed into the mic.

"We're about to have company, boys. What have we got so far?"

"Boss, we've got two Asian males and possibly the target...standby", the operator looked for the identifying marks—

"Yep, we've got the target, verified!"

Hollering in Spanish from the second floor and moving fast, several subjects could be heard moving toward the first-floor operators.

"We've got what we came for. Rear element move to suppress. Keep 'em upstairs if you can. Bravo and Delta, there are no friendlies on the 2nd floor. I say again, no friendlies on the second floor. Watch those upper windows and doors over", Greg ordered into his mic.

Three operators at the back of the stack, who had been covering Alpha's rear, moved to the edge of the living room, where a stairwell was leading to the second story of the residence. The second floor of the home had a half wall that looked out over the living room, and the operators could see the movement of multiple subjects running toward the stairwell. The suppressed rifles of the three operators began reporting in succession toward the stairs. The Spanish speakers got louder and began firing their unsuppressed weapons down into the den area, which became deafening. One of the operators pulled the pin on a flash bang grenade, quickly leaned out past his fellow operator who was actively engaging the second floor with fire from his rifle, and tossed the flashbang up over the half wall on the second floor. The one-and-a-half-second delay on the fuse caused the grenade to explode just as it made it over the wall. The gunfire from the second floor ceased for several seconds as the dazed Sicarios regained composure.

"Rodeo, this is Gunslinger. We're moving to the LZ with the package, over", Greg advised as he held the back of the robed Hispanic male's collar and moved down the hallway toward the residence's front door.

Senior Guirillo's hands zip-cuffed behind him, shuffling in his Italian slippers toward the front door through the house. One of the Alpha team operators quickly swept the room where the Hispanic male had been sleeping and saw a large plastic Pelican-type case, a cell phone, and a satellite phone. The operator quickly scooped up the phones and placed them in his dump pouch hanging on the rear of his combat belt. The operator opened the Pelican case and advised over the headset—

"I think I found whatever that photo was of ."

Greg quickly made a decision and spoke into his mic as he was moving past the operators laying down the suppressing fire, "Grab it and let's...Matt, you still got the Asian guys with you?" Greg said, changing the plan in mid-sentence.

"Roger that, boss!"

"Cuff em' and bring' em'," Greg advised, still moving with the target in hand.

"Roger that, moving.", came the reply from Matt Grayson as he and the other two operators' moved back into the hallway with their prisoners and began the egress toward the front door. The exchange of gunfire had not let up between the two floors of the residence and had become more intense. Smoke now filled the living room from the multitude of gunshots that had occurred in the confined area.

"Rodeo, we're moving to the canyon LZ. We now have the target plus two packages. I say again we have three total packages, over", Greg relayed to the Blackhawks.

Joey and Jim could just barely start to see the morning light on the Eastern horizon as Joey stayed on the glasses, and Jim quickly packed their gear and prepared to move to the top of the canyon to the secondary LZ for pickup. Joey and Jim could hear the distant thump of the rotor blades off to their Northern side. The crew chief onboard each Blackhawk prepared their miniguns in case they needed them during the extraction, which by now was sounding like it might be a hot extract listening to the chatter from the operators. Jim kept the glasses to his eyes and moved his head side to side, checking all the areas he could see for any potential threats to Gunslinger. Jim leaned onto his left side slightly to look further around to his right toward the mouth of the canyon and the one road leading in.

"Holy shit," Jim said aloud, never taking his eyes off the glasses.

Joey was kneeling, packing gear into his pack—
"What you got?"

"I've got several sets of vehicle lights entering

the canyon on the road," Jim exclaimed while keying up his radio—

"Gunslinger, this is Lariat. You're about to have company! I've got several vehicles at a high rate of speed entering the canyon, headed your way!"

"Gunslinger, this is Rodeo 1. We copy Lariats traffic. Trying to take care of that before it gets to you, standby", the Blackhawk pilot of Rodeo 1 said, looking over at his co-pilot, who had already switched frequencies and was relaying the situation to the Op-Cen.

The MQ-9 Reaper drone banked on its starboard side to maintain its altitude as it had for most of the operation over the target area where it could monitor the Arena LZ and the target canyon.

"Gunslinger, this is Rodeo. Keep your heads down. The Reaper's cleared hot, over."

Greg, his package, and part of the Alpha team were already moving quickly away from the ranch into the darkness of the canyon toward the designated LZ—

"Roger that Rodeo, we're still Oscar Mike," Greg advised over the radio, sounding out of breath and letting the helicopter pilots know that he and his men were on the move.

The vehicles were half a mile from the ranch when a large explosion rocked the canyon. As a warning, the Hellfire missile had impacted the road about one hundred yards in front of the moving vehicles. The vehicles came to a screeching halt as the large plume of smoke from the explosion masked them from Jim's view.

"HOLY SHIT!" Jim exclaimed as the shockwave and concussion from the blast startled him and caused him to pull the glasses away from his eyes. Jim quickly peered through his glasses toward the explosion as Joey, who had just taken his helmet and communication system off to adjust, was startled and said—

"Fucking warning would've been nice! Did they get em'..." Interrupting Joey mid—sentence, Jim said,

"No, I see some lights through the smoke. I think it was a shot across their bow."

Joey, snapping the buckle of his helmet back under his chin—

"Keep your eyes peeled, brother. These gomers are gonna want back what we just took!"

The balance of the Alpha and Charlie teams moved out of the residence, maintaining rear security and suppressing fire on the second floor. The explosion in the canyon caused a few seconds pause in the firefight allowing the remaining DEA operators inside the house to egress. Alpha and Charlie teams linked up with Bravo and Delta teams in the residence's front yard inside the adobe fence and near the dead dog. Charlie and Delta team leaders quickly paused in the yard to agree on an immediate egress plan, and Charlie team leader advised over his radio—

"Break contact at the residence and Peel, I say again, Peel! We've gotta get to the LZ!"

The Charlie team leader was referring to an egress tactic known as the Aussie Peel, which afforded the operators a way to maintain constant fire on their rear threat and effectively egress and put distance between them and the guards. The Sicarios had now moved to the second-floor veranda and second-floor windows of the residence to fire on the operators of Gunslinger. The last three operators still engaging the guards were in staggered formation already. Upon hearing the command, the rearmost operator in contact yelled into his mic—

"Peel! MOVING...LAST MAN...LAST MAN!" letting the other operators know he had run his weapon dry and was moving with his M-4 at the high ready rearward and at the same time changing his magazine.

As the operator slammed the magazine into the mag well, he passed his fellow operator patting on the shoulder and letting him know he had passed by. That operator moved fifty yards, spun around, kneeled, and waited for the other operators to pass by before re-engaging. The second DEA operator in the peel formation pulled the pin on a smoke grenade and tossed it as far as he could toward the fire coming from the residence just before the first operator passed him and tapped him on the shoulder. Each operator utilized this method, minus the smoke grenade, until they were safely away in the darkness, and only sporadic gunfire was seen and heard from the ranch.

Each operator had memorized, in detail, the area of operation. Greg was still holding Guirillo by the collar with his left hand and carrying his rifle at the high ready as they stumbled over the embankment into a small bowl on the canyon floor north of the ranch. One of the operators that had egressed with Greg—

"Boss, this is it. We should be at the primary LZ."

"Roger that! Throw out the fireflies!" Greg was referring to the infrared beacons that each operator carried. Each operator had the firefly beacons to note their position or to be able to mark an LZ. The small beacons were technically called Phoenix Junior, and they were the size of the top of a nine-volt battery. To activate, all one had to do was attach the small beacon to a nine-volt battery by snapping it onto the negative and positive posts. Once connected, the beacon immediately began blinking a light that could only be seen by night vision equipment.

The Blackhawk pilot banked and pulled slightly up on the cyclic to steer the helicopter over the mountains surrounding the canyon. The pilots had their NVGs flipped down in front of their helmets as they piloted the aircraft into the canyon and could see the infrared strobes each operator wore and the infrared fireflies that the operators had cast out in a square pattern to mark the LZ. The beacons were blinking bright white in the distance on the canyon floor. The medevac Blackhawk held up, stationary, just before dropping into the canyon to respond if needed and stay out of harm's way. The Blackhawks were slightly staggered as they swept onto the LZ. The Crew Chiefs of Rodeo 2 were operating their guns in the side windows of the Blackhawks. They could see the carnage that Operation Hammerhead had just dealt the Cartel. In his night vision goggles, one of the crew chiefs observed the smoke and fires rising from the ground from where the hellfire missile had struck moments before. He looked slightly to the left in his field of view and could see the ranch house and outbuildings in the distance. Small fires and lights were flickering in and around the ranch. As he gazed out of the gun port of the aircraft, he heard the smack of metal at the same time, realizing that some of the flickering lights around the ranch were gunfire, and the smack he heard was a round penetrating the metal skin of the aircraft. One hundred feet from the ground, the port side crew chief of Rodeo 2 excitedly yelled into the onboard communication system—

"We're taking fire off the port side. It's from a distance looks like it's coming from the ranch!

Gunslinger had almost entirely linked back up except for the last three rear security team members, who were only fifty yards further back when the first long burst of mini-gun fire came from the port side of the Blackhawk. It looked like a liquid fire spitting out of the side of the aircraft. The expended brass from the Blackhawks minigun rained down all around the operators making tink, tink sounds as some of the brass cartridges hit rock and wood. The loud buzzing sound of the mini-gun spitting out its lethal amount of projectiles was comforting to the operators on the ground below. One of the last three operators to make it to the Blackhawk had been slowed down by a leg wound on which he had paused to place a tourniquet. The LZ was half a mile from the ranch, but it would only take one lucky round from a Sicarios rifle to make it a bad day for everyone. The Blackhawk crew chiefs were not taking any chances. The operators of Gunslinger could no longer see the ranch, which was dimly lit by lights and a couple of small fires that had started from the firefight inside the ranch house. At ground level, the ranch had faded over the small knolls and hills between the ranch and the LZ. Both Blackhawks settled to the ground as the operators approached with their packages. Three detained persons plus whatever was in the Pelican case. Greg had made a battlefield decision to bring the extra packages that he felt might be important for not only DEA intelligence but military and DOD intelligence. Greg keyed up and advised the crew chief that all of Gunslinger was onboard. The pilots of each Blackhawk lifted off and made the short jump over the rim of the canyon to the secondary LZ to pick up Lariat. The operators, who had been on the ground, could now see the smoke still billowing up from the hole in the ground where the road once was and could see several vehicles attempting to navigate around the hole.

Joey and Jim looked like bushes moving across the off-slope of the canyon in the pilot's night vision goggles. Their infrared strobes could barely be seen bouncing in and around the foliage Joey and Jim had attached to their uniforms and packs. The pilots hovered several feet from the ground as Joey and Jim threw their gear into the open door of the Blackhawk, and their fellow operators helped them climb in.

"Whew…it's good to see you, boys! Hell of a show!" Jim exclaimed in his Mississippi accent.

Both Blackhawks swept wide around the backside of the canyon and linked back up with the Medevac helicopter. Once the Blackhawks were safely away from the canyon, they set down one last time at the Arena LZ to offload the wounded operator onto the Rodeo 3 Medevac helicopter. While offloading the wounded operator, Alamo communicated to Rodeo—

"Rodeo, this is Alamo. What's your fuel status, over?"

"Rodeo 1 to Alamo, we are currently at 5800 pounds."

One of the air analysts at the Op-Cen quickly translated the 5800 pounds to miles, and Alamo responded—

"Roger that Rodeo. IC1 is diverting your egress

route once you are feet dry to Ft Bliss, over." The pilot and co-pilot on Rodeo 1 looked at each other as they suspected each of the other respective pilots was doing the same and said—

"Roger that Alamo, we should make that a little before bingo, over." The pilot advised as the co-pilot figured out that the remaining fuel would get them a little over 690 more miles. Each Blackhawk lifted off and began their trek North.

CHAPTER 3

DRAGONS BREATH

Nick saw several familiar faces as he entered his old stomping grounds at the El Paso Intelligence Center. The Intelligence Center is known as EPIC and is located on the grounds of the Ft Bliss Army Base in El Paso, Texas. Military, federal, and local agency intelligence gatherers staffed the center.

"Well, what do we have here? Am I seeing things?" the guard at the front entrance asked as he stepped around the barricade to shake Nick's hand.

"Yes, sir. Good to see you, Donaldson.", Nick said in a smiling reply.

Nick only carried his computer bag over his shoulder. The two Agents who had escorted him from the airport carried his other small suitcase so they could get through security faster. The two agents did not stop at the guard station and continued walking toward the elevators attempting to subtly hint to Nick that there was no time for fraternizing.

"Apparently, I'm in a rush, Donaldson. I'll catch up with you later. How's the wife and kids?"

Since Nick no longer worked at the center, he was not afforded the security pass he used to have, but the guards knew Nick was an Agent.

"They're good, sir. Man, it's good to see you." Donaldson replied.

The agents escorting Nick picked up on Nick's apparent respect at the center from the employees that knew him.

The Agents led Nick to Dan's Office as if he did not know where he was going, and Nick said—

"Thanks for the escort, gentlemen."

"No problem, sir. Have a seat, and Agent Bryant will be with you shortly."

Nick had just sat down when the door opened, and the smiling face of Agent Dan Bryant emerged with an outward hand—

"Agent Bradshaw, good to see you," shaking Nick's hand and walking Nick into his large office.

"Nick, do you know Thomas Mayfield? Thomas is an Agent with DEA and Don Powers, you might not know, he's with the Department of Defense.", Dan said, introducing Nick to each agent. Shaking each of their hands, Nick said—

"No, I don't believe I know either of you, but it's nice to meet you both."

"Have a seat, Nick. How's Mitsy?"

"She's good. She just joined a small firm in Fredericksburg."

"..and the area, how do you like it in Virginia?" Dan inquired.

Laughing slightly, Nick answered—

"Colder than here, I can tell you that much! For some reason, though, I don't think I'm here about

Mitsy and the weather."

Don Powers turned and looked at Dan and said —

"I like this guy, ...straight to the point"

"Well, as you probably figured out from our phone call, we flew you down here because of your possible knowledge of this ....well, whatever it is! Agent Mayfield here also has some intel on this thing, and he ran across your name after we talked on the phone. Your name was in a DEA six that was written by an Agent who, by the way, is out of the country at the present time on an assignment. That six mentions a device and your possible knowledge of something similar from an interview you and the DEA conducted back several years ago.", Dan said, peering over his reading glasses and holding some papers in his hand that reference a DEA field report commonly referred to as a six.

"Well, gentlemen, the first thing that came to my mind when I saw the photos was that it was a thump gun. It was an experimental weapon system that, in theory, could be used to shoot down drones and possibly aircraft by emitting a beamed electronic pulse", Nick answered.

Don Powers leaned back in his chair, perked up, and said—

"I hate to interrupt you, Agent Bradshaw, but the DOD isn't very concerned about some Cartel guys shooting DHS drones down hovering over the Rio Grande!"

"Sir, I don't think you quite understand the concept of this particular weapon system. Yes, the weapon systems of this type, as we saw in Ukraine, are pretty much only capable of disabling small observation drones, but I don't believe that's what this is, sir. If this is the same type of system that I got intel on a couple of years ago, this thing could take down a passenger jet if aimed at the correct spot. Your basic EMP gun, like the ones in Ukraine, fires a directional high-intensity radio frequency that confuses the drone's gyro to force it to the ground."

Bradshaw paused and leaned in a little, tapping on the DEA six that he and the other Agent had written years prior, and continued—

"This Chinese-made system is what, back then, they were calling a thump gun. This weapon houses its own small semiconductor that fires an electromagnetic pulse directionally at its target and can fire multiple pulses. The last intel I had gave this weapon an effective range of half a mile or probably more now if they perfected it."

The other men looked on intently as Nick continued.

"The Chinese developed the thump gun prototype several years ago, and we intercepted some communications between the Cartels and the Chinese inquiring about it. During this same time, DEA made a mid-level bust on a Golfo Norte cartel member, and during the interview, the guy was asked about the thump gun, and he went deathly quiet and wouldn't answer any more questions, which gave me the answer I was looking for!"

"So, back when you wrote this report, you thought the cartels were seeking this weapon?" Mayfield asked.

"I believe a lot in the old adage, where there is smoke, there is fire, so, yes, I believed there was something to the intel. Then, when the guy clammed up when he was asked about it, that sounds more like fire to me!"

Don had been listening to Nick all the while thumbing through a manila folder he had pulled from a leather briefcase that sat on the floor next to him. Don located what he had been searching for, a photo taken at a street level, possibly by an undercover agent in China—

"This is a photo taken two months ago," Don said, sliding the photo across the table for Nick to look at more closely.

"So, is this real? Not just a prototype? Someone actually took this photo of a legit thump gun?" Nick asked, looking at the photo and then at the other Agents.

"Not only is it real, but one of these is on its way here as we speak! Also, the Chinese officially named it Dragon's Breath", Don advised, "other than that, we don't know shit about this thing!"

The President had been monitoring the operation from the situation room in the White House. The

President had been woken up early on this day as the Operators stormed the compound.

"Hedley, I knew your boys could pull this off!" the President said as he looked over from the monitor with a look of satisfaction.

The President had reached the situation room just before Gunslinger's egress from the compound. The President had listened to most of the chatter of the communications between Gunslinger, Rodeo, the AWAC, and the Operation Center.

"Yes sir, I think, so far so good sir," Hedley answered.

The Secretary of Defense, John Baker, had not liked anything about the operation and did not like the idea of a covert operation into the sovereign territory of a bordering country. Baker was an ex-military man and knew the bad things that could spawn from such an operation. He also knew the President and hoped that he would follow through with the operation. He knew politics was a funny thing.

The chatter went quiet for a time except for the pilots of Rodeo and the AWAC talking back and forth about terrain and pilot jargon. The observers in the situation room got a fresh cup of coffee and talked about other state matters.

It had almost been an hour since the President left the room. The radio chatter began to get louder, and stressed voices made the people in the situation room take notice and listen. The AWAC communicated—

"Rodeo, we have two fast movers about twenty miles South East of your location. We are jamming their radar, but they appear to be looking for you over."

"Roger that, we're maintaining course unless you advise otherwise, over." one of the pilots of Rodeo 1 acknowledged.

The two Mexican Air Force F-5 interceptors were dispatched to look for the Blackhawks and to force them to land. The President rushed back to the situation room.

"Rodeo, we show you 35 miles from the border, over ", came the chatter from the AWAC.

"Roger, we are max speed inbound, over," the Rodeo pilot acknowledged.

"The fast movers have changed course several times, but they're easing closer to your position, over," the AWAC advised.

"This is not a good situation, Mr. President," the Secretary of Defense advised.

"Well, it's a decision I stand behind," the President snapped back.

"Sir, if they force our birds to land or they cross into our air space after them, this is going to be disastrous," the Secretary of Defense complained.

"Neither of those things will happen, not on my watch! What air assets do we have to contend with this?" the President asked.

"149th out of Lackland, sir, They would be the closest fast-moving air support", the Secretary of

Defense answered.

"Get them in the air if those sons of bitches cross that river by one foot chasing our men; shoot them down. Get on the horn with someone that can communicate with those Helicopter pilots and tell them under no circumstances are they to land those birds on Mexican soil!" the President snarled.

"Yes, sir," the Secretary of Defense answered as he reached for a secure phone handset.

Greg was seated in the Blackhawk, listening to the chatter from the pilots. The three detainees were sitting in front of Greg on the chopper's deck. Each one was zip-cuffed behind their back. One of the Asians stared at Greg with a glare and a slight smirk. Each operator was stone-faced. Each operator's mind was still in the game until they were feet dry on American soil. Matt Grayson glanced over at the black Pelican Case he had seized from one of the rooms at the ranch and wondered what sort of toy he had found while trying to process the operation. After an operation of this nature, each man needed to decompress, but now was not the time. They were still flying over cartel territory or what combatants call behind enemy lines.

The two Mexican Air Force F-5 interceptors' radar systems were not working, but the pilots knew the general direction of egress that the American helicopters might take north. Their orders were to force the American helicopters to land, and they would wait on station. They would fly a menacing pattern, until local ground forces, in this situation also called Cartel members, could arrive and capture the American invaders. A phone call had been placed, and another call after that, and eventually, the buck stopped at the top of the Mexican Government, where that person's hand was forced to deal with the American invaders that had taken a cartel leader and his guests.

The sound of the rotors from inside the Blackhawks was loud, but the roar of the jet engines from the F-5 interceptors was much louder as both passed two hundred feet in front of the Blackhawks. Both jets banked in front of the Blackhawk helicopters attempting to intimidate them.

"Well, that's probably not good!" Jim screamed over the sound of the rotors as he looked at Joey.

In the other Blackhawk, the Asian male's smirk on his face got more prominent as he continued to glare at Greg—

"You do not know who I am, do you?" came the question in broken English.

"Don't know, don't care," Greg screamed and replied over the rotor noise.

This statement had not been entirely accurate, Greg now wondered who this guy was and what exactly he was doing in Mexico, but he knew someone above his pay grade could obtain that information. In Greg's mind, on this day, he had made a difference in the war on drugs and hopefully uncovered something more significant than what he had been authorized to deal with. The pelican case sat near the men, rattling with the rotor vibration of the aircraft.

"We are five clicks out from feet dry. We still have these bogies buzzing us. They appear to be fangs out, over!" the Blackhawk pilot exclaimed into the mic.

In desperation, Cartel Sicarios had made their way close to the Rio Grande River. They spread out over a couple of miles based on the relay of information from the Mexican F-5 Interceptors. In the distance and fast approaching, the Sicarios could see and hear the Blackhawks and F-5s nearing their location.

The lead Blackhawk pilot of Rodeo 1 quickly pulled the stick to starboard to avoid tracer fire coming from the ground several hundred yards ahead of them.

"Damn, that was close! This is Rodeo 1. We're taking ground fire from our front port side! Do we have permission to engage over? We can see dust plumes from multiple vehicles and tracer fire over." the Blackhawk pilot screamed into the mic.

The operations center deferred the hastily asked question to the situation room at the White House, which they knew was listening in on the operation—

"Rodeo, the ROE is only if the aggressors are non-military, over," said the voice referring to the rules of engagement.

The Rodeo 1 pilot looked at his co-pilot—

"How the hell are we supposed to see that at half a mile out?"

Rodeo 2, the dash two in the staggered formation carrying the elements of Lariat and three operators from Gunslinger, at the same time, experienced partial disruption in avionics and cockpit display as the ground fire intended for Rodeo 1 ripped into the airframe of the helicopter —

"Mayday...Mayday! This is Rodeo 2, we are experiencing a SNAG, over! INS is out, ...we are lights out as well, over!", the pilot of Rodeo 2 shouted over the radio, feeling the initial vibration in the pedals and seeing that the radar screen was black. The onboard inertial navigation system was malfunctioning.

Rodeo 2 began to have an engine failure. One of the crew chiefs of Rodeo 2 looked back at the operators onboard and motioned with both hands to tighten their buckles and pointed down in several motions signifying a possible impending hard landing. Jim had felt the projectiles hit the rear and upper airframe and pulled the straps on each buckle of his harness to tighten them down at the same time looking over at Joey's still camouflaged face and saying—

"If we hit hard, lift your feet when we hit the deck"

"Does that actually work?" Joey asked loudly, exchanging looks at Jim's still camouflaged painted face.

Smiling, Jim said—

"No idea, just thought it sounded good."

Joey shook his head at Jim making light of the situation. Air Group Rodeo was now less than five miles from the Rio Grande. Rodeo 1 and 3 heard the distress in the pilot of Rodeo 2's voice and knew what was about to happen. Rodeo 2 began losing airspeed and was trailing the other elements of Rodeo by several hundred yards.

"This is Rodeo 2. We are losing power and altitude, over! We are going to have a forced landing, over!" came the desperate call from Rodeo 2.

"Rodeo 2, this is one we will stay on station until SAR arrives, over", implying that his aircraft would provide air cover until search and rescue arrived.

"Negative, Rodeo 1, negative...get those two helos across that river! Too many black shoes and HVT on board, over ", came the reply from Alamo.

"We will get them across the river, over," came the additional reply from Alamo, knowing the pilot's concern for their brothers and sisters.

Rodeo 2 was in full collective pitch as it autorotated toward the ground. The Sicarios seeing that they had damaged and downed a Blackhawk, quickly sped toward the direction they had seen the Blackhawk descending toward over the crest of some distant hills. The Rodeo 2 pilot flared the nose of the aircraft the best she could to avoid the hard landing from pitching the helicopter forward end into the ground. The two crew chiefs and the five operators braced for impact. One of the crew chiefs had been slightly sitting on the edge of his seat, which caused one of his feet to turn inward. The hard impact caused the crew chief's foot to fold under, breaking his ankle upon impact. Jim, Joey, and the other three operators from Gunslinger were dazed and bruised, but nothing broke.

Rodeos 1 and 3 banked to starboard and made a large loop to ascertain Rodeo 2's crash site. The dust was still high when the Rodeo 1 co-pilot advised that he could see the crash site in a large plume of dust and smoke.

"I've got them! Rodeo 2, this is Rodeo 1. Do you copy over?"

Hearing the blatant disregard for the previous conversation, the IC1 at the operations center squawked on the radio—

"Rodeo 1 and 3 get those birds across that river immediately, over!"

The Rodeo 2 pilot, who was now unharnessed and attempting to determine her casualties and their mobility, was not waiting for another break in the radio chatter to relay Rodeo 2's situation—

"Rodeo 1, this is 2, we are banged up, we have seven walkie-talkies and one talkie, over", came the intercedent reply from the Rodeo 2 pilot as she took a head count and addressed that she had seven able bodies and one wounded non-walking personnel. The pilot of Rodeo 1 looked off his port side and could see multiple plumes of dust boiling up from the speeding Sicario technicals approaching the crash site—

"Chief, I see multiple technicals port side, make them reconsider!"

"Roger that, sir," came the reply from the crew chief as he readied the gun.

The crew chief pointed the multi-barrel gun toward the plumes of dust, flipped the arm switch, led the convoy a little, and depressed the high-rate button. The gun emitted a stream of copper and lead that blew up a cloud of dust throughout the Sicario convoy.

Jim and Joey jumped to the ground from the helicopter. The fuselage had nosed into the ground at a higher rate of speed than a landing is rated for, causing the aircraft to come to an abrupt stop. The damaged rotors were still slowly spinning from the crash. Jim reached up and helped one of the operators hoist down the crew chief, who was grimacing in obvious pain from his ankle injury. Jim saw the still helmeted pilot as she was inside the cabin, helping one of the operators whose harness was stuck. Jim looked over his shoulder into the sky as he heard the Blackhawks banking above and heard the prolonged burst of the minigun. Jim and Joey looked at each other, knowing what that sound meant. Danger close!

"Hey,.. ma'am, grab any weapons you have in there. We might need 'em. I think we're gonna have some company pretty soon!" Jim yelled into the cabin at the pilot.

Acknowledging only by action, the pilot retrieved a small pack from the cockpit. Jim heard the loud thumping rotors of the Rodeo 3 Medevac setting down in the gulch one hundred yards North of their location. Dust boiled up from the ground like a whirlwind as one of the medevac crew chiefs jumped to the ground with his M-4 rifle to cover and help the Rodeo 2 personnel into the helicopter.

The technicals briefly paused as the minigun rounds splashed around the convoy, disabling one vehicle but not hitting any Sicarios. Rodeo 1 circled above the crash site. They were attempting to cover the medevac as an excuse not to be court-martialed for disobeying orders to retreat the short distance to United States soil.

"I have a visual on the friendly's egressing Southeast from the crash site," the co-pilot of Rodeo 1 advised everyone else listening in on the secure transmission.

Greg had been fit to be tied in the back of Rodeo 1 as the events unfolded. Greg's multiple requests for him and his team to be offloaded to supply support to his downed comrades were met with negative results.

"Sir, there is no way we can offload you. We have multiple HVTs onboard, which is what the Sicarios are after. Command will take care of them, sir!" one of the crew chiefs advised Greg, who was now standing holding onto one of the handholds hanging from the aircraft's ceiling.

The three operators, co-pilot, and crew chief from Rodeo 2 each grabbed an appendage of the wounded crew chief and hauled him hurriedly to the Medevac. Jim, Joey, and the pilot had stayed behind to grab gear and communications equipment and attempt to destroy the mini-guns so that they would not fall into the hands of the Sicarios. Rodeo 1, circling above, began taking small arms fire from the technicals to include RPGs. The pilots took evasive action and deployed a string of flares out of the aircraft's rear in case the Cartels had acquired heat-seeking technology.

"We're taking heavy ground fire. Get that bird in the air Rodeo 3! Those technicals are close!" The pilot of Rodeo 1 exclaimed.

The technicals had gained a higher position than the downed Blackhawk and began firing into the gulch from several hundred yards away while still approaching the crash site.

"This is Rode 3. We've gotta get out of here. We're taking direct fire, over ", the pilot of Rodeo 3 advised as he looked back at the crew chiefs who had just helped load the operators, co-pilot, and wounded crew chief.

The Medevac lifted off while still taking small arms fire from the approaching technicals as one of the crew chiefs of Rodeo 3 jumped over to the mini-gun to provide his helo support so they would not end up like Rodeo 2. The operators on board the Medevac motioned and screamed at the crew chief to set the bird back down because they had left personnel on the ground. Unapprised of the situation degrading outside the helicopter, the DEA operators looked to the crew chief, who quickly motioned a flat hand under the chin of his helmet back and forth, signifying no good.

Jim heard the Medevacs engines' pitch change as they began lifting off. Thinking they had forgotten about them, he ran to the side of the aircraft's fuselage so that he could be seen and began waving his arms. Jim promptly observed why the Medevac was lifting off. Jim could see and hear the small arms fire directed at Rodeo 3 from the edge of the distant gulch. Jim ran around to the opening in the fuselage and yelled to Joey and the pilot—

"We gotta go. The bird lifted off! The Sicarios are close. Come on!" Jim motioned with his hands.

Joey and the pilot hurriedly threw their gathered equipment to the ground. The pilot quickly took off her helmet and grabbed the pack she had retrieved from the cockpit, and she and Joey jumped to the ground near where Jim was shouldering his pack.

"Hold up!" the pilot exclaimed as she pulled a white phosphorus grenade from her bag.

"We keep these just in case!" the pilot advised, pulling the pin and throwing the grenade inside the helicopter's airframe.

Jim, Joey, and the pilot began running to

put distance between themselves and the downed helicopter as the grenade exploded, and the cabin started to smoke more than it had from the crash. Rodeo 2 had crashed into a low, wide gorge that looked like an old riverbed. The three made their way across the expanse and over the lip of the gulch. They ran to a small knoll just seventy-five yards from the edge of the gorge. Jim, Joey, and the pilot knelt to catch their breath and began reconnoitering to get their bearings. Their main concern was for them not to get captured and to make it to the Rio Grande. Jim and Joey still had their full load-outs and successfully grabbed most of their equipment from the downed helicopter, not wanting it to fall into Sicario's hands. The pilot had a Beretta 9mm pistol, and she had grabbed her pack with multiple extra pistol magazines and a few pieces of additional gear inside. Jim heard the Blackhawks rotors that had been above them now fading away in the distance. They all knew that their comrades had not abandoned them and that they had too much at stake onboard their aircraft to stay on station. Jim, Joey, and the Pilot knew that the oaths they each had taken sometimes came with a price, and today that price might be the ultimate one.

Multiple Sicario technical vehicles came to a screeching halt one hundred yards North of the crash site near where Rodeo 3 had landed and taken off. The Sicario Saldatos offloaded and slowly approached the smoking Blackhawk. Jim crawled to the lip of the gulch to view the enemy position and get some better bearings. Joey pulled out the sat phone and re-dialed the op center. As soon as Joey heard someone pick up on the other end—

"Alamo, this is Lariat, we're plus one egressing 300 yards Southeast of the crash site, over!"

"Lariat, can you make your way to the border over?"

"Not sure, Alamo, we're danger close at the moment with little cover...is anyone coming over?" Joey asked in desperation for options.

"Negative, Lariat. You're on your own. We have orders from the top not to engage further. We can support you with directions and position only until you get the river over", came the reply from Alamo.

Joey pulled the sat phone away from his ear and looked disgustedly at the pilot—

"Directions...we don't need directions! We need fucking air support! Shit, this is about to get worse."

Jim crawled below the crest of the edge of the gulch and ran the short distance to the knoll where Joey and the pilot had held up. Out of breath, Jim exclaimed—

"They're coming our way on foot. We gotta get out of here!"

The Saldatos had cleared the wreckage of any American survivors and had located the bootprints leading Southeast. The Saldatos were spread out with their guns at the ready, slowly stalking in the direction of Jim, Joey, and the pilot. Understanding their situation, Jim and Joey readied their M-4s and strapped their equipment to themselves, anticipating a fight for their lives. All three knew with the limited scrub brush for cover and primarily flat land; they did not stand a chance if they made a run for it. They knew the technicals would catch up to them and kill or capture them in the flat terrain. Jim, Joey, and the pilot knew that their best option was to hold out on the small knoll and make this their last stand.

The downed Rodeo 2 Blackhawk helicopter exploded in a massive fireball. The destruction of Rodeo 2 caused residual explosions that killed and wounded multiple Sicario and Saldatos. Jim, Joey, and the pilot had been close enough to the blast to feel the shock wave as it radiated away from the fiery epicenter. The Reaper Drone had been cruising at 40,000 feet and monitoring the situation. The CIA Reaper pilot sitting in a secure facility in Langley, Virginia, who had been monitoring the radio communications, was not about to let the Sicarios take three Americans. He had released the last of the two hellfire missiles the Reaper had taken off with. The pilot passed it off as not wanting the Blackhawk helicopter and its contents to fall into enemy hands in a foreign country.

"Damn, that's twice that guy's scared the shit out of me in six hours! I'm not complaining! I'm not complaining!" Joey said as each of the three was surprised and startled by the blast.

They had been saved, and they knew it. Each smiled as the stress level lessoned, knowing someone above had saved their lives.

The remaining un-wounded Sicarios got the picture and ran for cover, not knowing how many more missiles might rain down from above.

The explosion had been felt and seen by the remaining Blackhawks and operators onboard the remaining elements of Rodeo. Each had hoped that the explosion had killed or at least delayed the Sicarios from locating their comrades that had been left behind on the ground.

"Does anyone have a visual of those fighters?" the Rodeo 1 pilot asked into the mic.

Rodeos 1 and 3 were about to cross over the Rio Grande back into the United States.

"Good morning, Rodeo. This is Gunfighter. We will be your escort to the office this morning.", came the reply over the radio from the pilot of one of the two F-16s from the 149th fighter wing.

"Good morning, Gunfighter. We appreciate the escort. The gomers must have bugged out when they saw you cruising the river, over!" the Rodeo 1 pilot replied.

The jubilation in the rear of each Blackhawk was not shared. The operators knew they had left boots on the ground.

CHAPTER 4

Egress

Bradshaw placed the photos back onto the table. Dan and the other two Agents looked on at Bradshaw as if they were waiting on an answer to this possible threat. In the awkward silence, Bradshaw asked—

"What is it exactly ya'll called me down here for? It seems to me we could've had this conversation over the phone."

Glancing at the other two Agents as if to get some sort of head nod, Dan said,

"Well, given your proven abilities in intelligence gathering and your ability to flip people into working for the government,.... we thought…". Bradshaw interrupted.

"I'm an instructor now. I haven't worked in the field in months…"

"Maybe he's right, Dan, he probably isn't who we need for this. I thought you said this guy used to be an operator?" Don Powers answered, sitting intently in his chair studying Bradshaws' mannerisms.

Dan put his hand out toward Don in a hold-on motion—

"Nick, you can do this. You thought enough of this as a threat that you placed a call based on an intel email. Now I know you're settled in at Quantico, but we need you here. Will you help us?"

Bradshaw picked up the photos again and studied them, looked up at Dan, and said—

"I'm in! What do you need me to do?"

At this moment Dan's cell phone began ringing. Dan answered his phone, got up, and stepped a few feet away. The expression on Dan's face changed, and the concern in his voice could be heard—

"Ok, when, how many? The HVT and the package? Thank you, yes. Be there in 30 minutes."

All eyes were on Dan as he finished the call—

"Well, gentlemen, things have escalated. Bradshaw, we need an answer. Now! Onboard or a no-go? Your call!"

"I'm on board!"

"Perfect, Bradshaw. Do you mind stepping out for a minute? Grab your bags. We have to be at the airfield in less than 30 minutes", Dan asked as he moved around his office, quickly gathering a few documents and referring to the airfield located on Ft Bliss which was almost walking distance from EPIC if it was not for the high fences and security.

"Sure, I'll be in the lobby."

Bradshaw left the office. Left behind were Dan, Thomas Mayfield, and Don Powers. Shaking his head in slight disbelief, Don said—

"I thought we were just going to consult with Bradshaw? Now he is essentially heading this investigation up? I disagree with this. There are a lot of other Agents, especially from my agency, that are far more qualified than this guy to handle an operation like this! This can potentially turn into something that requires a more tactical response."

Thomas Mayfield only shook his head in agreement with Don.

"I've known Bradshaw for a while now, and he's more than qualified and capable. You both are experienced Agents. Did you notice his ring? SRT! The eagle clutching the dagger and rifle. Before becoming a fed, he was a local guy and served on several different SRT teams. He's an operator, just like these guys. Maybe just the rapport we need, plus he knows enough about this weapon system to get us what we need. Geez, you boys need to do your homework!"

Don looked over at Thomas—

"Well, you mentioned that he had operational experience, but I didn't know that, but it still doesn't negate the fact that I think that the CIA should take it from here."

Still gathering documents and placing them into a leather satchel, Dan paused—

"You know if one of these Dragons Breaths falls into the wrong hands on this side of the border… I don't have to tell either of you the danger to the defense of the nation this poses. Some fanatic gets their hands on one, and power grids, planes, and anything with a computer or motherboard are in danger. Virtually everything we base our lives around is at stake. Bradshaw might be a little rusty in the tactical department but is fully capable."

The CIA had been behind the eight ball from the beginning. The CIA had only two pieces of paper and a handful of photos of a potential weapon system from China that had ultimately slid between the cracks. Now that this weapon system was this close to the border and one of them was on the way to Ft Bliss, it made it fair game for the other three letter agencies—primarily the FBI, the primary domestic anti-terror group. The CIA Special Activities Division had very little intelligence on the EMP handheld weapon system. Don Powers had been tasked with locating and destroying or seizing the weapons if they were the threat to the United States that the CIA thought they were.

Bradshaw did not sit down in the lobby. Instead, he paced while pulling the cell phone from his pocket and dialing Mitsy—

"Hello"

"Hey angel, I just wanted to call and give you an update," Bradshaw said, looking around and wiping his brow and trying to come up with the proper words to tell his pregnant wife that he was thrown right back in the fray.

"You're ok right?"

"Yes…yes, I'm fine. I'm probably going to be down here for a little longer than I told you."

"Please tell me this isn't about a new job back down there? I can't handle another move right now, babe. The baby is due in five months, and I've got a good Doctor up here...."

"No, nothing like that at all. I'm just going to be here handling something. Probably be home by the end of the week.", Bradshaw said, trying to comfort his pregnant wife.

"Please be safe. I know you!"

"I promise I'll be fine. Dan Bryant's here, and he says hello", Bradshaw responded, trying to comfort Mitsy with a familiar name.

"Oh, I love Dan! Please tell him hello. You both, please be safe. Whatever it is, you're up to. I love you!"

"I love you, angel. Take care of our baby! I'll call you later. Bye, I love you!" Bradshaw said, getting off the phone just as Dan and the others opened the door to Dan's office to leave.

The two operators of Lariat and the downed pilot took advantage of the confusion that the hellfire missile caused and traveled South. They moved quickly but quietly from clumps of the brush to dry creek beds. They hoped that they might buy some extra time by going South if the Sicarios believed they would have directly headed North for the river. The three could use an old creek bed to travel as Jim lagged a short distance behind, covering their bootprints and ensuring they weren't being tracked. About one mile and a half South of the crash site, they were able to locate a deeper draw with green brush and small trees growing near a flowing creek. The creek was only a couple of feet wide, but the water was trickling past, giving just enough nourishment to the surrounding foliage to stay green. Joey and the pilot stopped under a small tree that provided shade and camouflage from above. Both knelt to rest and waited for Jim to catch up. Joey took off his pack and began inventorying what gear he had. Joey had noticed that the name tab on the pilot's flight suit read, 'Fisher.'

"So, Ma'am, I guess I need to formally introduce myself since shit has officially hit the fan! Joey, Joey Keller DEA", Joey said, reaching his right hand out to shake.

"Carly Fisher, 2nd Lieutenant US Army, nice to meet you", Fisher replied, reaching out to shake Joey's hand.

The blue-eyed, sandy blonde-haired Carly Fisher had begun her military career in the ROTC program in high school. Carly had always known she wanted to join the military but had not thought much about making it a career until she got into Army aviation. Carly had entered the Army's flight school at Fort Rucker, Alabama. After completing her 32 weeks of flight instruction, Carly graduated at the top of her class. The war in the Middle East was boiling, and Carly wanted to use her skills to benefit and make a difference. Carly took her first post in the Army's 10th Aviation Regiment, attached to the 10th Mountain Division. In 2012 when Carly first deployed to

Afghanistan, she was a rarity in her line of work. Carly took the initial looks of having to prove herself to the male-dominated arena with a grain of salt. Her Texas laid-back attitude and tenacity in stressful situations emerged, and Carly became the pilot every soldier wanted to fly into combat. Carly had been deployed to FOB Shank, located in Logar Province. Carly had been shot at, and damage logged on the birds that she flew out of FOB Shank multiple times, but she had never been shot down. This was a first for her. The SERE training she had completed was just that...training, and it can never be as realistic as the actual situation. The instructors attempt to prepare you physically and mentally for escape and evasion, but they can never prepare you for that mental flip in that you are shot down behind enemy lines. Carly only confided in the fact that she was not alone. She had been dealt this lousy deck of cards along with two others at the table. *Two,* she thought, *two that, from all indications, know how to handle themselves in bad situations.*

Joey kneeling on both knees with the contents of his pack strewn out in front of him—

"Well, I have NVG goggles and binos, two and a half MREs, one full canteen, a couple of emergency water pouches, and my IFAK. Let's see,...one, two..", Joey was counting under his breath—

"six rifle mags, and four pistol mags, not counting what is in each gun"

Carly began looking through the small pack

she had retrieved from the cockpit—

"I have six pistol mags, one flare, one MRE, IFAK, and four water pouches. What does your partner have on him? About the same as you?"

Joey looked over his shoulder for Jim and responded—

"Yeah, probably so…about the same. Neither of us has fired a round yet in this whole thing so we still have our ammo load out."

Carly sat down on her rear end, same time ripping the top off of a water pouch—

"I've been in some pretty bad spots before, but this is a first for me!"

"You did any time overseas?" Joey asked, packing his gear back into his pack.

"Yes, sir, I did!" Carlys' attitude regresses a little to the early days in Afghanistan.

"I did a rotation in Afghanistan in 12. Logar Province."

Joey felt a little tension from the question he had just asked—

"Didn't mean anything by that Ma'am. I guess I should have worded that differently. I was over there also…in 14. I was in several small firefights. If it makes you feel any better…", Joey leaned over and half whispered, "this was my first helo crash also".

Both laughed.

Jim had now made his way to near where Carly and Joey had taken refuge under the small tree. Jim took his pack off and laid down prone, placing the field glasses to his eyes and scanning the horizon in the direction from which they had come. After several minutes Jim was satisfied that, at least to this point, they had not been followed. Jim got up, pack and rifle in hand, and walked the short distance down into the gully to Carly and Joey—

"Well, don't yall look comfy. I covered the bootprints best that I could. I didn't see any dust plumes or anything that looked like we were being tracked"

"Grab a seat brother, this is Lieutenant...", correcting himself and looking over at Carly, "sorry, 2nd Lieutenant Carly Fisher", Joey said introducing Carly.

Jim reached his hand over Joey's lap to shake Carly's hand—

"Nice to meet you, Lieutenant. Jim Cado, DEA. Well, I'd say we're in a pickle!" Jim said in his deep Mississippi accent.

"I'm sure the gomers are picking through the crash site. It's only a matter of time before they start looking for us. I looked through my gear a ways back, and I still have a pretty full loadout..." Joey interrupted—

"Same here, I am good on ammo, water, two and a half MREs..."

"Chowhound over here!", Jim exclaimed, as he cut Joey off looking over at Carly and thumbing toward Joey—

"I have three full MREs left."

Carlys' comfort in the bad situation was

furthered by the thought that these two operators had been around each other long enough to joke and make light of bad situations. A small smirk came across Carlys' face listening to the banter between the two operators.

Bradshaw had boarded the same black FBI SUV as Dan and settled back in the second-row seat to endure the roughly 12-minute ride through Ft Bliss to the airfield. Once underway, Dan attempted to get Bradshaw up to speed—
"Nick, I know you're wondering what the hell is going on, so I'm going to fill you in on what I know so far. Roughly forty hours ago, the DOJ and DOD launched a raid into Mexico to grab the head of the Golfo Norte Cartel. The operation is the brainchild of the President. He felt that the country needed to send a message to the cartels that we wouldn't stand for the blatant distribution of narcotics coming across our borders, so Operation Hammerhead was drawn up and executed. The advance recon team spotted and photographed the weapon system we sent the photo of in the secure intel email."
Bradshaw listened intently as Dan leaned over toward him and, with slight concern in his voice—
"That phone call I received in my office just before we left was informing me that one of our birds went down in Mexico!"
Bradshaw's expression changed—
"Oh my god! How many men did we lose?"

"I didn't get the full skinny on the phone, but they said we are missing two agents and a pilot. I just wanted to prepare you because some of these DEA guys are going to be pissed, distraught, or both about the buddies they were forced to leave behind. I was told they're bringing back the weapon system, and they have three detained"

"Who are the three detained? I thought you said they went after one?"

"I'm not sure. I know the operation was a snatch and grab of the Cartel head. Other than that, I can't say with certainty. The two remaining birds were diverted here to FT Bliss because they need us to figure this weapon system out and talk to these detainees. We were already working on this with the CIA, so the powers that be decided for continuity to let us take the ball. We will also help debrief the DEA operators handling the operation and the detainees. Nick, I have no idea where this will take us or how long. I know you agreed to help us, and ultimately your country will be grateful."

Nick had been staring out of the passenger side window. Silence filled the air as Dan waited for a reply. Nick thought for a few seconds and responded—

"You know, Dan, the last case I worked on before I left Texas was with a guy who, by all indications, was your average American. Guy had a family and a good job but somehow had gotten himself wrapped up with the Cartel. Blackmail-type stuff. He was given two hand grenades by the

Cartel that were smuggled across the border that were meant for a Federal Judge." Bradshaw had been looking out the window then turned towards Dan and said—

"I say that to say this, I took an oath, Dan,...an oath to defend this country from all threats, foreign ...and domestic. I'm here, Dan, and I will be here to see this through."

The jet fighter escort from the 149th flared off several miles outside of El Paso, wishing Rodeo a safe landing. Ft Bliss emergency personnel of the Army's 31st Army Service Hospital had been alerted to the incoming Blackhawks laden with their operators and detainees. Medical emergency personnel and Military Police rushed to Biggs Army airfield to intercept the wounded and help with the security of the HVT detainees that the soldiers had been advised were onboard.

As Rodeo 1 settled to the tarmac, Greg jumped to the concrete with a somber look on his face. Greg pushed his slung M-4 rifle to his backside and reached into the Blackhawk to help the three detainees down and out of the helicopter. Greg hollering over the noise of the rotors, said to one of his operators—

"You got 'em. Pass 'em off to whoever's in charge. I'm headed to check on Terrance."

Terrance, the operator who had taken a projectile to the leg on the egress from the ranch, was being offloaded from Rodeo 3, the medevac close by. Greg ducked to avoid the rotors and moved between the Blackhawks to the open side door of Rodeo 3—

"T, you got this, baby! You good?" Greg hollered at Terrance as he was being loaded by medical personnel onto a gurney.

"Yes, sir. They just winged me! I'll be good as new", Terrance advised, as he was not feeling any pain since the onboard medic of Rodeo 3 had administered a heavy painkiller.

"I'll check on you shortly once we get all of this sorted out," Greg said as he was turning to speak to the crew chief with the broken ankle—

"Chief, thank you. My team appreciates your sacrifice today. I'm sorry you ended up on the gurney."

The crew chief only nodded in the affirmative as he appeared to be in much more pain than Terrance. Both wounded men were wheeled away to awaiting ambulances that took them the short distance to the base hospital. Greg returned to Rodeo 1, where his operators gathered and secured gear. The pilots and personnel of Rodeo 1 were walking outside the helo, looking for the damage they might not have felt or registered during the engagement on the other side of the border. A Sergeant with the Military Police walked over to Greg—

"Sir, you and your men, please come with me. We have a secure area in one of the hangers for you and your men. Some people are on their way to speak with you."

"Some people, huh?" Greg snarled.

"I'm sure it's some suits comin' to tell us what we did wrong?" Greg inquired as he walked alongside the Sergeant.

"Not sure, sir. We're just told to take control of the detainees and ask you and your men to come to the hangar to debrief."

"No problem, son," Greg replied, patting the soldier on the back as they walked together.

The two dark SUVs were ushered through the Ft Bliss base escorted by MPs to Biggs Army Airfield to one of the hangars. Nick peered out of his window and could see the two Blackhawks that had just landed by the amount of personnel still frolicking around each helicopter. Nick and Dan exited the SUV, followed close behind by DEA SA Thomas Mayfield and DOD Agent Don Powers. The four men were escorted by one of the MPs inside the hangar to the back section, which had been converted at some point into what looked like rooms or offices. Nick could see several men standing around outside of the office area. The men loitering around wore camouflage uniforms; most had full beards or facial hair.

Nick had been around the DEA recruits and Agents his entire federal career. The DEA and FBI Academies are across the street from one another at Quantico. Nick always thought of the DEA recruits and agents as a rough-and-tumble bunch. They were not your lawyers and accountants that the FBI recruits. The DEA guys were generally men and women who wanted to be on the front lines of the drug war. A war that by any means was not clean and by the books. These guys mainly worked in covert operations. Most of the guys had either worked undercover or as cover agents for undercover narcotics purchases. They were masters at surveillance and intelligence gathering.

Nick deduced that these guys must be the operators who conducted the raid. Gear and rifles were lying in small piles close by to where the group of men was standing.

Greg noticed Nick and the other three agents walking in with the escort. He met them before getting to the offices and his men—

"I understand you gentlemen would like to talk with us and debrief, but before we start anything like that, I want to know if my men that went down in that chopper are being rescued? If not, I would suggest you fire one of those birds back up and let me and my men go get them!"

Dan held his arm out towards Greg and nodded —

"You must be Special Agent Greg Dean, I'm Special Agent Dan Bryant with the FBI, and yes, we're here to speak with you and debrief with you. I'm being told that your men and the pilot are alive and ok. Your men have been in contact with the Op-Cen and are making their way to the border".

Greg replied—

"I want to...." Dan cut off Greg—

"I'm going to put you in contact with your men the next time they call into the Op-Cen. I know this is a difficult thing to do, leaving your men out there like that, but we need to look at the bigger picture. Excuse me while I make this call"

"Tom, there has to be something you can do. Those are our boys we left over there!" Greg said while looking at Thomas Mayfield, who also fell within the DEA family and who Greg knew from conducting SRT operations within Thomas's AO.

"Who's this bean counter?" Greg asked, obviously agitated with the current situation and nodding toward Nick.

"I'm sorry Greg, this is Nick... Special Agent Nick Bradshaw with the FBI. Nick here might know a little about that device you and your men brought back."

Dan had walked away from the group to contact the operations center, and Nick attempted to break some of the tension in the air—

"Good to meet you, sir! I'm sorry about your men. It sounds like y'all might have uncovered something that needs a little attention. Agent Dean, did the guys you captured have anything to say on the ride in?"

Greg paused for a minute, attempting to change gears to a more civil conversation—

"No, not much. The only thing one of the Asian guys asked me was if I knew who he was. I told him I didn't know, nor did I care. Other than that small conversation, nothing to speak of."

Thomas introduced Greg to Don—

"Greg, this is Don Powers with DOD. Don's here for the military aspect of this shit show."

Greg, taking slight offense to the comment—

"Shit show? I think my team did an outstanding job, Tom! You tell me what other team could've pulled that shit off any better? Target, plus two HVTs and some sort of advanced weapon system! Sounds to me like a successful op."

"No offense Greg, I'm talking about dealing with this detainee situation. We don't know who these other two guys are or why they're 3000 miles from Asia. I was thinking out loud. I apologize, and you're correct! No other team could've done any better".

The late afternoon sun had heated the Mexican landscape and had just begun to cool off as the sun settled over the horizon to the West. The small scattered trees in the gully near the creek provided only modest shade but enough to make the temperature tolerable as the afternoon waned. Joey took the last shift on the gully's edge as a lookout. Joey nor the other two had seen any movement during their prospective guard duties except for some distant dust cloud around their helicopter crash site. The feeling was almost surreal for Joey as he could see the beautiful multi-colored horizon of the sun and feel what he and his comrades had just gone through. Jim and Carly had taken the earlier guard shifts and were now under the tree, attempting to nap. The three had agreed to move to the border near the river once the sun went down, and they could utilize their night optics. Joey knew that the peaceful afternoon was solace only because the Sicarios were more than likely strung out along the Rio Grande, waiting for them or an extraction team to cross in either direction.

As dark neared, Joey eased down the embankment to the tree—

"wake up, you sleepy heads, it's almost time to move"

Jim sat up, and Carly rolled to one side wiping her eyes with her thumb and index finger.

"Any movement out there?"Jim asked as he moved to one knee and began gathering his gear.

"Nothing other than some movement around our crash site. It's eerily quiet", Joey responded.

"You can guarantee that the gomers are up there waiting on us…maybe not here, but between here and that river. I guarantee it"

"Two US operators and a chopper pilot! They're looking for something to trade!" Carly said, interjecting her thoughts.

Jim pulled out the sat phone—

"I'm going to make this call and see what we're working with?"

Jim hit redial—

"This is Alamo, over.", came the answer on the other end of the line.

"Alamo, this is Lariat. We're still plus one. I

don't know if you have our pos, but we are about a mile south of the crash site in a gully in some trees."

"Roger that, we have your pos roughly seven miles from the border, over."

"Roger that Alamo. We are moving shortly to the border. It'll probably take us two and a half to three hours. Are we going to have a welcome party? Over." Jim responded with hopefulness in his voice—

"Roger, Lariat. We already have several partygoers near your crossing. We have an eye in the sky."

"Roger, can we expect any party favors for any party crashers over," Jim asked as he looked over at Joey and Carly.

"Negative, Lariat. We have orders for favors only if the party crashers cross the river after you, over."

"Roger that Alamo. We will activate our beacons once we start moving. See you soon, Alamo, over."

"Lariat, standby for a patch through, over." Jim looked at the other two with a puzzled look—

"They're patching someone through," Jim told them, shrugging his shoulders.

"Go ahead for Lariat, sir," came the voice from the Op-Cen.

"Jim, Joey, who do I have? This is Greg."

"SIR, this is Jim. Man, it's good to hear your voice!"

"Not as good as it is to hear yours."

"How are y'all fairing"?

"So far, so good."

"Jim, I don't want to burn your battery up. I'm being told you'll have support once you reach the river"

"Roger that, heard the same"

"Put Joey on"

"Sir,"

"Joey, I don't leave my men behind, and you know that, but I had no control, keep your heads down out there and make it to the river!"

"Yes, sir, it's not on you. Sometimes the chips fall like this. All good. See you on the other side"

"Nec Timeo Nec Sperno, over," Greg said, ending his phone patch-through with the DEA SRT motto.

"Lariat, this is Alamo. Your element needs to make it to the river before dawn, over.

"Alamo, we will make it over."

"Roger that Lariat, keep your heads down, and we'll be waiting for you, over and out," came the reply from Alamo.

CHAPTER 5

Evasion

Senior Sanchez Guirrillo had been led to a room in the hangar and now sat alone in a chair at a single desk in the middle of the dimly lit room. Guirrillo, still only wearing his long sleep pants, robe, and a pair of Italian leather slippers that no longer held their luster from being dragged through the canyon, sat with a disgusted and disgruntled look on his face. Guirrillo sat at the desk with both hands now in steel handcuffs strung through a metal ring screwed into the top of the desk.

The door to the room opened, and in walked Nick and Dan. Dan walked over to the opposite side of the desk as Guirrillo and sat in the only other chair in the room. Nick walked to one of the dimly lit corners of the room and leaned against the wall. Guirrillo looked up at both men as they maneuvered in the room and smirked and chuckled, looked back down at the table, and conjured up just enough saliva in his mouth to spit to the side onto the floor in disgust. Dan looked over at Nick, who had been watching Guirrillos mannerisms and only raised his eyebrows acknowledging Dan. Dan placed a folder and a notepad on the desk and pulled his pen from his shirt pocket when Gurillo began his interrogation in broken English—

"Do you have any idea who I am?"

Dan, with slight laughter in his voice and a twitch of his head to one side—

"Well, sir, we have a pretty good idea"

"I do not believe that you do. Because if you did, I would not be sitting here!"

"I haven't advised you of your Miranda rights, and seeing as how we have a federal indictment or...warrant for your arrest. I'm going to advise you of your rights before we proceed. You have the right to remain silent. Anything you say can and will be used against you in a court of law. If you do not have an attorney, one will be appointed to represent you before any questioning if you wish. Do you understand the rights as I just stated them?", Dan advised, staring into the eyes of Guirrillo.

"I do not have a cagar for your rights! You will soon see this was a very big mistake"

"Ok, chief, well, let's talk about how big of a mistake this is. You and every other cartel in Mexico have shipped hundreds of tons of heroin and fentanyl into the United States. We have proof of that, or we wouldn't have been able to obtain an indictment. Sounds to me like you're the one that made a mistake."

Guirrillo was upset and raised his voice—

"You will see very shortly who has made a mistake! Americans do not have the stomach for the type of warfare my organization is used to handing out. You come into my country, into my home, kill my men and take me hostage,"

Dan interrupted, leaning into the desk, and asked—

"What were the Asians doing at your compound?"

Gurrillo leaned back into his chair and looked at Dan and Nick—

"You are asking a question now that I think you already know part of the answer, or maybe the whole answer. I saw that you brought back one of the weapons I had just purchased?"

Nick uncrossed his arms and stepped toward the desk—

"ONE of these weapons? How many did you purchase?"

"Enough, my friend, enough, and you do not know the real answer to your question, so I am going to leave that as a surprise. I want my lawyer now and my phone call. You gringos will never understand this war. It is simple economics. Supply and demand. The people of your country demand what I can supply, and they ultimately pay me handsomely for it."

Dan and Nick left Guirrillo in the office and walked into the hall.

"This isn't good, Nick! This could be a disaster if the cartel had more of these weapons. Let's see what the Asian guys will come off of?"

Don Powers and Thomas Mayfield had been

watching the Asian male that appeared to be the one in the photos taken by Lariat and who appeared to be the head of whatever this was. Nick and Dan walked down the hall and met Powers and Mayfield—

"Guirrillo say anything? You weren't in there long." Powers asked.

"Lawyered up, but before that, he alluded to more than one of those EMP weapons," Dan responded.

"I'm gonna have to pass that up the chain while you talk to this Asian guy. This has turned into what's the word Tom used, a Shitshow!"

Don disappeared down the hall and into the open hangar, already dialing a number on his phone. Nick and Dan entered the room where one of the Asian males was similarly seated and cuffed to the desk. This time Nick sat at the chair opposite the Asian male, and Dan stood. The Asian male sat staring at Nick. Nick started the conversation—

"Good afternoon, my name's Nick, and I'm an FBI Agent. Do you speak English?"

The Asian male, head cocked slightly to the side, said—

"I speak a little English. Do you know who I am, or better yet, who you have kidnapped?"

Nick looked over at Dan with a 'here we go again look' and looked back at the male—

"No sir. That's why we're here to try and figure that out. My guess is you're Chinese. Other than that, I have no idea."

Laughing, now fully knowing that the Americans had no idea who he was looked up at Jim and said—

"My name is Zihao Chen. My father is General Tan Chen, the Defense Minister"

Nick asked, "Of the Chinese Government?"

Now smiling wider, Chen answered—

"Yes. You have just kidnapped the son of the Chinese Defense Minister."

Jim moved in a northerly direction, pack on his back and his M-4 at the low ready, meandering through the dry creek bed. The small tributary of water had stopped several hundred yards behind him. Jim paused and looked ahead into the green tint of his night vision goggles, which looked quiet. Jim looked behind him down the trail and could see the two green figures of Joey and Carly, who were staying about fifty yards behind Jim in case he made enemy contact. Carly was walking close behind Joey to mimic his footsteps because she did not have a pair of night vision goggles. Carly had failed to take the goggles from the top of her helmet in the haste to leave the Blackhawk. Jim and Joey had reapplied camouflage paint on their faces, and Carly had done the same to help blend in with the darkness. Jim continued, walking on the edge of the creek bank so that he could quickly jump to cover if he saw or sensed the enemy.

The dry creek bed that Lariat and the Lieutenant had chosen to mask their movement meandered a quarter of a mile from the crash site. The night was penetrated by the only light emitting from lights around the crash site. Jim ducked just below the lip of the creek bank and went prone to monitor for movement.

"Joey, hold up a few minutes. I've got lights at our crash site, just makin' sure they don't have any rovers out this far.", he said into his mic.

Joey reached behind him to hold his arm out to halt Carly—

"Roger that, holding here until you advise, over."

"He sees lights at our crash site. Just making sure we're clear to move past", Joey advised Carly, who had halted when she felt Joey's arm stop her in the dark.

"Ok. Sounds good"

The Lieutenant and Joey had been walking at the bottom of the dry creek bed and could not see the artificial light source. Both squatted down for a quick break, and Joey flipped up his goggles to rest his eyes.

"Lieutenant, I don't doubt that you can take care of yourself, and you know how to handle a pistol, but if things get bad, stay near Jim or me with these rifles. We can lay down a lot more direct fire with these."

"I already thought about that, Joey. I am sticking to you like glue."

A pause in the conversation allowed Carly to attempt to get to know one of the men she was undergoing this ordeal with—

"Do you have a family back home, wherever that is?"

"I do, wife, one kid...a little boy. He's seven. He loves to play ball, any kind of ball. If it's round, he wants to throw it or hit it", Joey said, laughing and reminiscing.

"As far as home, probably best we don't get too personal until we get across that river. I wouldn't want some Sicario showing up at my front door if we don't make it out of this. What about you, Lieutenant?"

"No family...I mean, no husband or kids. I have parents, of course. Home is Texas, and that's all I'm going to say for now. I love my Texas."

"Well, Lieutenant, by daylight Jim and I hope to help you see Texas again."

Joey could not see the smile he had put on Carly's face in the dark of the night.

"I think we're good. Let's keep moving", Jim whispered into his mic.

"Roger that," looking in the Lieutenants' direction in the dark—

"We're moving."

Both stood in the creek bed. Joey flipped his goggles down, looked around to ensure they had not left any gear, and began moving north. The three meandered in the creek bed for several miles in a northerly direction. Jim paused several more times throughout their trek to check their coordinates and ensure they were still headed in the correct direction.

Joey and the Lieutenant had activated their infrared beacons when they had begun their egress after dark. Jim, who was walking on point and more exposed, chose not to activate his beacon in case some sophisticated Sicarios had night vision optics. Unbeknownst to Lariat, a second drone had replaced the first drone, which had run low on fuel earlier that afternoon. The CIA drone operator had strict orders not to fire any weapons over Mexican soil. The President had backed off a little on his stance after receiving a scathing phone call from the Mexican Government wanting answers. The Mexican consulate in DC had sent the Ambassador to speak with the US Secretary of State. He demanded answers. The Ambassador scolded the Secretary of State for not consulting his government before sending aircraft and men inside his country to conduct a military-type operation. The Secretary of State corrected the Ambassador by telling him that Operation Hammerhead was not a military operation and that it was a law enforcement operation carried out to bring the heads of the Cartels to the US under federal warrants to stand trial for their illegal narcotics trades within the US.

The drone utilized its infrared sensors to track Lariat as they moved north. The CIA drone had been monitoring all activity between Lariat and the river. The drone pilot relayed to the Op-Cen that it had observed multiple technical vehicles and persons patrolling the hills on the South side of the river for several miles. The most disturbing intel was that numerous subjects were being dropped by vehicles on the US side of the river. Individuals were crossing the river, and some were staging on the US side in the hills above the river scattered over several miles. The cartels had called in all of their assets to attempt to capture Lariat and the pilot. The outpouring of Sicario activity from the US side of the border told the Op-Cen that this was more far-reaching and that if they could get Lariat across the river, the danger might not stop there. The several-mile stretch Lariat would choose a crossing was desolate on both sides of the border. There was not much cover and no roads for miles on either side.

Just after midnight, Lariat and the Lieutenant found themselves three hundred yards from the river. They were close enough now to see the tiny bit of light on the distant horizon from cities in Texas. Jim had halted Joey and the Lieutenant in the creek bed while reconnoitering ahead.

"Joey, do you copy" Jim whispered.

"Roger, I've got you"

"Gomers are close. I'm looking at two technicals spread out a couple hundred yards apart and maybe ten to fifteen gomers roaming around."

"Can we get across without them seeing us?"

"We can try. They're spread out but roving around."

"We gotta try, Jim"

"Ok, I'm coming back to you. It'll be after daylight if we double back to try and cross somewhere else."

Jim crawled back to Joey and Carlys' position and slithered down the embankment into the dry creek bed. Carly was removing the extra pistol magazines from her pack and placing them in the external pockets of her green flight suit for faster access. Jim and Joey both checked each other's gear. Joey pulled Jim close to him by the neck to where their helmets met in front of them—

"We got this, brother! Texas is right over that ridge. Move slow and smooth."

Jim only acknowledged by nodding, the first time Joey could remember the Mississippian not cracking a joke.

"Lieutenant, stay on me," Jim whispered to Carly as he motioned toward his rear end.

Joey led the three by crawling out of the creek bed and easing toward the crest of the ridge overlooking the Rio Grande River two hundred yards away. Joey and Carly were close behind, with Carly bringing up the rear with her Beretta pistol in hand. The three were on their bellies, crawling most of the way toward the cusp of the ridge. Joey froze mid-crawl as Jim reached up and grabbed his ankle. Jim had spotted a roving Sicario about fifty yards to the right moving in their direction. The only light that the Sicario could see was the dim light given off by the stars and the light from a city to the north on the Texas horizon. Jim could see that the Sicario was a twenties-aged Hispanic male carrying an AK-47 at the low ready. Looking down his sights, Joey tracked the Sicario with his suppressed M-4 rifle as he approached. All three watched as the Sicario walked toward them. Thirty, twenty, then ten yards in front of them and passed to their left. Murphy finally had his way with the operation as the Sicario passed, and one of the extra magazines Carly had placed in her chest pocket fell to the ground, sounding like a ton of bricks in the still of the night. The Sicario wheeled around and was bringing his AK-47 up to the ready when Joey fired two rounds from his rifle, dropping the Sicario. The three had been so intent on the one Sicario that they had not noticed a second Sicario approaching from further back from their right. The second Sicario had heard the muffled sound of the two rounds from Joey's suppressed rifle and began to yell—

"ELLAS ESTAN AQUI" At the same time advancing quickly and raising a pistol and firing in the direction he heard the suppressed gunshots.

Now only fifty yards from the crest of the ridge overlooking the river, the single Sicario approached the three at a trot. Carly being in the rear, out of pure reaction, spun and fired three rounds from her Beretta pistol sending the Sicario face-first into the desert floor. All three, knowing business was about to pick up, leapt from the prone position as they could hear distant hollering in Spanish and vehicles cranking up.

The CIA drone was feeding back images and information to the Op Center. The intel had been so concerning that the IC1 called the Administrator of the United States Border Patrol. IC1 explained the situation to the Administrator, only divulging enough information for them to understand the necessity for help. The Administrator responded—

"What do you need, and when do you need it?"

The phone at the duty desk for the United States Border Patrol Tactical Unit headquartered in El Paso, Texas, rang several times before someone answered. This specialized unit is commonly referred to as BORTAC and has quick reaction capabilities within the United States and other countries. The duty Agent ran to the fitness gym housed inside the same building and found the Special Agent in charge of BORTAC. The BORTAC unit prized itself on staying fit. They had to be! Chasing narcos and coyotes leading illegals into the United States along the Southern border required a certain fitness level. The heat and expanse of the border area were unforgiving, and the BORTAC unit understood this concept. Special Agent Bryan Thornhill had been on the bench press when the Duty Agent located him.

"Thornhill, I'm sorry to disturb your workout, sir, but we have a situation"

"What kind of situation?" Thornhill asked as he stood up from the bench, sweat dripping down his face.

The duty Agent explained, and Thornhill ran to the phone and contacted the Op-Cen. Thornhill quickly alerted the other eleven men on his BORTAC team and gave them one hour to prepare their gear and meet at the helipad.

It was now well after zero dark thirty as the helicopter lifted off and made its way to the southern border. The inbound Border Patrol Blackhawk was given the coordinates of the suspected river crossing of Lariat based on their Northerly movement provided by the intel gathered from the drone's multiple cameras and sensors. Thornhill and the Blackhawk pilots had been briefed in the preflight about the possibility of Sicarios being on the US side of the river and possibly armed with RPGs. The pilots elected to land the BORTAC team a good distance away from the Rio Grande River. The last thing the operation needed was another downed helicopter full of Agents. The Blackhawk, lights out, landed a mile and a half North of the Rio Grande and due North of where they believed Lariat would cross. The BORTAC team offloaded from the helicopter and quickly moved South toward the river. A half mile from the river, the BORTAC team froze in their tracks as they heard the distant gunfire. Each member of the BORTAC team looked at each other in silence, knowing what was happening up ahead. The BORTAC team began to sprint in full kit toward the gunfire.

Jim, Joey, and the Lieutenant jumped up and ran toward the river. They made it twenty-five yards from the bluff's edge when a technical sped over the lip of a distant ridge, approaching fast. Looking around in their goggles, Jim and Joey could see multiple subjects coming on foot from different angles and firing blindly in their direction. Joey stopped running and made a split decision—

"JIM! Get to the river and get the lieutenant across!"

"No way! I'm not leaving you up here by yourself." Jim replied as a projectile zipped past all three making a whizzing sound as it passed close by.

"We aren't all going to make it if I don't stall em'...I'm right behind you...GO" Joey yelled as he flipped up his goggles, turned to face the enemy, and went to one knee.

Joey pulled his M-4 up to his shoulder and began delivering effective fire on the approaching Sicarios. Jim and Carly ran to the edge of the cliff. Jim glanced back at Joey and saw him firing his rifle into the darkness at fast-approaching Sicarios. Another bullet zipped past their heads, and other projectiles were kicking up dust as they hit the ground between them and Joey. They both jumped to the steep embankment leading to the river on their rear ends and began the twenty-yard slide downhill to the river bank. Jim and Carly entered the river at a full sprint splashing water in tall spurts. Jim flipped up his goggles to have better depth perception in the water as they traversed the almost three-foot-deep current.

"We've gotta hurry. Let's go! Let's go! I'm gettin' you across and going back for Joey", screaming at each other as they crossed to overcome the noise of the water and the gunfire on top of the ridge—

"No way, I'm going back to!"

"No, ma'am, he's my partner...you cover us from the other side!"

Just as Jim and Carly reached the middle of the river, muzzle flashes began going off from the US side of the river, and projectiles began splashing in the water and zipping all around them. Jim planted his feet firmly in the muddy bottom of the River to brace himself against the current, raised his rifle, and began returning fire.

On top of the ridge, Joey fired at muzzle flashes as the Sicarios closed in on his position from all directions. Satisfied that he had temporarily stopped the Sicarios approaching on foot, Joey promptly turned his attention to the fast approaching technical with a Sicario over the cab firing a large caliber weapon. Joey heard the bolt lock back on his rifle for the third time. He pulled a fresh magazine from its pouch on his chest and seated it firmly into the mag well in front of his face to not take his focus from his work. Joey pulled the rifle down level with the approaching truck and emptied an entire thirty-round magazine into the cab. The truck rolled to an abrupt stop, obviously killing the driver and wounding the shooter on top of the cab. The truck held four more Sicarios seated in the rear of the truck, itching for battle. As the truck slowed to a stop, the four Sicarios in the truck's bed jumped to the ground. Joey had been focused on the truck and did not see a Sicario sneaking up on his left near the bluff's edge. The Sicario fired multiple rounds from his AK-47. Joey felt the first round penetrate his left side low, just above his belt line. The second round hit Joey on his posted left leg between his knee and waist, shattering his femur. Joey knew he had to protect Jim and the Lieutenant long enough for them to cross the river. The first realization that he might not make it out of this fight came across Joey's mind. His body was running on pure adrenaline, and he continued to fight!

Carly heard the sound of an AK-47 on top of the ridge and saw the Sicario firing in Joey's direction. Carly pulled her Beretta up and fired five rounds striking the Sicario and watching him disappear below the crest.

"MOVE LT, we're sitting ducks," Jim yelled.

Jim had been addressing the fire to their front and had not seen nor heard the firefight on the ridge they had just left. The infrared beacons that Jim and Carly wore were still activated and strobing for anyone wearing night vision to see.

Out of breath but driven by adrenaline, Thornhill and his team topped the ridge on the US side of the Rio Grande river and peered down into the heavily brushed draws leading the river bank. The BORTAC team could see the strobed blinking in the river through their night vision optics and hear and see the muzzle flashes in the draws to their front and across the river on the ridgeline. Thornhill hoped they would not get into a friendly fire situation, but they had no other option but to engage the Sicarios in the draws in front of them with hopes that Lariat would realize that friendlies had arrived. Thornhill and his men knew better than to enter the draw but chose to engage from the top of the ridge. Thornhill commanded to engage the fire directed from the draw and watch out for the strobes. The first BORTAC team member to engage the enemy fired his M-4 rifle with impunity into the draw at a set of muzzle flashes. The Sicarios on the US side of the River realized they were being fired upon from their rear and directed their fire at the BORTAC team. The lull in the gunfire directed at Jim and the Lieutenant made them realize that help had possibly arrived.

Jim and Carly had almost crossed the river when a Sicario emerged to their front at the river's edge. Carly saw the Sicario at the same time the Sicario saw them, and she lifted the Beretta and emptied the final rounds from the pistol's magazine. The Sicario melted into the foliage at the bank. Carly stripped the spent magazine from the grip of the Beretta, pulled out a new magazine from the top left zipper pocket of her flight suit, and slammed it into the grip of the pistol. As Jim and Carly stepped foot on US soil, they heard the loud English-speaking voice of Thornhill yelling—

"BLUE, BLUE, BLUE"

Sicarios had now made their way past Joey and onto the dirt and sand shore of the Mexican side of the river from both East and West. Jim quickly passed off the Lieutenant to Thornhill and the BORTAC team and turned and splashed back across the river to help his now-wounded partner.

"Where the hell's he going," Thornhill asked the Lieutenant.

Carly is out of breath and now feeling the after-effects of the adrenaline dump and pointing toward the opposite ridgeline—

"It's Joey...he is going to help his partner. He stayed behind to hold them off."

The BORTAC team had been under strict orders not to engage anyone on the Mexican side of the river, much less cross the river into Mexico. Thornhill toiled with the orders given to him by his superiors for only a split second—

"Carver, take four and go get our men!"

Carver and four others could still hear gunfire from the top of the ridge as they splashed across the river. They briefly paused to engage Sicarios that fired on them and Jim from the opposite bank. Jim was ahead of the BORTAC team by forty yards when he began scaling the steep embankment. Jim clawed at the embankment, trying to get to the top, his M-4 dangling off his back. Jim had lifted his NVGs from his face when he began to climb back up the embankment but noticed that he could faintly see in the dark that was lit up by a small fire nearby once he had topped the embankment. Jim made it over the ridge and saw Joey lying on his left side, struggling to rack a fresh round into his Sig Sauer pistol on the back heel of his boot. Joey's left leg, shattered from the AK round, lay limp under his left side. Jim saw movement past Joey. A single running figure approached and yelled into a handheld radio in Spanish. The Sicario was about seventy-five yards when Jim shouldered and fired his rifle. The high-velocity five-five-six projectiles zipped through the darkness of the Mexican landscape, striking the Sicario in the lower chest, collapsing his lungs, exiting out of the right lumbar region, and spattering blood across the short grass blades and dirt. The Sicario disappeared in the brush. As Jim rushed the few short yards to Joey, he could see the carnage from the battle that had taken place on the ridge. A truck crashed a short distance away with a small fire underneath the chassis. Sicario bodies lay all around, scattered in low brush that covered the hillside, one as close as ten feet. Jim could see bodies that looked like scattered mounds of earth in the faint light. The smell of burnt cordite and smoke from the brush that was on fire, and the oil leaking from the damaged truck hung in the air. Joey had expended hundreds of rounds of ammunition, and it was evident! Jim's mind was trying to process quickly, and he could see spent brass and magazines all around Joey's position.

"Joey, it's me..it's me, brother!" Jim exclaimed, out of breath, as he dropped his M-4 next to Joey and attempted to help his friend.

The smell of burnt cordite quickly changed to include the smell of iron. Jim realized Joey had lost a lot of blood. Adrenaline had been the only thing keeping Joey alive. When Joey saw that it was Jim who had come back for him, he dropped the Sig pistol and reached for Jim, pulling him close. Blood was trickling down the side of Joey's mouth as Jim tried to assess his wounds. The five members of the BORTAC team topped the hill at the river's edge behind Jim and Joey and could not believe their eyes. The team ran to Jim and Joey and quickly set up a security perimeter as Carver attempted to help Jim patch up Joey's wounds—

"Sir, we have to move. We have to move fast", as he tried to help Jim place a tourniquet on Joey's left leg. Jim knew the wound looked fatal. Joey had lost too much blood. Jim looked at Joey as his life faded —

"I'm sorry, brother, I shouldn't have left you!"

Joey could only slowly shake his head from side to side, not wanting Jim to think that his death had been his fault. Joey knew what he had done when he chose to stay on the ridge alone. One of the

BORTAC members on the perimeter security yelled —

"I have a technical speeding our direction! We need to MOVE!"

Jim had been holding Joey's hand and felt Joey's grip go limp.

CHAPTER 6

Conspiracy

The night drew on in the hangar at Ft Bliss. At the same time that Nick was interviewing the operators and detainees, the two phones that had been acquired from the bedroom of Senior Guirillo during the operation were in the process of being forensically analyzed by a man and woman that had shown up in the hangar with some computer type equipment at the behest of Don Powers. The forensic analysis of the cell phones took two hours to compile and break down. The analysts immediately began combing through the data derived from the Grey Key and Cellbrite programs. A portion of the data was transferred to ZETX, which compiled the GPS data from the phone and allowed for an easier translation on a map. The mapping from ZETX showed that the phone had been at several other locations known to the CIA and DEA as Golfo Norte Cartel buildings and structures and ultimately tracked the phone past Juanit's store and into the canyon where DEA SRT later seized it. The tracking information was not the concern. The two analysts from the CIA, one of which was a fluent Spanish Speaker, began word-searching the text messages on Guirrillo's phone.

What she found was important enough to call Don Powers out of a midnight meeting with Bradshaw and Dan. The female analyst ran down the hall to locate Don.

"Sir, I need you to come with me to look at something we found"

"Alright," Don said as he stepped out into the hall, closing the office door behind him and leaving Bradshaw and Dan to mull over the situation.

Don walked the short distance to the office where both analysts had set up to work on the phones. A guard had been posted outside the office along with a small desk and a Faraday bag rested on top. Don stopped by the guard, took his phone out of his jacket pocket, and placed it inside the Faraday bag along with the phones that belonged to the analysts.

"Do not answer that if it rings!" Don told the guard jokingly as he rolled the top down on the bag.

Once inside the secure office, the female analyst handed Don a printout from the Grey Key program that had an exchange of text messages in Spanish. Before Don's CIA employment, he had served his country as a 7th Special Forces Group member. After selection, Don received advanced language training in Spanish and completed several iterations of live environment training in South America. Don read the several pages of printout, handed them back to the analyst, and rushed back out of the door. Almost forgetting his phone, Don turned and snatched the Faraday bag, unsealed the roll-down velcro enclosure, sifted through the contents, and plucked his phone out. Don jogged down the hall, made a left at the intersecting hallway, and slowed to re-enter the office where Bradshaw and Dan were interviewing and debriefing members of the DEA SRT team.

"We need to place a call to the White House situation room immediately!" Don exclaimed to Dan as he entered and pulled the door shut around him.

"Ok, Why?"

"I can't say here. We need a secure room and phone", hastily walking to the door.

Don located an MP and advised him that he needed a secure room and phone line if the base had one. After several minutes, the MP radioed his superior, who commanded the MP to bring the three men to the Major General's Office on the other side of the base from where they were currently located. Dan and Mayfield stayed behind at the hangar to finish the debriefing of the DEA SRT team.

It was now well after 02:00 as the MPs ushered Bradshaw and Don across the base to the Major General's office, who had also been awakened and summoned to his own office by this time—

"What's this about gentlemen?" The Major General asked as he walked past the three men waiting outside his office in the hallway.

The Major General had hastily thrown on his class B uniform consisting of fatigues and his cover in hand. Entering the office behind the Major General, Don pleaded—

"Sir, we apologize for the inconvenience, not only for this instant but for any inconveniences we might have caused on your base."

The Major General, now standing behind his desk, motioned for the men to sit in the chairs spread out in front of it.

"We believe we might have a matter of national security on our hands, and we need to use your secure line to call Washington."

Laughing, the Major General asked—

"You want me to place a call on my secure line to Washington…at 02:00 in the morning? Have you lost…," Don cut off the Major General—

"No, no sir, I'll place the call. I just need your secure line. I have the number and a code."

The Major General, looking perturbed, picked up the phone from his desk with the secure line and handed it to Don, who placed the phone back down on the desk facing him and Nick. The Major General, who possessed the same clearance level as the others in the office, leaned back into his oversized leather office chair and placed both hands on his head, waiting to see how this call to the 'boss' played out. The phone rang, and the individual at the Whitehouse switchboard picked up. Don exchanged several codes and numbers and was placed on hold. The Major General now smirks like a father watching his kids about to get in trouble. Don had placed the handset back on the phone and pushed the speaker button so everyone could hear.

"Sir, hold for the situation room." came the reply from the silence on the phone.

"Yes, Ma'am."

The Secretary of Defense had been in his office at the White House working late after the day's events had unfolded. The Secretary of Defense and the President were summoned to the situation room. Bradshaw and Don sat patiently waiting as if they were waiting to hear their punishment from the school principal.

"Alright, go for the situation room. You have the SecDef and the President on the line.", the official at the Whitehouse advised.

"Yes sir, this is Agent Don Powers with the CIA..." at the same time, Bradshaw snapped his head over to Don and whispered—

"You said you were DOD!" Don shrugged and mouthed, "Sorry."

Don continued in the background—

"...sir, I know you've been kept abreast of the situation down here on the border."

"This is the President, yes, yes we've been kept in the loop, and we're doing everything we can to get your men over the border...," Don cut the President off mid-sentence—

"Yes sir, and we do appreciate that fact, but that's not the reason for this call. During the operation, one of the operators seized two phones from the bedroom where they located Guirrillo, and I had two analysts flown here to dump the phones. What they found on one of the phones is pretty concerning, sir...."

"Son, we've already been briefed on the drone killing weapon they brought back...."

"No sir, It's more than that. There were messages, sir, messages between the Cartel and members of the Chinese Government about not only the drone weapon, sir but...the acquisition of suitcase-sized dirty bombs." A few seconds of silence was followed by—

"Oh my god, are you certain it was the Chinese and,...and how do you know they are talking about a nuclear...", the Secretary of Defense was interrupted—

"No sir, not Nuclear, both the drone-type weapon and the suitcase bombs are EMP in nature!" Bradshaw blurted out, not being able to contain himself.

"Who was that?" the President asked.

Don looked at Bradshaw to reply—

"Bradshaw, sir, Nick Bradshaw FBI."

The silence on the other end of the situation room lasted a few seconds—

"Agent Bradshaw, what're you trying to tell us?" the President asked, obviously closer to the microphone now by the volume of his voice.

"Sir, if the suitcase bombs that are referred to in these messages are similar to the other weapon, we have a pretty big problem on our hands. The handheld weapon that was brought back is a big enough problem. It houses its semiconductor to produce multiple directed EMP beams at an object. If the suitcase EMP is something of the same,... if it were not located, it could continue to emit pulses after things were brought back online after the first outage."

"Ultimately keeping us in the stone age? Is that what you are getting at Bradshaw?" The President asked.

"Yes sir, something like that." He looked over at Don as his voice faded.

The Major General now leans forward, listening intently and realizing the importance of this phone call.

"Sir, I believe you've been advised that one of the Asian males detained by the DEA is not only Chinese Intelligence but the son of the Chinese Defense Minister?" Don asked.

The Secretary of Defense said,

"Yes, we were still digesting that information before this call...standby one, we have another call."

The call was placed on hold by the officer in the situation room. The Major General did not say anything, but the look on his face had changed from when the gentlemen had originally entered the room. Don looked at Bradshaw as he had one elbow on the desk with his chin on his fist—

"Well, this changes things."

After several minutes the line was live again with the voice of the Secretary of Defence—

"Well…I'm at a loss for words. We just received a call notifying us that the three US personnel left behind in Mexico are now across the Rio Grande River. They also informed us that one of the three is KIA."

"Oh, my God! Who was killed, sir? What happened?"

"I'm not sure, son. We're still getting information."

"This is the President! Bradshaw, are you still with us?"

"Yes sir. I'm here"

"I want you and Don to locate the other weapons or at least find out if more weapons exist. Go to Mexico if you have to. We can't sit by on this type of information and not do something about it. The lives lost in this operation were one too many! If these Cartels have more of these weapons and they have conspired with a foreign government to undermine this great country, then I want you to get to the bottom of it!"

"Yes, sir. Excuse me, sir? Under what authority am I acting, FBI, CIA…I just…" Nick questioned.

"You are acting under the direct authority of the President of the United States and any actions taken shall be justified under my authority to protect the people of this country. From here on out, you both answer to the Secretary of Defense. I'll speak with the Attorney General and make sure you're squared away, Bradshaw."

"Yes, sir."

"Agent Powers, I hope you'll be conveying a plan of action to your superiors to track this down?"

"Yes, sir. I was just thinking about several options from here, sir. We will take Guirillo and the two others to the Bureau office here in El Paso. We might have a little more luck questioning them there."

"Ok. Do what you need to do. You boys, be careful out there."

"Yes, sir."

The phone line went dead and awkward silence lay in the room. Everyone was still stunned by the news of a deceased operator or pilot, and now they had been officially given the football. Bradshaw and Don thanked the Major General for using his office and offered their condolences for having to hear classified information that could now not be unheard.

Bradshaw and Don were promptly escorted across the base to the hangar, where Dan and Mayfield were still debriefing team members. Besides basic tactical information, the operators could not provide any information about the weapons system they had brought back with them. More than one operator told them in their debrief that the two operators that might have told them more had been left behind in Mexico. Jim and Joey had observed and taken photos of the weapon and its delivery and could provide far more than the assault team.

CHAPTER 7

The Weapon

It was late the following morning when the convoy left the base at Ft Bliss. The convoy consisted of four FBI SUVs. The day's weather called for sunshine and mild heat, with a high of 83 degrees. Nick and Dan were onboard the SUV second from the front of the caravan, along with Chen, a driver, and a front passenger that was an FBI agent. Don had offered to ride in the third SUV in the caravan along with Guirillo and the same agent makeup as their unit. The fourth and last SUV in the mix had Chen's guard and two agents onboard. Nick and Don decided to take the three detainees to the FBI field office in El Paso, where there were multiple interview rooms with audio and video recording capabilities and not to mention more agency-friendly amenities. The Caravan sped out of the front gate of Ft Bliss. The caravan took Liberty Expressway, then Interstate 10 West, to get to the field office as fast as possible.

Nick was seated in the back passenger seat closest to the window, Chen was placed in the middle seat with Don sitting on the other side by the driver-side window. The SUVs sped through the morning traffic. Nick had been a part of multiple close protection details as an agent and as an SRT operator with his local agency before joining the Bureau. The phrase " never let your guard down " constantly ran through Nick's mind in this scenario. *Keep your head on a swivel.* Nick thought to himself as he looked out of the side window and then looked out of the front window past the driver. He was looking for threats. As the caravan approached the 18B exit on Interstate 10, Nick noticed cars begin to slow in the traffic all around the SUV. The FBI driver of Nick's SUV began to cuss—

"What the hell's wrong with this thing? Fucking government vehicles! I'm pushing the pedal. Nothing's happening."

Santiago Morales had grown up in south-central Mexico to a single mother who had provided the best she could for her only child. She worked three jobs to pay the rent and provide the measly amount of food placed on the table each day. It was inevitable that Santiago fell for the smooth-talking recruiters of the Cartel at the early age of fifteen. At first, Santiago's mother opposed the life that Santiago had grown to depend on until he had been promoted within the cartel and was bringing home more money in a week than she could provide in a month. Ultimately the cartel won out by giving them the lifestyle they had wanted for all their lives. Santiago was now thirty-two years old and had advanced his way through the ranks of the cartel and proved himself to be one of the Golfo Norte Cartels most trusted by his compadres and feared by their enemies. Santiago was now Guirillos, top Lieutenant. Santiago had been conducting a business deal on the Eastern Mexican coast when the operators had assaulted the ranch and taken his boss. When he heard of his boss's kidnapping, he set measures in motion to get him back. Santiago began by calling the Mexican Secretary of State and demanded that the American helicopters be intercepted and stopped by the Mexican military. Santiago had been the radical voice in Guirillo's ear, planting the idea that the cartels needed to join alliances against the United States and any type of incursion by the United States into Mexico. This came in the form of dealings with the Chinese Government, which the cartels would side with in providing any means to undermine the United States. The cartels had been acquiring ingredients for their illegal narcotics from the Chinese for years. Now, Santiago had personally met with the Chinese on behalf of the Golfo Norte Cartel to purchase weapons. Unconventional weapons. Santiago had orchestrated the arms deal in China by delivering half of the money in US currency, with a promised delivery date of the weapons. The delivery date had been bad luck on the side of Guirillo and the Chinese when it had been planned to meet and exchange the other half of the money and the delivery of the weapons at Guirillos remote weekend home in the mountains North of

Lamadrid.

The black Land Rover crunched the tiny bit of loose gravel as it drove up the slight incline dodging several large potholes on C Orquideas road. The Land Rover pulled over to the side of the road in a span of open ground between the homes in the neighborhood. Santiago Morales rolled the passenger side window down to check the view. This would do! He could see over the wire fence separating the US from Mexico and beyond US Highways 375 and 85. From this vantage point, Santiago could see down into the deep concrete embankments of US Interstate 10 for a two-hundred-yard stretch as both lanes traversed under the overpass of Porfirio Diaz Street. This particular Land Rover and two others in the Golfo Norte Cartel had been retro-fitted with nickel and copper inlay fabric. The cab, main compartment, and every component under the hood had been encased and surrounded for protection. Each of the three Land Rovers was essentially made into mobile Faraday cages. Santiago opened the front passenger side door and stood up in the doorframe so that he could get a few more feet of height to watch the events he had set in motion play out. He pulled the binoculars close into his eyes to see the full breadth of view within the glass. The Americans had been dumb enough not to put Chen's phone in airplane mode when it was seized at the ranch, and Santiago had been able to track the phone to Ft Bliss, he thought!

Santiago had sent two carloads of his best Sicarios to watch the base and shadow any vehicles that left. The Sicarios saw the SUVs leave the base and were unsure if the boss was on board, but someone important was, or the Americans would not have been traveling in multiple vehicles. The Sicarios now followed the Government SUVs and blended in around them with the traffic.

Two truckloads of six Sicarios each had been following Santiago around the streets of Ciudad Juarez near the border. Juan radioed that the government SUVs were leaving Ft Bliss. The two trucks sped to the border fence on the Mexico side of the wall and offloaded. One of the Sicarios jumped from the back bed of the truck, bolt cutters in hand, a Beretta pistol stuffed in the back of his pants. He ran the short distance to the fence, followed by the other eleven Sicarios. The chain link fence was cut like butter under the crimping of the jaws of the bolt cutter. He cut 30 links in under one minute, pulled the fence apart, and crawled through. The eleven other heavily armed men followed.

Santiago jumped down from his perch in the crease of the door and walked to the back of the Land Rover, opened the back hatch, and pulled the large, black Pelican case from its resting spot. Santiago walked to the front of the vehicle, swung the Pelican case onto the hood, unbuckled the four safety latches, and opened the box. Cursing in Spanish and placing the words Estados Unidos within the phrases, Santiago began flipping switches and bringing the Pelican case to life. Santiago's driver opened the driver-side door and quickly closed it behind himself, remembering that the weapon could disable their truck if he left an opening inside the vehicle. In Spanish, the driver—

"Hey, boss? Juan radioed that they're getting close."

Santiago was focused. Listening, but focused. He had heard his driver and acknowledged by glancing at him and then flicking the red switch inside the Pelican case to *Arm*. The *Arm* switch had the word written below in Chinese. Luckily, the switch was shown to Santiago during Santiago's visit to China to negotiate the original arms deal. Every switch and knob within the Pelican case had been shown to Santiago and translated to what it did in his language.

Everyone in the FBI SUV was silent except for the driver. Nick frantically began to look around and out of each window in the vehicle. Craning his neck, knowing something was not right, he noticed the large computer display in the center console of the SUV had gone dark. The driver saw that the other cars in lanes around him were coming to abrupt stops, some crashing into one another—

"Call this in on the radio. I'm not sure what's going on. Tell 'em we're almost under the crossover at Porfirio Diaz Street!" The driver firmly stated, asking someone in the SUV to use a radio to call in their position and send help.

"Radios not working. The phone isn't working either!" the agent in the front passenger seat advised.

Almost in slow motion, the totality of the situation added up to Nick. He looked to his left arm, where his smartwatch was strapped to his wrist, and noticed it was not working. Nick knew —

"EMP! It's an EMP! Stay in the vehicles." Nick was looking behind them to ensure none of the other people had gotten out of the other SUVs.

Some civilians had gotten out of their cars and were milling around the interstate, and some were inspecting damage from lite wrecks. Cars were honking, and the distant sounds of cars crashing into one another could be heard as the domino effect of the stalling cars filtered east and west from the EMP blast.

The first projectile penetrated the lead SUV's driver-side window, barely missing the FBI driver. A loud crack-boom was heard—

"Was that a gunshot?" Nick said as he expressed concern.

Chen, who had been sitting in his seat, silent, without much of a demeanor, perked up and began looking out of the windows. Nick had a bad feeling in his gut. Knowing deep down what was coming for them. Nick noticed two dark SUVs moving in their direction through the stalled vehicles. Dodging people were now outside of their cars, meandering in and out. A terrible feeling came over Nick.

Don Powers, guarding Guirillo in the other SUV, reached under his untucked dress shirt and felt for the grip of his Glock 19 pistol. He kept his hand on the hilt for only a second before realizing the situation required him to draw the Glock from his waistband. Greg, who had been seated on the rear passenger seat along with Guirillo and Don, holding his M-4 at the low ready, tightened his grip and placed his thumb on the safety selector switch as he craned his neck and looked out of his side door window.

Juan and the Sicarios, who had been slated for the mission to shadow the Americans and to get their boss back, sat at the ready in the retro-fitted Land Rovers. Santiago and his men had essentially turned their vehicles into mobile Faraday cages. Juan was driving in the far left lane of I-10. He was keeping the caravan of American government SUVs barely in sight. Juan did not want to be the one that compromised the mission to get the boss back. Juan radioed Santiago's driver and the other Sicarios that had been staged that the caravan was approaching the target area. Juan and the other Sicarios tasked with the mission knew once Santiago set off the EMP, it would disable their handheld radios. They had quickly planned to attack the Americans, recover their boss, and return through the hole in the border fence before the Americans could react.

The first projectile that penetrated Nick's SUV missed its target and was followed closely by several more rounds from the overpass one hundred yards ahead of where the caravan had stopped. Don looked over his left shoulder through the back glass of the SUV and saw one of the black Land Rovers approaching.

"GREG! We got a vehicle approaching fast to our rear!"
The black Land Rover was weaving around stalled and wrecked vehicles and coming at a fast rate of speed.

"We staying or getting out? What are we doing?" Greg responded as he turned to put eyes on the approaching threat.

"We're sitting ducks in these dead vehicles! We need to move and find cover!"

"Roger that!" came the agreeing reply from Greg. The driver and front passenger operator under Greg's command nodded in agreement. Guirillo, who had been sitting quietly, now began to process the brevity of the situation. Guirillo knew what was happening was probably a rescue mission to get him back, but he also knew that one wrong move and he might end up killed or wounded in the firefight that appeared to be imminent. More rounds began striking the SUVs.

Civilians milling around trying to figure out what was going on now found themselves screaming and running for cover in all directions. The steep concrete embankments of the Interstate created a fatal funnel with the only possible directions to run away to the East and West. The chaotic situation played havoc on the approaching Land Rovers attempting to get as close as possible to the government caravan before offloading and taking their boss back.

Both passenger side doors of Don's SUV flung open. Don bailed out, Glock in hand, ducking down and reaching back into the SUV with his outstretched left hand to pull Guirillo out with him. The FBI SUV convoy had been traveling in the far right lane of the four-lane interstate. The operator, seated in the front passenger seat, was now out and reaching back in to help the Special Agent climb over the center console to exit the passenger side, away from direct fire from the overpass. The Special Agent had just reached the passenger side when a round entered through the front windshield and struck the Special Agent under his left armpit. Falling limp out onto the operator trying to help him get out. Don dragged Guirillo out of the vehicle onto the ground—

"Fuck, we're in a funnel!" Greg exclaimed, looking around and seeing the steep sides of the concrete embankments on each side of the Interstate.

The operator dropped his M-4 rifle, which fell

and hung by the tether attached to his kit, and attempted to render aid to the lifeless FBI Agent—

"Drivers dead, we gotta move,...find cover!" as he looked around for any semblance of a bastion.

The lead Land Rover screeched to a halt three car lengths away from the back driver-side quarter-panel of the government SUV. Three doors to the Land Rover opened quickly, and Juan and two of his Sicarios jumped out. The first Sicario jolted to the right behind a four-door Camry and knelt behind the bumper. He looked down at his AK-47, reached with his right thumb, and depressed the safety selector switch down to the middle notch signifying full auto. The Sicario did not carry any extra magazines. He had taped a second thirty-round magazine upside down to the one already seated into the receiver of the AK-47 rifle and hoped that would be enough.

The second Sicario and Juan ran to a Ford Explorer that had stalled in the lane next to the government SUV. Juan slowly walked, hunched over, down the driver's side of the Explorer while gripping his Beretta 92 with both hands. Juan held the pistol as he had been taught during his short stint in the Mexican Army. Thumb over thumb gripping the pistol grip with both hands wrapped around it. Thinking of the imminent gunfight, Juan reached behind his back to the pocket of his blue jeans with his left hand and felt for his two spare seventeen-round magazines. They were there! The second Sicario had followed

Juan, crouching and slow walking, AK-47 at the ready. Juan looked to the overpass bridge already spewing bullets, knowing that one of the Sicarios posted on the bridge had snuck an RPG launcher through the hole in the border fence that had been hastily cut just before Santiago had punched the button. The RPG launcher and its rockets had been wrapped in Faraday cloth to camouflage its smuggling through the fence and to counter the EMP blast. Juan hoped that his Sicario with the RPG was not trigger-happy and did not release the rocket at the wrong target or time.

Santiago and Juan had gone over the intricate plan with each Sicario. Until they knew if Guirillo was in the SUVs, and then once they knew, to place careful shots at the American employees guarding their boss. They did not want to chance killing or wounding the boss. The Sicario behind the Camry could hear commotion around the closest SUV and leaned out and looked around the back passenger side quarter panel to see. He caught a quick glimpse of Guirillo as Don dragged him out to the ground and attempted to reconnoiter. The Sicario shifted his weight to the other leg and still squatted and jumped into the lane where Juan and the other Sicario could see him. In a half screaming and whispered—

"El patron, el patron," the boss, the boss, as he pointed at the SUV through the Camry.

Juan heard the commotion behind him and looked back to see the Sicario pointing at the SUV just on the other side of the Ford Explorer he had crouched behind for cover. Juan peeked over the hood from the abandoned driver's side of the Explorer and could see the operator, still wearing his multi-cams, through the driver's side, moving around on the front passenger side.

Don had placed Guirillo on the ground, sitting on his rear end next to the rear passenger side tire and rim for cover. Greg was now out of the SUV and squatting near the rear of the SUV, motioning with his hands, trying to get the attention of the other Agents in the two SUVs that had stalled behind them. Don looked around and saw that the only way out of this concrete funnel was to backtrack east on the Interstate about one hundred yards to the off-ramp for Porfirio Diaz Street.

"Greg, we need to get to the off-ramp! It's our only point of egress."

"Roger that, let's grab this bag of shit and go!" referring to Guirillo.

Greg had finally been able to get the attention of the Agents from the other two SUVs that had stalled behind them and used the knife hand motion for them to move toward the off-ramp.

The second Land Rover had stopped just short of the last FBI SUV, twenty yards to its rear. Four Sicarios jumped out of the Land Rover and took cover behind two stalled vehicles. Santiago's plan to fire the EMP and stall the American convoy in this spot, where it was virtually a concrete bathtub, had worked perfectly!

The Special Agents and Operators were now facing 19 Sicarios with heavy weapons on the open Interstate. The Agents in the rearmost FBI SUV immediately found themselves in a firefight as the Sicarios from the second Land Rover opened fire on them. The Agents had been attempting to get out of their SUVs on the passenger side along with Chen's bodyguard when rounds fired by the Sicarios struck the Agent holding the back of Chen's bodyguard's collar as he led him away from the caravan. The 7.62 caliber bullet from one of the Sicarios' Ak-47s struck the Agent two inches to the right of his spine, traveling through his trapezius into his chest cavity, clipping his heart, exiting the ribcage, and striking Chen's bodyguard in almost the same spot. Both men fell to the ground. Neither moving, one of the other Agents stopped and knelt to give life-saving measures as another Agent, standing guard above them, pulled the trigger on his Glock pistol firing four rounds toward the Sicario that had fired the successive shots in their direction. *The situation had officially turned to shit.* Don thought as he observed the situation playing out in front of him.

The traffic on I-10 and the highways and roads surrounding and overlapping it had reached a standstill. The electromagnetic pulse had gone almost one mile in all directions, including on the Mexican side of the border in Ciudad Juarez. The El Paso police department and Texas Highway Patrol were getting hundreds of calls for service for some sort of anomaly on the south side of El Paso. They were now hearing the sounds of the gun battle raging on the same stretch of Interstate being called in. Outside of the affected area, police, fire, and ems radios were abuzz. The traffic had been so congested when the EMP attack occurred that no first responders could get to where the gun battle was taking place. The radio rooms at DEA and FBI El Paso, housed in the same building but on different floors, began chattering. The Duty Agent for each respective agency called their SACs. Knowing this was the route the inbound Special Agents for each branch had taken to bring the detainees was alarming to them. The phone rang in the DEA radio room—

"Hello? Yes sir! No sir, I tried them on the radio, and I tried the agents' cell phones that were with the convoy, no joy sir! Yes sir, I will call them now sir" the duty agent hung up with his SAC and began calling every number he had for the Agents assigned to the SRT team from their office. The problem was the majority of the SRT operators in the El Paso Field office had been assigned to the operation in Mexico. This part of the country was El Paso's AO, or Area of Operation, not to mention the majority of the Agents belonging to SRT were of Spanish descent or Spanish speaking. Their operators were still at Ft Bliss, and the only good news was that the DEA operators were already assembled and somewhat geared up and ready for a gunfight.

Jim had been reunited with his team. His debrief had taken longer than the other team members. The loss of his friend and partner had taken an immense toll on him. His teammates had given him some breathing room and did not want to crowd him about his experience and what happened to Joey. Jim and the other operators had been brought to an area of the hangar where their personal gear had been brought and placed. Cell phones, paddle holsters, blue jeans, and polo-style shirts. The daily attire of a DEA Agent.

"Hello?" Jim said awkwardly, looking at the receiving phone number and recognizing it was the office.

"Jim, this is Mark! I'm the duty agent. Have you or any of the other guys heard from the convoy bringing the detainees to the office?"

"No, why?"

"We aren't sure what's going on, but there's a lot of local chatter that something has happened on I-10 and several reports of some sort of gun battle."

"Holy shit! Ok, we're headed that way!" Jim said as he stood up and began snapping his fingers to get the attention of the rest of the team, who had been milling around stowing gear and changing.

Jim had already changed into a pair of

blue jeans but had just taken off his Multicam compression shirt when had received the phone call. Jim's muscular build sported a tattoo on the left shoulder that depicted the DEA SRT team's patch of a Roman centurion's helmet encapsulated in a shield pattern with the words *Nec Temio Nec Sperno*, meaning in Latin, I will not fear nor hate. Jim ran to where Agent David Ponder and the balance of the operators were stowing gear in the DEA SRT van for the short trip back to the office. The DEA SRT van had been upgraded to hold most of the team and equipment for transport. The bench seats of the 15-passenger van had been taken out and retro-fitted with custom bench seats that spanned, on each side, along the entire back of the van except for the portion where the double doors opened. Seated in the van, each operator could face the other and have their gear in the middle of the van that could be easily picked up and exited with.

"David, we've got a problem, possibly a major problem! No one has heard from the convoy headed for the office."

"Shit, that ain't good!"

"That's not all! Radio room says there's a ton of local first responder chatter and reports of a gunfight on I-10 south of the city."

All the operators had paused what they were doing to listen to Jim's report. Instantly, the operators came to the same conclusion in their minds. They all began grabbing weapons and plate carriers that held extra magazines and loaded them into the DEA SRT van as fast as they could. Several operators had changed into civilian clothes, and others still wore their multi-cams.

The gunfight was now in its seventh minute, with no way for the Agents and Operators to communicate they were in a dangerous situation. In the back of Nick's mind, he knew they were on their own. Pieces of glass and metal shrapnel were sporadically flying around the area of the SUV. The Sicarios' bullets had found their mark on the SUV and the pavement around it. Smoke from the discharged firearms and vehicle oil smoke from wrecks intermingled to make a foul odor. *No quick reaction force, no SWAT team was coming, and not even a uniformed patrol unit could do much good for them at this point*, Nick thought. Luckily the driver of Nick's SUV was a female FBI Agent who was small-framed and able to crawl across the center console into the passenger area and get out that way of the direct fire being poured on them from the overpass. Several projectiles had found their way through the SUV but had not made contact with a person.

Nick depressed the magazine eject button on the left side of the pistol frame, pulled the magazine out halfway, and saw that his round count of ammunition was seven. He had already expended half of a pistol magazine, realizing he only carried one extra magazine. He chose to pick his targets to conserve his ammo. Nick looked to the east, and only a couple of car lengths away, he could see Don and his group huddled on the passenger side of the SUV. He could see Greg leaning out, firing his M-4 rifle to the rear of the vehicle, and the other Operator was in the crease of the open front door frame exchanging gunfire in the direction of the overpass. He and Don locked eyes, and Don's hand motioned that his group was going to try and make a run for the off-ramp to the east. Nick looked to the west in the direction of original travel, looking for a way out of the concrete bathtub they had been ambushed in. Nick saw only concrete embankments. It would have been suicide to go that direction anyway. The Sicarios were all over the bridge that crossed the Interstate in that direction. Nick could hear words in Spanish being yelled back and forth above them and to their front on the overpass seventy-five yards away. Nick peered around the open front passenger door, which had been kept open for any semblance of cover, and saw a Sicario moving to get a better angle on his position from on top of the bridge. Nick extended his arms out, gripping the Sig Sauer, placed the moving target of the man in the sights, and squeezed the trigger multiple times. The three 9mm rounds from Nick's pistol flew toward the bridge. The first two struck the wire cage that kept people from falling off and was deflected from hitting their target. The next round found its mark, striking the Sicario in mid-stride, sending him face-first into the concrete pathway, out of sight of Nick.

Smoke from car crashes and gunfire was heavy enough to block portions of sunlight and cast fast-passing shadows on the ground around Nick. The sound of sporadic gunfire and screams coming from close and distant fleeing civilians was almost deafening. Over these sounds, Nick heard an unfamiliar one, a whoosh sound. The high-explosive cased rocket spun across the sky with the smoke trail emanating from its starting point on the overpass. As Nick realized what he was hearing, it was too late to warn anyone as he jerked his head around to see the contrail of smoke as if it were in slow motion. The rocket's internal fuse had automatically begun to burn ten feet from where it exited the launcher on top of the overpass. The rocket did not reach its maximum distance of two-hundred meters before it slammed into the concrete interstate in front of the SUV that Don and the others were on the passenger side of. The rocket's nose, which holds the impact fuse, did not touch the concrete, and the rocket skipped and traveled another twenty feet before its nose impacted the concrete barrier. The explosion of copper, plastic, metal, and concrete sent hot shards of itself flying into the air. The explosion had happened closest to Don and the operator from his SUV and sent their bodies violently into the vehicle's front passenger side, instantly giving Don a concussion and the operator nearby writhing on the ground. The explosion had caused Greg, who was nearest the passenger side back fender, to lurch forward and fall onto the ground. Guirillo fell over onto his right side. His hands were still cuffed behind him.

Juan, who had been exchanging potshots with Greg and the other operator, flinched and drew back when the rocket had flown past his position heading for its target. Juan peeked over the hood of the Explorer and could see Greg lying on the ground, attempting to get up. Juan took a step back from the Explorer, steadied his stance, and aimed down the sights of his pistol. The explosion had rocked Greg, but he was still able to function. As he gathered his wits and attempted to get back on his knees, the bullet from Juan's gun ripped through his back right shoulder, sending Greg back down to the ground. Juan knew this was their opportunity!

"Let's go! Get the boss. Get him now!" Juan screamed in Spanish to the Sicario, who had been using the explorer for cover along with him.

The Sicario, who had been behind the Camry, now stood up, pulled the empty magazine from his AK-47, flipped it around to the loaded second magazine he had taped to it, seated it back in the AK receiver, released the bolt which seated a live round in the chamber of the rifle. He shouldered the AK-47 and began advancing on the rearmost SUV, firing while moving. This provided enough cover fire for Juan and the other Sicario to run to the back bumper of the FBI SUV that Greg lay wounded next to. Juan peeked around the rear corner panel of the SUV and could see his boss, Guirillo, the beast, trying to get off of the ground and having trouble because of the handcuffs. A smirk came across Juan's face. He knew he would be a hero, a legend in the cartel, for bravely rescuing Guirillo.

Juan quickly reached out over Greg, who was now immobile on the ground, and drug Guirillo to the back of the SUV—

"Grab the American! We may need him!" Jaun told Sicario next to him in Spanish.

Juan picked up Guirillo by one of his arms with his left hand and ran back to the waiting Land Rover. Greg was in great pain but kicking and trying to grab at the back of the Ford Explorer as he was being drugged past it by the Sicario, leaving a bloody handprint on the back quarter panel. Greg knew what was going to happen if he was taken captive. He kicked and cussed—

"You motherfucker! Nooo! Get off me!" Greg yelled and screamed as Juan and the other Sicario pushed and shoved Greg into the back seat of the Land Rover.

"You get yours now gringo!" Guirillo said in broken English, smiling and now sitting on the other side of the back passenger seat of the Land Rover.

Nick and Dan had both been dazed by the explosion of the rocket. Nick had been knocked to the ground and was lying on his side and now had a sideways view of things. Nick could see several of the Sicarios' feet and legs moving through the stalled vehicles toward Don's SUV.

"They are taking Greg! They got him!" Dan screamed, trying to gain footing and stand up to fight back.

Bullets were flying around Greg, Dan, and the female Agent from the sporadic gunfire coming from the overpass and the few Sicarios littered throughout the stalled vehicles. A second rocket from the same RPG was now in the air, attempting to cover the retreat of the Land Rover containing Guirillo and Greg. The only Americans left to return fire after the initial rocket and the taking of Guirillo and Greg came from the rearmost SUV that had stalled the farthest away and to the East. The SUV was almost at the rocket's maximum fuse range. The fuse burned down and caused the rocket to explode before the nose of the rocket impacted around the front driver-side tire of the rearmost SUV and exploded, rocking the SUV and causing the Agents on the opposite side to dive for cover.

The Sicario behind the Camry fired the last couple of rounds from his AK-47 as he slowly walked back toward the Land Rover, trying to cover Juan and Guirillo. His eyes were still trained on the rear-most FBI SUV he had just emptied his second 30-round magazine into when he felt a punch to his left rib cage. He turned his head quickly to see who had punched him and realized a bullet had hit him. He looked down and saw his blue t-shirt turning red on his left side. He glanced up and saw the female FBI Agent approaching and firing her pistol. The second round to hit the Sicario hit him a little higher in the chest than the first. FBI Agent Kelly Develand was the last thing he ever saw. Kelly had seen the situation unfolding and had exposed herself to enemy fire from the overpass, dead set on not letting Guirillo escape, much less allowing an American to be taken, prisoner. She was hunched slightly over, moving meticulously. Her head leaned in to see the sights of her weapon more clearly. She approached the Sicario, firing at him, striking him twice until her gun ran dry. Seeing the slide on her pistol lock back, meaning that her weapon was empty, Kelly's training took over. She knelt to make herself a smaller target, reached with her left hand into her waist, and pulled a fresh magazine from its carrier, keeping her pistol in front of her face and scanning for targets. Kelly seated the new magazine into the gun, pulled the slide back to release it, and locked a live round of ammunition into the chamber.

"Go, Go, Go!" Guirillo yelled at the driver of the Land Rover in Spanish as he observed through the front windshield and could see the female FBI Agent approaching and engaging one of his men.

The driver placed the gear shift into drive position and floored the Land Rover. Juan's door was still partially open and almost fell out as the

Land Rover careened past the first stalled vehicle in front of them, striking the rear quarter panel of the stalled car with the passenger side front fender.

Kelly quickly stood back up as the Land Rover sped off. Kelly heard the whizzing sound of a bullet passing close by her as it passed her and lodged into a stalled car that was nearby. Kelly took a firing position behind the Ford Explorer that Juan had recently used for the same purpose. Her adrenaline was pumping through her veins as the auditory seclusion she had been experiencing left her, and the sounds of gunfire faded. She peeked over the hood of the Explorer toward the overpass, smoke billowing up and blocking a portion of her view, but she did not see any targets. The gunfire was now gone, and Kelly could hear the moaning of her wounded fellow Agents and the desperate screams of civilians.

Two Land Rovers had made the rescue attempt on the American side of the border, but only one could be driven away. Juan's Land Rover sped the short distance to the hole in the border fence that Santiago's men had cut. The Land Rover had crossed the median into the Eastbound lane of the Interstate, traveling only about one hundred yards before making a sharp right turn going the wrong way up the on-ramp to the Interstate from the overpass. The Land Rover took another hard left turn going eastbound on the service road, where it quickly turned into a dirt cut-through road that went by the El Paso County Transport bus yard. The Land Rover traveled over three sets of train tracks running east and west and stopped one hundred and fifty yards behind the bus yard. Juan quickly exited the SUV and ran to the driver's side to help his boss exit the vehicle. Guirillo hopped out of the SUV with Juan's help and turned to watch Juan drag the wounded and bleeding Greg across the back passenger seat and onto the ground. The Sicarios, who had been on top of the overpass, now made it to the hole in the border fence and helped Guirillo and Juan drag Greg through the fence to the awaiting Land Rover that Santiago had now pulled up near the Mexican side of the fence. The Land Rover and the truck filled with Sicarios and the wounded Greg faded into the nearby streets of Ciudad Juarez.

The operator-laden DEA SRT van sped through the now almost impassable traffic. Interstate 10 in El Paso was at a complete standstill. The operator driving the van could see the smoke rising from the Interstate several miles ahead of them.

"Fuck, we gotta' find a way around!"

"Fuck it! Get on the shoulder, median! Whatever, just go!" David Ponder, one of the operators, yelled from the back.

The driver scooted over onto the right-hand shoulder, weaving in and out of the right lane and back onto the shoulder for the next mile. The van approached a section of the Interstate that appeared to be even more congested than they had just traveled through. As far as the eye could see, there were cars askew in lanes of travel, vehicle collisions in all lanes, and civilians running in all directions.

"What the fuck! This is crazy!" the driver said out loud as he pulled the steering wheel to the right to avoid a female civilian running in his path of travel, bloodied and crying.

"We can't go any further! This is it! Last bit's on foot, boys."

Agent Ponder and the other eight operators jumped out of the van from the sliding side door on the passenger side and the two doors on the rear. Each man was trying to figure out what was going on. Ponder, one of only two operators who had been able to change into civies entirely, pulled back the charging handle on his M-4 rifle as his feet hit the concrete Interstate. Ponder and the other operators ran the last miles of the Interstate, past several hundred stalled and abandoned vehicles and hundreds of civilians. The operators were focused on the smoke billowing into the air ahead of them.

"Blue, blue, blue!" Ponder yelled as he approached the rearmost FBI SUV and could see the carnage. The Sicarios were long gone but Ponder and the others were unaware of this fact, nor did they care. Protocol as operators deemed them to secure the area and look for work! The many special operations schools the operators had attended over the years had all taught them to look for work or scan the surroundings for bad guys. Ponder, now the senior DEA operator in the approaching group, yelled for the operators to spread out and set a defensive perimeter. Agent Jeremy Long, the DEA team's medic, had thought to bring along his A-Bag. The A Bag stood for an advanced medical bag that contained medical equipment to take care of more life-threatening wounds. Each operator and most FBI and DEA Agents carried an IFAK, or Individual First Aid Kit, for this event, but the IFAK contains limited supplies. Jeremy immediately ran to the downed FBI Agents who were on the ground on the passenger side of the SUV. Grimacing in pain and obviously in shock, the two wounded Agents still clutched their semi-automatic pistols, wide-eyed. One of the injured Agents had not realized his pistol was out of ammunition and was still scanning for threats as he lay wounded, with the slide locked back, which meant the pistol had been run dry. Matt Grayson had been in the second from the rear FBI SUV and had only been dazed by the RPG rocket. He had been trying to administer first aid to one of the wounded FBI Agents from his SUV when he saw his teammates running to them through the stalled vehicles.

The Secretary of Defense had only been at the White House for forty-five minutes and had been working on an evaluation plan for the presentation of troop movements by the Russians in the Balkans. *Probably just an exercise,* he thought as he jotted down notes for the upcoming briefing. The Secretary of Defense had not gotten much sleep from the night before dealing with Operation Hammerhead. The Attorney General had been in his ear most of the morning as he readied for work, talking about the operation in Mexico. The Attorney General was unhappy with how the DOD handled the joint operation between the Agencies.

The phone on his desk rang, which startled him. He sighed, reached over, and picked up the handset—

"Yes?"

"Sorry to disturb you, sir, but we have a situation in Texas."

"What kind of situation?"

"The kind that requires your attention, sir. It's bad."

"I'm on the way." he hung up and thought *what now* as he quickly took his White House ID lanyard from next to the documents he had been working on and placed it around his neck as he exited his office.

"Meeting in the boss's office." the Deputy Secretary of Defense advised as she ran into Baker leaving an office into one of the many hallways of the White House.

"Figured that! What's this about?"

"I don't have all of the intel yet, sir, I was just told to come over for a meeting, but it sounds like the FBI Agents escorting that Cartel leader and the other guys they detained were ambushed on the I-10 in El Paso"

Baker stopped in the hallway—

"Did we lose anyone?"

"Again, I don't have any details. This just developed, but I do believe there are casualties sir. That's not all sir, …"

"What, what is it, Eileen?"

"Whatever happened, shut down a large portion of south El Paso."

"Ok, so? I'm sure it did. Gunfire and bullets tend to do that, Eileen!"

"No sir, whatever happened was like a blackout. No communication or something like that is what I got from the phone call, sir."

"Oh, my God! Bradshaw. He was right!" Baker muttered under his breath.

"Sir?"

"Bradshaw," Baker said, "Special Agent Nick Bradshaw, was his name mentioned in what you received?"

"No sir, I…I don't know who that is?" looking a bit quizzical.

CHAPTER 8

Matters of National Security

One of the Nurses in the emergency room of Las Palmas Medical Center walked to room 103B to check the pulse-ox monitor. The Nurse monitoring the multi-bed ER unit had received a beeping notification that the monitor in room 103B was not reading the patient's pulse and blood oxygen levels. The El Paso County Deputy Sheriff stood by the door of room 103B and nodded at the nurse as she entered the room. The nurse was a bit on edge as she entered, wondering why her patient's monitoring system had alerted the nursing staff. The Nurse quickly realized why her patient was not registering—

"Agent Powers, what are you doing? You need to lay back down and relax, sir." the Nurse said caringly as she rushed to the bedside just as Don was attempting to stand up. Agent Don Powers clad in a hospital gown, had set up in the bed, let the guard rail down on the right side of the bed, and swung his legs around to get up.

"Where am I?"

"Emergency room at Las Palmas, sir."

"What happened? Where is everyone else?"

"Some of the people you were with are here, and some went across town to Kindred." the Nurse said, referring to Kindred Hospital about two miles Northeast of Las Palmas.

"Where did you think you were going, Agent Powers?" she said as she adjusted Don back in the bed, lifted the right side guard rail back up, and placed the pulse-ox monitor back on Don's finger.

"Don't know, just trying to figure out what happened. How many men did we lose?"

The Nurse ignored the question—

"You do have a gentleman outside waiting to see you, Agent Powers…whenever you feel up to talking?"

"I can talk. Send them in, please."

Special Agent Nick Bradshaw entered room 103B.

"You look like shit!"

"Speak for yourself. You obviously haven't looked in a mirror, asshole!" Don replied with the best smirk he could conjure up, given the circumstances.

"What the hell, Nick? What happened out there? How many Agents did we lose, and how were they able to get the drop on us like that?"

Nick, who had sat down in a visitation chair on the right side of the hospital bed and had been looking up at Don, looked down—

"Three. Four, if you count Chen's bodyguard. The rest of us were wounded, every one of us! Not one of us came out unscathed, Don." Nick said as he reached up with his left hand and felt for the bruising and stitches sewn into the left side of his head.

Don shook his head in disbelief as he tried to compute what was being told.

"Um...that's not the bad news."

"What are you talking about? What could be worse?"

"It's Greg Don..." Nick was cut off mid-sentence —

"Shit, don't tell me he's one of the dead."

"They took him, Don! When they grabbed Guirillo, he was right there by him, and they took him!"

"What the hell! He was right by me, and then I don't remember anything until here."

"Nothing you could've done, Don. I saw it happening, and I couldn't get off the ground from the explosion. It was like it all was in slow motion. The female FBI Agent that had been with me in my SUV wasn't as shaken up and tried to stop it, but she couldn't get to him in time. It all came out of nowhere. We couldn't have expected the Cartel would've gone to this extreme. They used it, Don! They used an EMP on us, on our own soil! We've gotta figure this out. We've gotta go get Greg."

"We're gonna get Greg and get those weapons!" Don concluded with anger in his voice.

"I'm headed to the field office for a debrief and probably a call to Washington in there as well."

"The hell you are! Not without me!" Don exclaimed as he started pulling his sheets back and unhooking wires.

"Hold up, Don! You stay and let them take care

of this. You took a nasty lick to the head when you hit the side of the SUV."

"I'm fine...little dizzy, but I'm fine. You're not leaving here without me!"

Nick reached out and put his hand on Don's leg —

"Ok, ok, give me a minute. Let me talk to the Doctors and Nurses and get you outta here."
Just then, Nick's cell phone rang and buzzed in his pocket. He pulled it out and saw Mitsy on the incoming call screen.

"I gotta take this. Give me a few, and I'll get you out of here." Nick said as he quickly walked towards the door to exit and take the call.

Nick slid the green button on the screen to answer the ring as he walked down the hospital corridor away from people to talk.

"Mitsy!"

"Nick, you're in El Paso, and I just saw the news on Facebook. Please tell me you weren't involved with that." Mitsy said frantically.

"More than involved, honey. It's complicated, and I can't talk about it. I'm ok." Nick said, talking in a low tone.

"There was a video showing smoke and vehicles all over the Interstate, and someone had commented about a big gunfight between the Cartel. Where are you now?"

"Las Palmas Hospital."
Mitsy gasped!

"I'm ok, babe, I'm ok. They just brought me

here for some stitches. I'm fine." Nick's voice began quivering slightly.

"Three Agents didn't make it! I tried to help. I couldn't get to them."

"It's not your fault, Nick. I'm sure you did what you could. I'm being selfish in wanting you away from there, but I know that's not you. It's ok. I know what I married into and who I married, was Dan with you? Is he ok?"

"Banged up like me, but he's ok." Still talking low and glancing around to ensure there was no one within earshot.

"Thank God you are both ok!"

"They took one of our men."

"What? Who?"

"You don't know him. I have to do what I can to help get him back."

After a few seconds of silence, Mitsy now with a firm voice—

"Get him back, Nick! I don't care what you have to do. If it were you, I would hope and pray someone like you would go after my husband or father or whoever he is to someone. Get him back, Nick!"

Nick had been leaning against one of the walls in the ER hallway. His cell phone to his ear, he looked over and saw the ER Doctor at the Nurse's station.

"Angel, I need to go. I love you. I promise I'll call soon. Take care of the baby."

"I love you, Nick. Please take care of yourself. Do

what you have to do. I love you."

Nick ended the call and walked to the Nurse's station. After a few minutes of fast talking and using the words *matter of national security*, Nick convinced the Doctor to release Don into his care.

The FBI field office in El Paso is a shared government building with the DEA. The hospital ER had been extremely busy, but Nick had found an FBI Agent in his unit and begged him to take him and Don to the field office. Nick and Don hobbled into the office's third-floor conference room, which they had been told had been made into a makeshift command center. The SAC, or Special Agent in Charge, stood when he saw Nick and Don enter the room.

"Special Agent Bradshaw!" the SAC said as he walked across the room to shake their hands and help them each to a high-back leather chair nudged up to a large oval-shaped false wood conference table.

"Sir, do we have any word on the DEA Agent who was taken?"

"Nothing yet. We've got our ears to the ground. DEA has sources in the area of Ciudad Juarez, beating the bushes as we speak. We've got a conference call with the SecDef and Attorney General in 20 minutes, so we're trying to get as much intel on this situation as possible. What do you two have to share since yall were boots on the ground?"

"Sir, no disrespect, but I'm not sure whether or not we can disclose everything we know about what might have happened unless the Attorney General, SecDef, or President gives us permission to speak freely."

The SAC, who had been standing near where Nick and Don had sat at the table, tapped his fingers on the conference table several times and sighed—

"Well, if that's the way you feel, son. We're just trying to get a leg up on this."

"I understand, sir, but we would feel better if we were granted permission to speak about this," Don cut off Nick.

"I also mean no disrespect, sir, but I have instructed your Agent here not to speak about what we know of this issue. We'll need the SecDef to permit you to hear it."

"Alright, I don't think we've officially met." The SAC reached out to shake Don's still trembling hand as the meds were still rumbling through Don's system.

"Agent Don Powers, DOD."

"Devin Thompson, I'm the SAC for El Paso. DOD huh? You sure you don't need to be in a hospital? You don't look so good."

"I'm fine, Special Agent Thompson. I've been in worse shape than this."

The conference room was walled on three sides with standard office sheetrock. The side of the conference room that spanned the hallway was all glass. Special Agent Devin Thompson had been sitting on the edge of the conference table with one ass cheek on the table and his right leg extended down to support himself from the floor. He looked up from speaking with Nick and Don to a person motioning through the glass.

"Looks like our phone call is waiting, gentlemen," Devin said, standing erect and glancing at the Cisco conference phone system in the middle of the conference table. Devin looked back towards the glass wall and motioned for the two Agents in the hallway to come in for the meeting.

The phone on the conference table began to ring. Devin reached across the table and pushed the button on the phone with the symbol of the speaker—

"Good afternoon, this is Special Agent in Charge Devin Thompson"

"Agent Thompson, this is Secretary of Defense John Baker, along with Attorney General Wayne Bradwell, Deputy Secretary of Defense Ileen Marksfield, your boss -Director of FBI Benjamin Hudson, and DEA Administrator Doug Hedley on the line."

"Yes sir, we also have in the room on our end Special Agent Kim Jeauro, Special Agent Richard Pearson, Agent Don Powers, and Special Agent Nick Bradshaw," Devin advised as he glanced around the room, accepting nods from each one as he announced them.

"Bradshaw! Can he hear me?" The SecDef

exclaimed.

"Yes, sir, I'm here. I can hear you." Bradshaw leaned in toward the center of the table and closer to the microphone.

"My God son, you were the first one I thought of when I heard about this. Are you ok?"

"Yes, sir, a little banged up, but I'm good to go, sir." looking around the room as he felt the stairs from everyone who was now probably wondering what the connection between Nick and the Secretary of Defense was.

"Bradshaw, I need you on point for this! Are you sure you're up to this after what you just went through?"

"Yes, sir. I'm fine. How can I help, sir?"

"The weapon systems you spoke about at our last conversation. Were you or your team able to recover the one they hit you and the escort team with?"

Looking over at Don and scrunching his eyebrows while answering—

"No sir. They hit us before we knew what was going on. We're not even sure where they deployed the weapon from, sir."

"I need you to use whatever means necessary to locate not only this weapon but to find out if they have any more and how many if they do. Do you understand?"

"Sir, I..." Nick was interrupted while attempting to come up with an excuse.

"Agent Bradshaw, this is FBI Director Benjamin

Hudson, the Secretary of Defense has asked me to assign you to this case permanently until you can locate these weapons. The Attorney General and DOJ have already relinquished the jurisdiction of Operation Hammerhead to the DOD. Administrator Hedley has been asked for the DEA's full cooperation in the investigation and to provide you with any manpower or intel from that end. Special Agent Thompson, are you still in the room, sir?"

"Yes, sir, I'm here."

"The El Paso field office is to provide Special Agent Bradshaw with the same, understood?"

"Yes sir, understood."

"Sir, may I ask a question?" Nick held up his right hand as if they could see him on the other end of the phone.

"Go ahead," came the reply from the SecDef.

"What about Special Agent Greg Dean? Are we sending a team to go get him?" Nick asked in concern.

"No, son, unfortunately, we are not..." the SecDef was interrupted by Administrator Hedley —

"This is Administrator Hedley. We don't know much at this point. We have no idea where they took Special Agent Dean, nor do we know if he survived the attack. My understanding is that Agent Dean was wounded in the attack, and we don't know the extent of those wounds. We will wait and see if they ask for a ransom or somehow give up a location. For now, it's out of our hands. The President will make that decision once we gather more intel. As the Secretary of Defense stated, this operation now falls under DOD protocols."

"Gentleman, for the time being, we have been advised from the top to shut down all operations involving any incursions into Mexico. The President has a delegate speaking to the Mexican Government as we speak to gain Special Agent Dean's release. While we are on the subject of releasing people, the President has ordered the release of the remaining two Chinese Nationals. They are not under arrest, we do not have any viable reason to hold them, and the President does not want World War Three started over these two arms dealers. It's bad enough that one of them was killed in the rescue of the Cartel leader. At least he was killed by a Cartel bullet, and not one of ours!" the SecDef followed up.

"What do you want us to do with them, sir? Do we need to provide transportation?" Special Agent Devin Thompson asked.

"No, let'em walk out the front door. They can figure out how to get back to China.", was SecDef's response.

Nick now stared at the phone in the middle of the conference table, his face turning red, still stuck on the fact that they were leaving Greg in Mexico and to the perils of the Cartel—

"So, we're just gonna sit back and leave this

man behind? That's what we're doing here?" Nick said as his voice elevated. "That man doesn't Deserve this!"

"Special Agent Thompson, could you clear the room for me? I'd like to speak only to Special Agent Bradshaw and Agent Don Powers if he's still in the room?"

Thompson believed Bradshaw and Powers were about to be reprimanded—

"Absolutely, sir!"

The sound of whispering and moving around could be heard on the end of the phone line from SecDef's end. There was silence on the phone line as each room on either end of the phone line was cleared until the only remaining people on the line were the SecDef, Bradshaw, and Powers.

"Is everyone out, gentlemen?" came the question through the silence from the SecDef on the phone.

Bradshaw and Powers looked at each other like schoolboys waiting on the principal to thrash them with words for the conduct Bradshaw had just displayed.

"Yes, sir, It's just us, sir."

In a slow, methodical voice, the SecDef was obviously closer to the phone microphone—

"I want you both to listen to me and listen carefully. The President has suspended all operations South of the border. His exact words were, *no more boots on the ground south of the border until this blows over.* The President has lost his stomach for this fight, gentlemen. Calls from the Chinese and Mexican consulates have made him rethink his position. Normally I would agree with him. This thing with the recovered weapon and the Chinese has turned into a shitshow. The President cooked up this operation against the Cartels to help our nation. Still, he didn't bargain on the team finding Chinese-made unconventional weapons and the Chinese operatives that brought them. I disagree with him on leaving one of our own across the border to the torture and God knows what else at the hands of the Cartel."

The SecDef was somewhat of a history buff and thought hard momentarily.

"I want to tell you two a story. In 1519 Cortez sailed across the sea from Spain with eleven ships and 600 men to conquer a new world. The trip was long and painful. When Cortez and his men landed in what is now South America, he got wind of a mutiny by some of his men that had lost their stomachs and did not want to continue the mission. Cortez gave the order to burn the ships. There was no turning back after that. Gentlemen, burn the ships! Finish this mission! I'm placing this burden on the two of you. Go get our man back! I don't care what you have to do, where you have to go, or who you must coerce to do it. Powers, I'm giving you free rain on this, but this needs to be covert, not overt, understood?" Don attempted to answer but was cut off by the continuing speech.

"If the two of you or any others you recruit for this mission get compromised on the wrong side of the border, it won't just be Special Agent Dean that needs rescuing. There is no contingency plan. You are the only contingency plan! Do you both understand me?"

"Yes, sir. Understood." Nick and Don acknowledged in unison.

"I'm about to make a couple of phone calls and open up the pipeline for whatever assets and gear you need. Bradshaw, find these weapons. If you and Powers fail, we'll be looking at another disaster like the one in El Paso somewhere else in the US. Put a small team together, whatever you need to do. I'm authorizing you to do this, and I'm sending an email to this effect to both of you immediately. I'm taking on the burden if this goes south. I'd rather get fired and sleep well at night than the contrast. Put a tail on the Chinese if you think you need to. Whatever, just get the job done! Powers, your boss could not attend the meeting today because of a health emergency, but I'm sending him a memo advising him that you'll be working directly under my direction for a short time. The DEA's operation in Mexico a couple of nights ago was Hammerhead. Let's finish Operation Hammerhead!

"Yes sir!" came the reply in unison from Bradshaw and Powers.

CHAPTER 9

The Border

Nick sat behind the wheel of one of the FBI El Paso's cool cars. The vehicles the federal and local agencies used to conduct undercover operations were called cool cars. The cool cars had been cleansed of government ownership and registered to fake entities. The gray Honda mini-van was parked in a parallel slot at the St. Francis Xavier Hall on Findley Avenue in south El Paso. Nick had both hands on the steering wheel and glanced over at his left arm to see the time on his MTM Warrior. It read 13:07, or 1:07 P.M. The SAC at FBI El Paso had given Nick the MTM watch after the conference call the previous day when he saw Bradshaw kept looking for the time on his non-functional smartwatch that the EMP had taken out the day before.

FBI Special Agent Kelly Develand sat in the front passenger seat next to Nick. The SecDef had given Nick free rein to pick a team, and pick he did! After witnessing Kelly's exemplary actions on the interstate two days before, he knew Kelly was the type of Agent he needed for this operation.

Kelly Develand was a Marine. She had joined the Corp straight out of high school. Kelly served in Afghanistan for one tour assigned to a Female Engagement Team, or FET team. She had been attached to an infantry unit and was no stranger to challenging situations with bullets flying. Upon leaving active duty, Kelly used her GI Bill to go to college, where she finished in criminal justice. With her military background and education, she was a shoo-in at the FBI at twenty-nine.

Kelly had her long brown hair in a ponytail, and her brown eyes were concentrated on the end of Findley Avenue. Nick and Kelly had tailed the black Mercedes for several miles around El Paso. This was the second heat check the Mercedes had done since it left the area of the FBI building in El Paso. The heat check is when a person being followed will turn abruptly onto side streets and make several other turns to ensure they do not have a tail. By doing this, they hope to see if the identical vehicles they believe are following them will turn with them to keep them in sight.

"There it is!" Kelly exclaimed, pointing with her right hand, seeing the Mercedes pass the side street traveling South.

"Good eye! We'll give them a few seconds to feel comfortable, and then we'll get back behind them." Nick replied.

The Black Mercedes had picked up Chen and his one remaining bodyguard a few blocks South of the FBI office after they had been processed and released. *Right out the front door!* Just like the SecDef had stated. This was stuck in Nick's mind, but he now saw that the SecDef might have had a master plan. The SecDef knew that once Chen was released, he would not be on the street long, and he was correct. Nick had slowed the FBI paperwork process to release Chen on purpose. This gave him enough time to set a few things in motion, including inciting the help of Kelly, who had been more than willing to volunteer once asked.

Nick backed out of the parking slot and drove to the end of Findley Avenue. He and Kelly looked in the direction they had seen the Mercedes traveling—

"There it is!" Kelly exclaimed again, almost like she was playing a game of hide and seek.

"Old eagle eye over here! Good job." Nick commended.

Nick had a feeling that the Mercedes was trying to get across the border by the direction it was traveling and the way it was trying to ensure it was not being tailed.

"You've got your passport, right?" Nick asked.

"Yep, got it in my bag."

"Ok. I think they're trying to get back across the border. Chen has unfinished business with the Cartel. He never got paid! It would probably be hell to pay if he showed back up in his country without the money. We're gonna have to figure our way through this on the fly. Reach back and grab my passport outta my bag and grab yours too. I think we're gonna need them sooner than later."

"Ok. You're probably right." Kelly said while

reaching behind them and unzipping backpacks on the floor in front of the first passenger bench seat.

Nick kept the Mercedes seven to eight cars between them and swapped lanes often. He did not want to not stay in the same spot on the interstate to draw attention. Finally, the Mercedes exited from Highway 62 onto Interstate 10, traveling south. This gave Nick and Kelly a bit of anxiety since the incident involving the shootout the day before had occurred on Interstate 10.

"Yep, that looks like where they're headed," Kelly noted.

"Our names don't match, so we'll have to be girlfriend and boyfriend for a few minutes. When we get close, hold my hand. I have no idea if they know who we are. This can only go two ways." Nick replied.

Nick could feel the cold steel of his nine-millimeter Sig Sauer pistol under his shirt pressing against the skin in the back right side of his pants. Nick was not sure where Kelly had her weapon stowed, but he knew she had it, and better yet, he knew she knew how to use it.

Nick rolled the window down on the driver's side and leaned out just enough to see past the Ford F-350 that had gotten in between their Honda and the Mercedes. Nick could see the Mercedes nine cars ahead of him as it pulled up to the Mexican Federale' guard at the Puente' Internacional Co'rdova de las Americas which was the port of entry into Mexico from this part of El Paso.

After a brief exchange of words and documents, the Mexican guard retreated to the guard shack and appeared to be making a phone call.

"I can see the guard makin a call. We'll see what happens." Nick said, giving the play-by-play to Kelly.

The Mexican guard hung up the phone and walked out of the guard shack back to the waiting black Mercedes. The driver-side window was rolled down, and Nick saw an elbow on the seal. The Federale guard was conversing with an individual through the driver-side window, and after a few seconds, the guard handed the paperwork back to the driver and waved the Mercedes through the port.

"Damn! They were waved through pretty fast for Asian Nationals. Their passports should be Chinese or maybe diplomatic. If not, some pretty good fakes!" Nick said as he tucked his head back inside the car.

"We're gonna lose 'em if this line doesn't speed up!"

"I can see them in the distance. Still on the Interstate. I don't see any other cars shadowing them." said Kelly, craning her neck and head almost into the visor of the Honda as she tried to maintain sight of the Mercedes.

The other eight cars filtered through the

checkpoint without any delay. The gray Honda was next up. Kelly reached across the open area between the captain's chairs in the front of the Honda and grabbed Nick's right hand. Nick's left hand was on the steering wheel. Kelly held his hand, which made Nick remember that he was married and almost made a basic undercover mistake. His wedding ring!

"Damn, my ring!" Nick dropped his right hand below the line of sight of the guard, quickly pulled the wedding ring from his left ring finger, dropped it into the center console, and picked Kelly's hand up from where it had been on his armrest.

"That was close!" Kelly said.

"If they pay attention, it could've been close," Nick responded.

Nick's driver-side window had still been rolled down as he drove slowly up to the white-painted mark on the street to stop.

"Good afternoon, officer"

"Hello, what's your reason for visiting Mexico today, sir?" the Federale asked in slightly broken English.

"Well, my girlfriend and I are headed into Ciudad Juarez. We booked one of those romantic tours and a night on the town." Nick explained, smiling ear to ear and holding Kelly's hand.

Kelly leaned over the arm of her captain's chair toward Nick while holding his hand and smiling back at the guard.

"Passports, please?" the guard asked while

looking past Nick into the cabin of the Honda.

"How long are you staying in Mexico?" while accepting the two passports handed out the window to him by Nick.

"Just tonight, sir. We'll be coming back to the States tomorrow afternoon."

The Federale' looked closely at both passports and then glanced at Nick and Kelly. Seeing that the photos matched and the pair of love birds were on their way to a lovely evening in the Ciudad Juarez, he handed the passports back to Nick—

"Welcome to Mexico. I hope the two of you have a good time tonight in the city." he said as he waved his hand in a passing manner.

"Thank you. Have a good day, officer." Nick replied, nodding since he still held Kelly's hand and the other was on the steering wheel.

Nick pushed the gas pedal on the gray Honda minivan and sped south on Highway 45, known in the city of Ciudad Juarez as Avenue Abraham Lincoln. Kelly pulled up the map on her phone—

"Looks like if we stay on 45, it'll make a hard left several miles ahead. If they stay on 45, we should be able to catch up to them."

"Good deal. Can you reach into the bottom of my pack and hand me that sat phone?"

Kelly dug around with her hand in the bottom of Nick's pack, found the phone, flipped the antenna out to the side, and checked for a signal—

"It's searching...alright, you're good to go!" She said, handing the phone to Nick.

Nick had preprogrammed several numbers in the satellite phone earlier that morning when it had been issued to him. He scrolled to a particular number and pushed the dial button.

"Hello,"

"Hey, brother! Well, we ended up in ol' Mexico. They're not far ahead of us. We're on 45 now, trying to acquire the target."

"Roger, that brother! If that's where you're telling me they're headed, I'll not be far behind you. Keep me updated, and We'll be on standby."

CHAPTER 10

Covert, not Overt

Don Powers hung up from the call on his satellite phone with Bradshaw. Bradshaw was already where the President had expressly said he did not want them, and Don knew he would soon be there. Don had utilized half of the day to prepare for this operation to scrounge up the gear and recruit a few insubordinate individuals like himself. Each person that volunteered for this operation knew it was highly covert, meaning there was no getting caught!

Don had been recruited by the Special Activities Division of the CIA after he had gone inactive from the Ranger Battalion. Don had three tours in the Middle East, along with numerous other missions and operations. Some missions had been in South America, and even one operation in Somalia to disable suspected boats and small watercraft used by the pirates. The operation had been conducted during the night, and they had only encountered small resistance from guards who had been posted near the docks. Don's team had managed to disable or destroy eleven boats and did not take any American casualties.

After Don had been recruited and passed selection to the CIA Special Activities Division, he spent months in further training on paramilitary operations, ambushing, sabotage, and unconventional warfare. Ranger School had taught Don these same tactics, but the CIA greatly expanded his knowledge base. The Special Activities Division had trained Don not only to take the fight to the enemy but to make the enemy regret they were ever in the fight in the first place. The Special Activities Division had plenty of work worldwide when the United States was not in an active war. Still, since that was not the case, Don and his team had gained an exponential amount of experience completing covert operations around the globe in the war on terror.

The pain was almost unbearable. One arm is tied to the other behind his back. The bullet had traveled straight through. Hitting only skin, ligament, and muscle was extremely painful nonetheless. The makeshift bandage had been applied by Juan not as a life-saving measure but as a life-preserving measure. Greg opened his eyes. The sunlight was brighter in his left eye than in his right. The blindfold allowed enough light through the fibers of the fabric to see the light difference in one eye from the other. In his pain, steered by grogginess, Greg realized he was lying on his right side in a moving vehicle. He could hear a song playing on the vehicle's radio with a female singing in Spanish. Greg knew he was in a dire situation and wished he had not awoken from his pain-induced sleep. *Were they going to ransom him, torture him, kill him, or some version of all three*, he thought?

The black Land Rover sped over the bumpy gravel and dirt road, causing a plume of dust cloud to boil in its rear. The tall trees lining the road that the Land Rover was traveling on seemed out of place. Thirty and forty-foot-tall tropical-type trees and green grass lined the gravel and dirt road as it meandered through the drought-ridden arid climate toward a distant compound.

"He has to have underground irrigation in this type of climate! He is wasting his money on water for trees." Guirillo said as he thought aloud.

The compound had a large black iron gate with two armed guards standing next to each pillar. The gate was affixed to a ten-foot-tall white stucco wall surrounding the property. Inside the stucco wall were several large white, stucco, and stone buildings, with the largest of the three in the middle facing the inner portion of the iron gate. The roofs were orange terracotta clay that expanded over the porches and side entrances. Armed guards roamed within the stucco walls of the compound carrying automatic AK-47s and some with AR-15 assault rifles.

The black Land Rover quickly slowed to a halt just before the iron gate and guards. The dust cloud caught up with it and engulfed the vehicle, making the guards cough slightly. The driver-side window of the Land Rover lowered as the guard approached.

"Senior Sanchez Guirrillo. You should be expecting us." the driver advised in Spanish.

"Let them through!" was the reply as the guard motioned to the other guard to open the gate.

The other guard ran to the gate hinge and lifted the bar keeping it in place. The guard swung the gate to the outside as the Land Rover drove through. The Land Rover traveled the short one-hundred yards to the circle drive, dodging a roaming peacock crossing the driveway. Guirillo again shook his head in disapproval at the ridiculous manner his dear friend spent his money. The circle drive in front of the residents held a large flowing fountain in the middle ground with colorful flowers planted throughout. The Land Rover came to a halt straight out from the residence's front door. Roaming guards halted and watched the Land Rover enter the compound and stop. The eight-foot-tall double doors of the home opened, and an older Hispanic male and a younger thirty's aged Hispanic male walked toward the Land Rover with giant smiles—the older man with outstretched arms to welcome his guests.

The Golfo Norte Cartel and the Rio de Polvo Cartel had been allies for over five years. Senior Lucas Perez had founded the Rio de Polvo Cartel fifteen years prior when he was in his late fifties and was able to topple the then-floundering leader of the region's Cartel. It had been a lucky strike by Lucas when he had weaseled his way into the prior Cartel and found that the head of the organization had been strung out on his product and mismanaging the business. Lucas's son, Thiago, was now thirty-three and was following in his father's footsteps with plans soon to take over the day-to-day operations of the fortuitous empire. The Golfo Norte Cartel and the Rio de Polvo Cartel had expansive areas to manage as their own, but each location was arid and sparsely populated. This meant it was hard for the Cartels to recruit new employees and difficult to watch and maintain their territory. The two Cartels had made a truce and a pact to help one another in the form of security for their respective shipments. If a narcotics shipment needed to go across the other Cartel's territory and through a port they each controlled, a deal could easily be made. It had been highly lucrative for both Cartels.

Guirrillo exited from the front passenger side door first, leaving the door open and walking with outstretched arms to hug Lucas and Thiago. In Spanish—

"Ahhh...the beast has arrived! We weren't sure if we would ever see you again, and yet here you are! Great to see you, my boy!" exchanging hugs with Guirrillo, who was twenty years his junior and clutching his upper arms with both hands.

"I had faith, Senior Perez, faith! I knew I knew our men would look for me and come get me. I did not know your men, and mine would go to such lengths. I owe you."

"Nonsense! You would've done the same for my son or me. I know it! So, I hear you come bearing a gift.

"I do, in fact. I appreciate you and your family accommodating us so far from our home. We only need to rest and get a few things in place to move the gringo to a more suitable location. If you know what I mean, Senior? I understand you could not acquire your weapons from the Chinese because of this unfortunate mishap at my ranch. I assure you that you will be made good on the delivery. Your weapons are in a safe place until we can find somewhere to meet out of the eye of the watchful Americans. Now that they know we have this technology, they will try to take it from us. As you probably heard from your men, the weapon was used quite successfully in El Paso to effect my escape."

"Yes, we heard that the weapon performed magnificently! The plan to help the Chinese has come to fruition on a shorter timeframe than originally expected, but this sort of thing has to be figured in."

"Yes, besides, we had to test the system out. At least it was tested for a good reason, Senior. I am glad I was the good reason." Guirillo said, laughing.

"So, this business of Mr. Chen on his way to finish the deal? What exactly do we need to provide him? You have the money owed him, correct?" Lucas said as he cut the cap off a cigar with a pearl-handled pocket knife.

"Yes, I do not have his cash with me, but it will be delivered here or wherever he prefers. As you and I agreed on the phone, Chen will come here, and we can all sit and figure out the best course of action to get his money and to get Chen and his bodyguard to the Chinese consulate in Mexico City. The border guard cleared Chen through the border at the Abraham Lincoln Avenue port a little while ago, so we should be expecting him in the next couple of hours. I would suggest having the money brought here to exchange with him. He will be expecting that."

"Perfect! We will solidify this deal and keep this channel open for further business." Lucas advised, now smoking the Cuban Suprema No. 2 cigar.

The gray Honda Minivan sped south, then east and south again on Interstate 45 as it meandered through Ciudad Juarez in a southerly direction. Nick and Kelly sat up straight in the captain's chairs of the Honda and craned their necks as they scanned into the distant moving traffic for the black Mercedes.

"Is that it?... Nope! Damn! I thought we would've caught up to it by now. How fast are you going" Kelly asked.

"75"

"I think I see it. I've got a black four-door far right lane. Slow down. slow down. Son of a bitch!

Newer Camry!"

"We're gonna find them. I feel like they stayed on 45. I just can't see them getting off in Ciudad Juarez. Where would they be going unless they are meeting Guirillo or some of his guys in the city to follow?" Nick said as he swapped lanes and looked for the Mercedes up ahead.

Nick and Kelly were still southbound on the Interstate and fast approaching the outskirts of the next city as they passed the exit to an International Airport.

"You don't think they drove all the way to Mexico to catch a flight back to China, do you? Kelly asked.

"I doubt it. Stranger things have happened. Hold up! Middle lane five cars ahead. You see it?"

"Yep, that might be it!" Kelly exclaimed, leaning closer to the passenger side window to see around the cars in front of them.

"That's it! Back off a little, Nick. That's definitely it!"

"I'm slowing down. I'm going to drop back as far as we can. Let me know when you can barely see it."

"Right there, Nick! I can see if it changes lanes. I can't believe we found it in all of this traffic! Where do you think they are headed?"

"Not a hundred percent sure, but I am guessing it has something to do with not getting paid for the weapons. That's just a guess, but I bet it would be frowned upon if he showed back up in China without the cash."

The black S-class Mercedes sedan cruised in a southerly direction on Interstate 45. Chen had been used to the finer things in life. He had grown up as the son of a career military father and politician. His father had spoiled him: the most expensive automobiles, fine food and drinks, and the best designer clothes. Chen had not wanted anything growing up. The only thing Chen wanted was more! More of everything. The only thing Chen's father required was that he join the military and excel at it, and excel he did. Chen had garnered high-ranking military leaders to do his bidding because of who his father was. They had been afraid to say no to any request by Chen. Chen specialized in foreign intelligence and garnered himself as a James Bond type. Even though a Western ideal, James Bond was a hero of Chen's. He had visited Mexico numerous times to develop a collective ideology to infiltrate the United States in whatever manner his country could imagine. Chen met Santiago Morales while visiting Mexico City, and they struck up a friendship of sorts. More of a business venture. Each had something the other desired. The Cartels had plenty of money, and the Chinese had plenty of weapons, some conventional and some unconventional. Chen had been in the Chinese Navy and was a Chinese Naval Special Operations Force member. This allowed

Che'n to play with current and experimental weapons systems that the Chinese were developing. Chen had seen the value in the EMP-style weapons and kept close contact with the developers when he left the Navy. After leaving the Navy, Chen joined the Chinese version of the Americans Central Intelligence Agency—the secret police. Undermining anything the United States had a hand in was his primary goal as an officer in the secret police. The Chinese had supplied not only fentanyl but the ingredients to mass-produce methamphetamine for the Mexican and Colombian Cartels for years. Chen worked a new deal. The deal consisted of providing unconventional, experimental-style weapons to the Cartels. The Chinese weapon developers could not think of a better way to test the validity of new weapons systems—live targets. The Cartels had been pressured to figure out new methods of securing their loads of narcotics into the United States, and the Chinese had been looking for methods to undermine any part of the security and government of the United States. The Cartel was the perfect avenue for unconventional and guerilla-type warfare against the United States without getting their hands dirty.

Don had spent a few hours after the phone conference with the SecDef gathering gear and making calls to get as many assets as he could to help not only get Greg back but to help him and Nick find and destroy the EMP weapons. Don had placed a call to two other Ground Branch Agents with the Special Activities Division that was on his immediate team. Ground Branch was the designation of all personnel operating on the ground for the Special Activities Division. Don explained the type of mission this was before asking the other two, and both volunteered before Don could get through his speech about it being for God and Country.

On the second morning after the Interstate attack, a Blackhawk Helicopter summoned to a small private airfield eleven miles southeast of El Paso settled to the asphalt of the airstrip. The Blackhawk was solid black and did not display any markings. Don had been leaning with his back on a navy blue Ford Taurus that was a loaner from the FBI El Paso Field Office. It was 07:00, and the sun was half of itself on the horizon. Dew was on the grass between the tarmac and airstrip and began to whirl around and glaze the immediate surroundings of where the helicopter set down with a thin layer of moisture. The helicopter's skids touched the runway. The port-side door of the aircraft slid open, and a tall, muscular man jumped to the ground out of the helicopter's open door. The man was wearing Costa sunglasses. His shoulder-length brown hair was swept back, a long sleeve blue shirt with the sleeves rolled up to his elbows, blue jeans, and wearing a pair of Salomon Speedcross shoes. He strolled toward where Don was leaning on the car near one of the several small dome-shaped hangers.

Don reached down and grabbed a green military duffle bag that had been at his feet as he heard the deep voice yelling through the long brown beard of the man approaching him from the helicopter as the sound of the Blackhawks twin General Electric T700 turboshaft engines roared in the background—

"Good to see you boss!" the man reached his hand out to shake Don's hand.

"Greaver, it's good to see you too. A fabulous day for a business trip, don't you think!" Don said, smiling ear to ear.

Greaver grabbed the duffle bag that Don had slung on his shoulder.

"James is in the bird, sir. You know him! He's double-checking gear and shit." Greaver yelled to Don as they both hunched down and walked under the rotating blades of the Blackhawk.

Don laughed and acknowledged Greaver by nodding. Greaver and Don climbed into the Blackhawk and slid the door back shut. Greaver looked at the co-pilot and nodded that they were onboard and ready to lift off. Greaver was a handsome thirty-eight-year-old ex-Navy Seal. Greaver was the silent type. He did not say much but preferred to listen and take things in.

The Blackhawk's flight time to the next stopping point was less than thirty minutes. During that time, Don briefed Greaver and James on Operation Hammerhead and got them up to speed with Greg's hostage situation. All three changed clothes while en route. For the second time in less than twenty-four hours, Don was going against the President's wishes. The Air Branch of the Special Activities Division was also breaking that wish. Don had given the Blackhawk pilots GPS coordinates. The coordinates, once punched into the computer system of the Blackhawk, took them across the border into Mexico. The pilots had been briefed on Operation Hammerhead before taking off and were given further information once in the air by Don.

The three Ground Branch Agents onboard the aircraft could do terrible things to the enemy. They had been trained to do so. When the gloves of the United States military and federal law enforcement agencies had to stay on, the Ground Branch Agents took the gloves off. If the Cartels wanted to play the unconventional warfare game, they had picked a fight with a group that excelled at it.

CHAPTER 11

Black Ops

"Where the fuck are these guys going?" Nick stated as he thought out loud.

"No idea. I don't think they know where they're going, either. If we stay around them much longer, we'll have to switch cool cars. I gotta piss too!" Kelly responded.

"We're gonna have to stop for gas soon. The tank on that Mercedes must be huge. Parading us around El Paso and now almost two hours into Mexico has about run us dry. I can't help but believe they're headed to meet up with Guirillo. Wherever Guirillo is, and hopefully, we'll find Greg." Nick spoke about what he was thinking to Kelly.

Kelly was beginning to feel the taxation of straining her eyes all afternoon and evening, keeping the Mercedes in sight. Kelly rubbed her eyes with her thumb and index finger, then opened her eyes wide to try and re-focus.

"If we find Guirillo, maybe he'll also have the EMPs with him," Kelly added.

"Damn the EMPs! Right now, our focus is getting Greg back. The EMPs are secondary. I don't know Greg well, but he seems like the kind of guy that would do the same if it were us in his shoes right now. I just hope Don's plan works."

"You think that's his real name?" Kelly asked.

"Who, Don? Hell no! When I met him, and he said who he worked for. I knew then he was into some shady shit and that Don was probably a ghost name."

"You know...at the FBI, we call that a clue!" Kelly said, smirking under her breath.

The Mercedes was approaching the outskirts of Chihuahua, Mexico, and the traffic on Interstate 45 had picked up the closer they got to the city lights that were glowing on the night horizon. Ten miles outside the Chihuahua city limits, the brake lights lit up, and the Mercedes turned off of the Interstate onto a dirt and gravel road heading east. Nick drove the Honda van past the dirt road without turning. There were no other vehicle lights on the dirt road. Nick and Kelly wondered if the Mercedes was just conducting another heat check or if it intended to travel down the road. The terrain was flat, and the tail lights of the Mercedes could be seen for a great distance. Nick pulled the van over on the side of the Interstate a quarter of a mile past the turn-off and cut the van's lights out. Nick and Kelly watched the Mercedes's red tail lights and occasional red brake lights moving across the tundra in an easterly direction.

Nick reached and picked up his cell phone and pulled up the mapping application. The light from the phone screen lit up the front cabin area of the Honda van. Kelly peered over at Nick's phone screen, squinting, trying to see the map as Nick used two fingers to move the map and zoom in.

"Looks like that road winds around and travels near a bluff for a few miles." Nick used his fingers to zoom in on the screen ahead of the eastward traveling road and could see a large compound.

"Wonder what that is," Kelly said as Nick zoomed in on an area of buildings on the map.

"Mmhm, it looks like maybe a large residence or business complex. Look at that wall surrounding it. I'm only a mediocre FBI Agent, but that looks like a Cartel compound. It's large enough to protect if they're hiding something or someone, that's for sure!"

"I agree. I bet they've got surveillance on that road somewhere along the way. Maybe, cameras or lookouts. Either way, I'm guessing it isn't for a picnic wherever that Mercedes is headed! What's the plan, boss?" Kelly added.

"Well, as soon as those tail lights disappear, we're gonna drive down that road a little piece and turn off and find somewhere to park this jalopy, and we'll see if we can figure out what they're up to. I hope you're wearing your walking shoes! That compound looks like it's a couple of miles further east."

The Mercedes tail lights disappeared, and Nick gave it a few minutes to ensure it was not doubling back. Nick cut across the median and turned around north. The Honda turned down the same road the Mercedes had been on. Nick drove a half mile and turned off the main road onto a dirt path that looked like it might have been used by farmers sometime in the past. The only semblance of a path was the two small dirt ruts that tire tracks had left behind, possibly from an old rancher. The Honda bumped up and down in the ruts causing Kelly to grab the handle above the passenger side door. There were several large sage bushes in a clump that was just tall enough to hide most of the van behind. Nick stopped and moved the shift knob to Park.

"Let's get that gear bag out of the back and see what Don left for us."
Back in El Paso, Nick had attempted to gather some guns and ammunition and had been stopped by Don, who promised Nick he had taken care of that.

Before departing the FBI motor pool in El Paso, Don told Nick that he had placed a duffle bag of gear that he and Kelly might need in the back of the van. Don had covered the duffle bag with two colorful suitcases filled with clothes from the local Goodwill Store to disguise it from any prying eyes.

Nick walked to the back of the van and pushed the button to lift the back hatch. The hatch slowly opened, and Nick reached in and grabbed both colorful suitcases, and tossed them over the back bench seat of the van to get them out of the way. Kelly was still seated in the front passenger seat with the door open so that it would provide her light to change from her running-type shoes to a pair of black Salomon Quest boots.

"I'm liking Don more every minute!" Nick exclaimed from the rear of the van.

"Whatcha got back there?"

"I think he robbed a gun store. You want the M-4 or the MP-5? Take your pick!" Came the muffled voice of Nick as he was looking through the bag at the back of the van.

Kelly finished tying the laces on the last boot and quickly walked to the back like a kid excited to see what Santa had brought for Christmas.

"Whoa! I don't even know him, and I like him already! I'll take the MP-5."

"I was hoping you were gonna say that. Here's four extra mags too. Do you know how to use this thing?" Handing Kelly the MP-5 machine pistol and four extra magazines filled with 9mm ammunition.

Kelly took the MP-5 and four magazines from Nick, reached up on the left-hand side of the weapon above the forward-hand guard, grabbed the charging handle, and slid it to the rear, checking for a round in the chamber and locking the handle back into a groove. This left the bolt of the machine gun open. Kelly grabbed one of the four thirty-round magazines she had set to the side and slid it into the magazine well, seating it by hearing it click. Holding the pistol grip of the machine gun with her right hand, she reached out with her left hand. She slapped the charging handle out of its position in the groove, which made the bolt of the weapon slide forward, picking up a live round from the freshly seated magazine and sliding it into the chamber of the weapon where it waited to be fired.

"I'm impressed!" Nick exclaimed as he looked on in astonishment.

"Looks like you get the suppressor too." He reached out toward Kelly, holding a round black steel cylinder that Nick had removed from a thick round cardboard tube it had been housed in that had *9mm* stamped on the side.

Kelly took the suppressor from Nick and began threading it onto the end of the MP-5 barrel. Nick dug further into the bag and pulled out two pairs of black, multi-pocket pants, one in a lady's size four and the other in a man's size thirty-four. Matching multi-pocket tight-fitting light jackets were folded underneath, which was also in both of their sizes.

"I'm not even gonna ask how he knows our sizes," Kelly said sarcastically as she picked up the clothes and walked to the front of the van out of the sight of Nick to change.

"CIA shit, I'm scared to ask anything else he might know! There're two pairs of NODs in here too." Nick said, referring to two pairs of night vision optic devices with head straps he had pulled out of the bag, holding one in each hand.

Nick and Kelly changed into the provided dark clothing, and both lifted the chest rigs with bullet-resistant ceramic plates over their heads and dropped them onto their shoulders by the straps. Both reached back, grabbed the velcro straps on each side, pulled them to the front of the chest rig, and pushed the velcro in place. Each chest rig had a pouch on the front that held four extra rifle magazines and four extra pistol magazines. Nick filled the pockets with metal thirty-round AR magazines and four extra Sig P229 magazines that he had retrieved from his backpack between the van's captain's seats. Nick placed the head strap over his head and buckled the buckle under his chin. Nick walked over to Kelly, who was struggling with her head strap, and helped her buckle and tighten the straps on her optics head strap as she stood there looking like a peewee football player whose coach was trying to fix their helmet. After adjusting Kelly's head strap, she handed him the optic, and he slid it onto the rail system of the head strap and locked it in place. Kelly reached up and pulled the NODs down in front of her eyes, reached on top of the device, and turned the switch on. The dark arid surroundings lit up green in the view screen in front of each eye.

"I haven't used a pair of these since Afghanistan," Kelly said as she smiled and looked through the darkness at Nick, who was digging around in his backpack, his NODs still flipped up on top of his head. Kelly made minor adjustments with the knobs to focus.

"Been a while for me too...there it is!" Nick

pulled the satellite phone from the backpack, turned it on, and waited a few seconds for the phone to locate satellites for service. "I'm letting him know our coordinates and that we might have located Greg." Nick scrolled with his finger and pushed the redial button. The phone rang two rings—

"Hey, brother. I'm about to send you our coordinates. Yep, they disappeared east of our position about half an hour ago. There's a compound of some type at the end of this road, according to the satellite photos. Our boy might be there. The coordinates I'm sending you are where the van's parked. The compound's about two miles east of those digits. By the way, thanks for the goody bag! I'll have the sat phone, but it'll be off. Ok, sounds good. We'll let you know something shortly if we're able to see if Greg's there. Stay safe!" Nick pushed the end button, turned the phone off, and returned it to his backpack.

Nick and Kelly scrounged some of the loose scrub brush from the surroundings of the van and placed them on top of and around the van to camouflage it from the naked eye. Nick had not been as concerned about the van being discovered at night, but if they were still not back by daylight, the last thing they needed was someone stealing their ride.

The ravine that the Blackhawk had set down in

was one hundred and seven miles southeast of Ciudad Juarez. Don had gambled that Greg and the EMP weapons would have been taken back to the area operated by the Golfo Norte Cartel. With limited resources and working in a foreign country, Don had devised a plan to have Nick and Kelly determine if the Chinese would lead them back to Greg and the weapons or if they were only attempting to flee back to China from Mexico. At the same time, Don and his group would stage in Golfo Norte territory to get a jump on things in case they received information that Greg or the EMPs had been taken back there.

Don hung up from talking with Nick. He had jotted down the coordinates Nick had given him on a small waterproof notepad he kept in his top right jacket pocket. He tore out the page and handed it to James, who was seated in the Blackhawk, pecking away at a laptop running a specialized CIA program that disseminated information and intelligence. James was trying to gather any information from all likely and unlikely sources through chatter on public forums and social media that might help them locate Greg, which he also hoped would ultimately lead them to the weapons.

"Here...they might have something. These coordinates are where Nick parked their van. The Chinese headed east from these digits toward a possible compound. See what you can dig up."

"Roger that, boss, on it!" James replied as he

reached and grabbed the small piece of paper from Don.

Don walked over to Greaver, who was about forty yards from the aircraft standing on the ravine's edge, looking out into the flat terrain with his night vision binoculars.

"Anything?" Don asked as he approached.

"Nothing, boss."

"Good. Nick called. They might have something near Chihuahua. He gave us the coordinates of their van and some compound a couple of miles east of that."

"They got a pos ID"

"Not yet, they're working on it. Look, ever which way this goes, that Blackhawk is all of our tickets home. Nobody is coming for us, so we have to protect that bird. We'll have to figure out a way to get in and out of wherever this takes us from a distance."

"You mean ingress and egress from a distance because of the EMP?"

"Yep. We don't want another situation like those other poor bastards were in a few days ago, humping it across this shithole of a desert back to the States with half of Mexico looking for them."

"I'm with ya, boss. I guess James is gonna have to leave his toys on the bird. He ain't gonna be happy!" Greaver said, laughing and staring out into the darkness.

"For sure. The fewer electronics we can take, the better, in case they see us coming and activate that EMP again." Patting Greaver on the shoulder. "I'll let you know something when I hear back from Nick. Keep your head on a swivel and be ready to move." Don said as he walked back toward the Blackhawk.

Nick and Kelly moved across the night landscape in the direction they had seen the Mercedes tail lights disappear to the east. The night air had become cooler as the night lingered on and made the double layer of shirt and jacket feel comfortable to Nick and Kelly as they quietly moved across the flat landscape, dodging the occasional scrub brush. Nick and Kelly had agreed to stay clear of the road in case there was some sort of counter-measures for trespassers. The night was pitch black to the east, in the direction they were walking. To the west and behind them, the night sky faded into the glow of the distant city lights of Chihuahua.

CHAPTER 12

Knife Play

The black Land Rover was going well over the speed limit to travel along a major interstate in central Mexico. That did not matter to the occupants. They were untouchable, or so they thought. They had just issued an ass-whipping to the American Agents on their soil in the United States. The cheerful banter within the Land Rover had now been going on with the singing and bolstering of the recounting of the story of the ass-whipping handed out a few days earlier. Santiago sat in the front passenger seat, focused and staring out the side window. He allowed his men to have a good time and let their hair down a little because he would need them focused when they got to their destination.

Santiago stayed behind for a couple of days in Ciudad Juarez, watching over four of his men that had been wounded and made it back across to Mexico. Once he felt they were all stable and in good hands, he communicated with his boss, Guirillo, by satellite phone to see where the boss needed him and his men. Santiago's Land Rover now traveled south of Ciudad Juarez in the middle of the night, headed for the residence of the Golfo

Norte Cartel's trusted confidant, Senior Lucas Perez. Santiago had been to Senior Perez's home only twice in the past. Both times he had been tasked with the head of security for Guirillo. He knew the layout of the compound backward and forwards. Like any great head of security, Santiago was superb at his job.

The Land Rover turned off of I-45 onto the gravel and dirt road that disappeared in the Land Rovers headlights in an easterly direction. The Land Rover drove past the Honda van that sat off the road two hundred yards to their left. The van had passed the nighttime camouflage test. The Land Rover turned slightly to the right as the road wound in that direction and bumped up and down as its wheels crossed over dips in the washed-out portions of the road.

Nick and Kelly were moving slowly and surveying their surroundings as they moved as if they were on foot patrol in some province in the middle east. Nick paused and whispered loudly to Kelly, who was several feet to his right—

"Get down!"

The Land Rover's lights bounced up and down on the road as it quickly traveled one hundred yards away to Nick and Kelly's left side. Nick and Kelly were both face down on the ground, their weapons held in front of their prone bodies, their heads moving slowly from South to North as they watched the lights pass by in the night vision optics that each had flipped down in front of their faces. The Land Rover's tail lights disappeared in the direction they believed the Mercedes had gone.

"Looks like we've got another party crasher," Nick whispered to Kelly.

"Roger that, boss! Business is picking up." Kelly responded in a whisper.

"Switch on your radio. Make sure it's on the channel Don programmed in to work off of." Nick said as he reached down to the radio pocket of his chest rig, turned the knob to on, and heard the beep in his earpiece that meant the radio was on.

"I'm on. Can you hear me?" Kelly asked.

"Yep, gotcha!"

Nick and Kelly lay on the ground in their position for several minutes allowing for the night's silence to encroach back to normal after the vehicle had disrupted the silence. After they felt comfortable that no patrols had come past or any other anomalies, they stood back up and began slinking in the direction that both vehicles had gone.

As the Land Rover approached the front gate of Senior Perez's residence, the driver turned the radio down, and the three men that had been celebrating became quiet. Santiago appreciated the respect of his men, like a father that looks at his children when they are doing something wrong. A look is all it takes. The gate and the compound beyond were lit up with the orange glow of the lights affixed to the poles every fifty yards. The guard shifts had changed to the night time shift. A new guard walked to the Land Rover as it approached. They had been called by Thiago Perez and told to expect the black Land Rover containing Santiago and his men. In Spanish—

"Good evening, sir. We've been expecting you. Park in the circle in front if you don't mind, please." The guard said as he motioned to the other gate guard with his left hand in an underhanded waving motion to open the gate.

"Thank you," Came the reply from the driver of the Land Rover.

Santiago sat silently in the front passenger seat with his arm resting on the rolled-down window sill. The Land Rover traveled through the gate and across the compound yard to where the circle drive began. The driver saw their boss, Guirillo's, black Land Rover also parked in the center of the circle drive. Santiago and the other three men exited the Land Rover. The headlights were still shining in front of the vehicle and onto the back of Guirillo's Land Rover as Santiago walked by in the headlights. He looked down, noticing something out of place on the ground near the back hatch of his boss's Land Rover. It was Blood. Santiago paused as he looked down at the large spatter of blood droplets on the concrete and a cobblestone circle driveway, and a smile came across his face. *This must be from his old gringo friend.* He thought as he began to get excited about the torture session he knew was inevitable.

Santiago and his men walked toward the large front doors to the residence. The tall, thick, wooden double doors opened, and the light from inside the home showed outward, casting shadows behind the men as they approached. Guirillo wanted to welcome Santiago personally. There had been many heroes on the day of Guirillo's rescue, but none matched the wit and grit Santiago possessed to pull off the rescue operation. In Spanish—

"When I personally hired you as a boy, I knew one day you would prove to be a great addition to this organization. Thank you, thank you from the bottom of my heart. You will always have a place in my organization." Guirillo said admirably as he clutched Santiago's right hand with both of his shaking it up and down as he spoke.

"Thank you, boss. It was the least I could do."

"Come in, my boy, Senior Perez and Chen are waiting to see you. You know Senior Perez has already asked me if he could hire you at double the salary. I told him, no, but that means you get a raise."

"Again, thank you, boss. Not expected, but thank you."

The entourage continued inside, where pleasantries were exchanged between the new group and Senior Perez, his family, and Chen. Chen had been as grateful as Guirillo and promised Santiago that he would make it up to him somehow. Thiago Perez had been the head of his father's security since he was twenty-one. He had met Santiago on his two previous visits when they exchanged security protocols and bounced ideas off one another over the phone numerous times. The group sat in the large living room of Senior Perez's home. There were rugs on the floor from multiple animals that the Perez family had hunted and killed and several made from cow hides that had been harvested from one of the family's large cattle farms. The walls were adorned with the same type of trophies, Sitka deer, water buffalo, mule deer, and an American bison shoulder mount were on the walls and surrounded the plush leather sofas and recliners in the room. The coffee and end tables were made by German engineers from marble harvested out of quarries in Italy. Adjoining the living room was a glassed-in room shelved from the floor to the ceiling with some of the finest wines of the world and two shelves containing bottles of almost every sort of whiskey and rum one could imagine. The only people allowed to sit in on the conversation in the living room were Guirillo, Chen, the Perez family, and Santiago. Santiago had not devised a bold plan to rescue his boss from the idea that he might get a promotion or more money. He had done it because it was his job. Guirillo recognized this and, at least on this night, had put Santiago on a pedestal. The recognition by Guirillo's men that Santiago was well respected by the boss meant more to Santiago than anything. The group sat in the living room until after 11:00 P.M. Thiago had gotten up from the living room conversation and had walked to the glassed-in room with the whiskey and wine. There were two leather chairs with footrests and one coffee table in the glassed-in room, and Thiago had made one of the leather chairs his destination. Santiago followed Thiago after several minutes.

"Do you mind?" Santiago asked as he opened the glass door to the room and motioned toward the extra leather chair.

"By all means...sit. Better yet, pour you a glass of something and sit." Gesturing toward the whiskey.

Santiago walked to the bar counter near where the whiskey was, poured a glass of Four Roses Bourbon whiskey, and then sat down in the leather chair. Thiago watched Santiago pour the whiskey, and as Santiago sat—

"American whiskey, huh? You know they say you can tell a lot about a man by the type of whiskey he drinks."

"Really? Well, this isn't just any whiskey. It's Bourbon."

"Whiskey is whiskey," Thiago commented.

"On the contrary, do you know that whiskey can't hold the title of bourbon whiskey unless it's made in Kentucky? Anything else is just whiskey. So, what does that say about me, my friend?"

Chuckling, Thiago responds, "A lot! It says to me, you're a risk taker! I'm not saying that's a bad thing. Obviously, it worked in your favor this time, but that cowboy bullshit is only good in certain situations."

"Well, I'm glad we can agree to disagree. That brings me to my next question. Where is the gringo?"

"Ahhh...well, he is in one of the outbuildings chained to the floor. My mother doesn't like father doing the dirty work inside the house. You want to go see?"

"Absolutely! I thought you'd never ask?"

Thiago and Santiago passed through the living room, and Thiago bent over and whispered into his father's ear that he and Santiago would pay the gringo a visit. Senior Perez nodded in acknowledgment and addressed Guirillo and Chen about what his son and Santiago were up to. They were almost out of the living room when Guirillo spoke up and held his glass of wine up as if to toast Thiago and Santiago—

"Have fun!"

The men exited from the side door of the residence through a door that was not much smaller than the front entrance. They sauntered across a manicured courtyard with a fountain trickling in the background. A guard posted near the door stood up straighter as the two passed him.

"We aren't sure what to do with him yet. My father asked about ransom or bartering for one of our own from an American prison, but the Americans aren't much on giving in to demands, no matter that the prisoner is an American Agent.

Your boss wants to torture him but keep him alive and then maybe sell him or give him to the Chinese if they'll take him."

"I agree with my boss. Torture is the best medicine. I don't care if the Chinese want him or if he dies during torture. I don't care if he even talks. He will bear the torture for all the gringos that attacked my boss's residence and for the men they killed. I hand-picked those men. I knew their families." Santiago stated as they stopped shy of the door to the outbuilding to finish their talk.

Thiago asked for the door key from the guard sitting in a chair to the right of the door, but who was now standing? The guard handed a key attached to a long chain around his neck to Thiago. The door opened inward into what looked like a small jail. There were three cells with bars from the ground to the ceiling, with a barred cell door to each cell. The expanse between the door and the three cells held a metal office-type desk on the left and a coiled-up green water hose on the floor near the desk with a chair that was scooted up under the desk. In the two prior visits, Santiago had not been in this building and thought maybe it had been a guest house, and in a manner of speaking, it was a guest house. The coiled-up water hose connected to a spigot with a turn knob on the inside wall of the room was perplexing to Santiago until he looked down and saw the drain grate in the center of the room. *To wash the blood away*, it dawned on him. *Genius*! He thought. Santiago was taking a mental note of future building ideas for Guirillo's compound three hundred miles East of their present location. In broken English, Thiago stated—

"There he is...wake up Gringo! I have a friend of yours here to see you." Thiago said in broken English as he spits in the direction where Greg lay on the concrete floor.

Greg had been lying on his left shoulder, the only good shoulder he had now. He could feel shivers coming over him as the cold concrete transferred into his body, attempting to reduce his body heat. Greg lifted his head from where it had been resting on the floor and tried to focus on the two individuals speaking to him through the cell door. The bandage on Greg's right shoulder had begun to have seepage, and the dark blood had stained parts of his bare chest and back as it succumbed to the laws of gravity.

Thiago walked over to the metal desk and grabbed a key ring that held three large gold-colored keys, one to each cell and a single smaller silver-colored key that unlocked the chain secured to the prisoner. Thiago walked back over to Greg's cell, shoved the key in the keyhole, and turned it clockwise. The latch clicked, and the door opened quickly under the tug from Thiago. Santiago walked across the few feet of Greg's cell to where he lay on the floor and picked him up by his good arm. The thick steel links were connected at one end to a steel plate affixed to the wall with bolts, and the other had a metal clasp locked to Greg's left ankle. The weight of the steel chain and clasp had already begun to leave its mark on the thin skin around Greg's ankle bone. Thiago bent down and wiggled the silver key into the keyhole of the clasp, and the pin fell to the floor from its weight. Thiago and Santiago picked Greg up from the floor by supporting him under each arm. Greg grimaced in pain when Thiago grabbed him under his wounded shoulder.

"Ooh...sorry about that Gringo. That's nothing compared to what is about to happen to you." Santiago stated.

The terrain Nick and Kelly had been walking through had been without tall trees and much in the way of green foliage until now. Nick and Kelly stopped in their tracks and looked at each other in the darkness through their optics. Kelly had drifted in the dark away from Nick by about fifteen yards. Nick reached up to his rubberized radio button clipped to his chest rig and depressed it to speak—

"You seeing this?"

"Yep, that's some crazy shit! Who plants fifty-foot-tall palm trees in the middle of the desert?"

"These assholes! The closer we get, the more I think we're in the right spot. You see the lights up ahead through the trees?"

"Yep," came the reply in Nick's earpiece.

"It looks like we're getting close. Let's tighten

our formation and stay frosty!"
Nick and Kelly moved toward the lights that showed through the trees. The closer they got, the brighter things became in the night optics. The area ahead of them was now bright, as if the sun was beaming down in the middle of the day. It was now well after midnight, and the vastness of the Cartel compound revealed itself to the eyes of Nick and Kelly. They were still one hundred yards off the main road moving slowly, scanning the distant walled compound for movement and personnel. Nick stopped and knelt on one knee, and Kelly mimicked him a few feet away. Now close enough to one another to whisper without using the radio —

"Guards! Looks like two of 'em at the gate by the road."

"I see 'em."

"I don't see any other way in on this side, do you?"

"Nope. There's gotta be another way in and out of this place. Maybe on the backside."

"I agree. Let's move slow around this side to the back."

"Copy, I'm on your six." Kelly acknowledged that she would stick close to Nick's backside as they progressively moved forward away from the light sources and sticking to the dark areas of the landscape.

Nick moved further away from the right side wall of the compound to help keep their visibility down. Now almost two hundred yards off the right side of the wall, Nick kneeled again—

"You see that? It looks like light is coming from the side wall."

"I see something. I can't tell what it is, but yeah, I guess."

Nick craned his neck from side to side, trying to pierce the darkness around the trees with the night optics. Nick took his pack off his back, unzipped the main compartment zipper, and began rummaging around. Nick pulled out his pair of black, rubber-armored Steiner binoculars. He reached up, flipped the night optics from his face to the upward position, and brought the binoculars to his naked eyes. It took Nick's eyes a few seconds to adjust from the night optics to the normal lighting. Kelly looked on as he did so.

"It's some sort of an entrance. I don't see a guard on the outside, but I'm betting there's one on the inside." Nick said as he stared toward the wall where the light was emanating through a small sliver of the wall.

"You hear that?" Kelly said, cocking her head to the side to hear better.

Nick pulled the binoculars from his face and listened hard.

"Yeah…it sounds like someone whaling."

"It sounds like someone's in pain."

"Fuck! That has to be Greg! Chen's here, and we've seen other people show up, and this place is heavily guarded. It's gotta be Greg!" Nick excitedly whispered as he placed the Steiners back in the pack and felt around for the satellite phone.

"You makin' the call?"

"Yep, calling in the cavalry."

Sleep was hard to come by in the world of special operations, so you take it when you can. Don had fallen asleep almost upright, sitting in one of the fabric and metal bench seats in the rear of the Blackhawk. His head was resting on one of the bench seats' support pillars. James had taken a second watch, and Greaver rechecked his gear. This was his third time checking his equipment since they landed. The pilot, co-pilot, and crew chief were all asleep in the Blackhawk. The vibration disrupted a dream that Don had been in the middle of and woke him up wondering for a split second where he was. He quickly realized the vibration was from the satellite phone in his pants' side cargo pocket, plucked it out, and pushed the green answer key.

"Yeah"

"Don, I think we found him! We are a couple hundred yards off the side wall of the compound, and we can hear sounds like someone is being tortured." Nick whispered into the satellite phone. This got Don's attention, and he stood up and jumped to the ground from the doorway of the Blackhawk. Don had the phone to his right ear as he walked to the closest crew member asleep and kicked him in the side of the leg. Don cupped the phone's mouthpiece as he looked down at the now awake but groggy crew chief—

"We need to get movin'. They've got him!"

The crew chief awoke the others and passed the word as they all frantically began gathering the gear they had drug out of the helicopter.

"We're on the way...probably take us half an hour. We'll have to hump a few miles on foot not to spook 'em with this helicopter. Give us max two hours and keep your radios on. We'll see you when we see you." Don said, pulling the phone away and pushing the end button.

"Let's move, boys...they're torturing him as we speak, c'mon, gather your shit, let's go!"

The early night conversation and drink between the family of Senior Perez, the Chinese, and the Norestre Golfo Cartel had now turned into a late-night business meeting. Old cigar smoke and the faint smell of whiskey lingered in the room. Chen and the Cartels had unfinished business. There was still a large sum of money owed for an already delivered product, the EMPs. The lady of the house, Senora Julieta Perez, had retired for the night before the gentlemen got down to business. After several minutes of her exit, Julieta re-entered the living room where the men had just begun to discuss more serious matters, walked to where Lucas Perez was seated and bent down, and whispered into his ear—

"I don't think I need to remind you that the

cries from your prisoner can be heard in our bedroom. I would appreciate some sleep."

"Of course, my love. I apologize." Lucas acknowledged, at the same time standing to his feet and excusing himself from the room.

Lucas Perez opened the large side door to the residence and immediately heard a loud moan of a male voice coming from the outbuilding. Lucas shook his head from side to side as he walked across the short span of the yard toward the building's door. Lucas opened the door to see Santiago and Thiago standing over Greg, who had been stripped of his shirt and now sat in the chair they had removed from behind the desk, his arms zip tied to the backrest. Blood dripped down the right side of Greg's mouth, and a pool had begun to form below on the floor several feet from the drain. Lucas noted that Greg's bandage had been removed from the bullet wound in his shoulder to reveal a nasty hole that had now turned dark red, almost black from the onset of infection.

"Thiago!"

"Yes, sir?" Thiago answered as he and Santigao turned to see Lucas standing in the open doorway.

"Your mother has asked that you keep the noise down. You know she doesn't like to hear all of this! At least turn on the radio. Do not kill the American. We might need him or keep him around for a while."

"I apologize, Senior Perez," Santiago said, feeling a little embarrassed that he might have awoken the lady of the house.

"Hey Gringo, how has your stay been so far? I hope you enjoy the room service! Maybe if we make a good enough example of you, your American friends will think twice about kidnapping one of us again. Too bad you won't live long enough to see the chaos we plan to deliver to your country." Looking back at Thiago, "Clean him up when you're done. We don't need him dying just yet, and turn the radio on to mask his screams, please."

"Yes, sir," Thiago said as he looked over at the older radio that looked like a 1980's style boombox sitting on the back of the desk.

Nick and Kelly had moved twenty yards closer to the opening, where the light showed through the high-security wall. They had set up a makeshift perimeter with Nick lying prone on the ground looking toward the opening in the wall and Kelly lying flat looking in the direction they had come from to the Southwest.

"I don't know how much more of this I can take! If I have to hear him much more, I'm marching in there and killing some people." Kelly whispered to Nick.

"Yeah, same! Don needs to hurry the hell up." Just then, the sound of a Hispanic male could be heard singing along with a cantata of instruments. "What the hell is that? Are they having a party or somethin'?"

The faint sound of music now drowned out the midnight torture session.

The Chinese bodyguard that had survived the kidnapping in Mexico and the gunfight on the Interstate now had been tasked with counting the money in the large black Pelican case handed to Chen in the middle of the meeting. Chen had passed it to him and ordered him to count it. Chen was slightly upset at the whole situation. He had traveled thousands of miles to perform a duty for his Government and to pad his pockets. Chen had never been in combat and was so sheltered in his service that the situation now took him aback. He wanted to get this night over with so that he, his bodyguard, and his driver could be on their way first thing in the morning to Mexico City, where he would gain transportation back to China through the Chinese consulate.

"I hope that we can secure more business with you and your Government Mr. Chen. The unfortunate events surrounding this transaction will be avoided in our future dealings. Thanks to you and the delivery of these weapons, extra precautions will now be in place. We now not only can make sure technology is not in play near our future transactions, but we can also now wreak havoc on any mass technologically occupied city in the United States." Guirillo said in an apologetic and reassuring tone.

"I appreciate the consolation. I'm sorry for how

this transaction began, but I'm satisfied, as is my Government, with the outcome of this business deal. I hope in the future, whether it be myself or another, that your security is improved and the lives of my men and I can be guaranteed safe. The relationship between your organizations and my Government has been advantageous for all parties, and we look forward to providing you with any items that would benefit the People's Republic of China in undermining the Government of the United States." Chen replied as he sipped the last bit of whiskey in the bottom of a thick round crystal glass where a tiny bit of ice resided.

The bodyguard closed the lid to the Pelican case and snapped the four hinges shut, which garnered Chen's attention. Chen glanced over, and the bodyguard nodded in the affirmative, signaling that the funds were correct.

The time was now just after 02:00, or 2:00 A.M. Nick and Kelly were still in their same position on the right side of the compound, about two hundred yards off the side wall. Nick had taken the first watch and agreed they would each nap for thirty minutes or so before the other would relieve them. The second watch was underway with Kelly lying prone on the now cool ground, MP-5 machine pistol out in front of her. Kelly had balled up her fist and set it on the shoulder stock of the gun to make a soft place to rest her chin as she watched and listened for any changes around their location.

The crackling in Kelly's right ear startled her as the earbud came to life and words filtered through —

"Nick, do you copy over?" came the male voice. Kelly had not been the only one startled, and Nick quickly raised his head from the ground where his head had been resting on both hands for a pillow. Nick promptly reached down to his chest and depressed the button to activate the bone-conducting mic in the earpiece that rested over the back of his ear.

"Roger that, Don. We got you over."

"Where are the fucking keys to this van?"

Nick looked over at Kelly, both with puzzled looks wondering why they would need the keys to the van.

"Behind the front driver-side tire. What's the plan, over?"

"We're driving in the front gate."

"Y'all are gonna do what?"

"We're going to drive right through the front gate, over."

"How close are you and Kelly to the wall?"

"About two hundred yards, we think we have an opening on the right side of the wall. So we're gonna try and get through the wall that way."

"What's your plan other than driving through the front gate over?"

"You and Kelly get close to that opening. As soon as yall hear the fireworks up front, make your entry. You think you'll know about where Greg is?"

"General area, we've been listening to them off and on for a couple of hours. They're drowning out the torture session with music for some reason, so we'll go for wherever that is coming from. We can hear the music playing as we speak."

"Roger that. Watch for friendly fire, don't kill one of us, got it?"

"Good copy Don. See you on the inside."

Greaver, hearing the conversation between Nick and Don in his earpiece, knelt by the front driver-side tire, reached behind it with his left hand, and felt for the keys. James was already pulling the brush from on top of and around the van that had been used to camouflage it and was casting it off to the side into the dark. James heard the door locks of the van all click at once when Greaver pushed the unlock symbol on the remote. All three men had jogged almost two miles from where the Blackhawk had dropped them off to the West of the van just over the top of a set of small ridges. Greaver, James, and Don all carried a heavy pack of equipment and weapons.

James tossed the three heavy packs each had lugged with them into the passenger side sliding door of the van and pushed each pack up to the far side. James had already removed the M-14 rifle from its protective backpack case. The M-14 rifle had a long history in the United States military as a precision semi-automatic rifle that fired 7.62x51 rifle rounds with extreme stopping and dropping power when used on humans. The premis for the M-14 semi-automatic rifle came from its famous cousin, the M-1 Garand. The M-1 Garand rifle found its mark on history during World War two when it was extensively usd by infantryman of the United States military. The M-14 James used had a Nightforce 20x50mm scope mounted onto the top of the receiver. James had used the same type rifle in Iraq as a designated marksman for his platoon.

James pulled multiple metal M-14 twenty-round box magazines from one of the packs they had brought and began placing them into the oversized magazine pouches on the front of his black chest rig. James, Greaver, nor Don said a word to each other. They each knew exactly what they were doing and how to do it. Greaver finished loading out his vest and tossed the van keys to him through the air as Don walked towards the driver's side door. Don reached out, caught the keys, and placed them in his pocket. Don pushed the button on the van's dashboard, and it cranked up just as James slid the passenger side door closed. Don reached down and keyed up his mic after looking at all the displays on the dash—

"Nick, you copy over?"

"Yep, got you."

"You think you ahh… could have left us a little more gas in this thing?"

"It's a Honda…you can go a long way on half a gallon. We didn't have a chance to stop for gas."

Nick said, depressing the button for his mic to pick up his voice as he whispered.

Nick and Kelly had already begun to move slowly toward the compound wall before Don's radio transmission. They stopped to receive the communication and then kept moving forward in the shadows of the tall transplanted grove of trees.

"We're about to be rolling out…are yall set?"

"Negative. Give us about five minutes, over."

"Good copy, five minutes"

Greaver pulled back the charging handle of his Sig Sauer XM250 light assault rifle, and a live round moved into the firing chamber from the one-hundred-round belt of ammunition that was strung into the box pouch container attached to the underbelly of the machine gun's receiver. Greaver slung a black satchel over his left shoulder and across his body that contained four more one-hundred-round pouches of ammunition, giving him five hundred rounds of light machine gun ammunition. He felt on the side of his chest rig for the three 40mm cartridges, which gave him a total of four, counting the one he had loaded in the chamber of the H&K M320 launcher he had hung from a tethered sling from the shoulder of his chest rig. To most, this loadout would have been too much weight, but Greaver was built for this type of load and had trained and operated with this loadout many times.

Don had turned the headlight indicator knob on the dashboard, turning off the exterior lights of the van, including the running lights. He pulled the gear shift to Drive and began driving back toward the dirt and gravel road. Don pulled the van onto the road and was driving while he looked through his night vision goggles. The van made the first turn in the street and began to buck and jerk.

"What the hell!" Don keyed up the mic on his vest, "Damit, Nick, we're out of gas!"

"Sorry, brother," Nick replied in Don's earpiece.

"We'll be humping it from here. Gonna be a few extra minutes." Don said, lifting his finger off the mic button and looking over at Greaver and then back at James, "Sorry, fellas!"

"Wouldn't have it any other way, boss!" Greaver said, shaking his head and smiling as if he knew Murphy's law would wreck their plan.

James slid the passenger side sliding door open—

"Well shit! I had just caught my wind from the last sprint!"

"Always complaining…glass half full," Greaver said as he opened his door and stepped out into the darkness of the road with gear hanging off all of him.

"Like two old women bickering! I'm gonna have to separate you too!" Don said, shaking his head in the dark and walking to the back of the van.

Nick and Kelly had made their way to within twenty yards of the wall. They had not seen any roving security guards on the outside of the wall the entire time they had been surveilling it. They had been able to get close enough to determine that the sliver of light they had observed from a distance was, in fact, a slim doorway possibly used to enter or exit in case of an emergency. The opening matched the color and texture of the wall, but the light from the compound's interior pierced the edges, and the square doorway was obvious from the outside.

The three Ground Branch operators had arrived at the front entrance of the compound. They could now hear the faint sound of Hispanic music coming from somewhere inside the compound's walls. They could see two guards at the main gate and a roving guard or two as they passed by the small entrance of the main gate they could see through. The three only used hand signals as they looked around, observed the guards, and ascertained their approach. Don quickly formulated a plan. Don looked at Greaver in his NVGs. He held up two fingers to signify the two guards. Don Knife hand motioned forward, for he had Greaver move forward on the opposite side of the wall. Don gave the hand signal to use their knives.

Don had already pulled the Randall knife from its leather sheath as he moved silently down the wall toward the guard on his side of the gate. Don had been given the Randall knife by his father upon graduating Ranger selection. This had not been the Randall's first encounter with a bare neck. Don had used the knife several times in the Middle East and once in an Eastern Bloc country to immobilize a guard.

The guard on Greaver's side of the gate only felt the cold steel on his neck as he awoke from his nap. Too late to do anything about it, and no wind in his windpipe now to scream. He only struggled for a second or two as Greaver drug him backward down the wall and into the darkness of the underbrush.

Don, simultaneously with Greaver, had utilized the razor-sharp edge and the tip of the Randall knife to thrust it deep into the upper chest of the guard at the same time while reaching around his shoulders with his left arm and placing his left hand over the guard's mouth to squash any last bit of air that might have formed a noise out of the guard's mouth. Don also silently drug the guard back into the brush.

Chewing on a piece of spearmint gum, James had been watching from his prone position in the edge of the grove of trees lining the road leading up to the gate from one hundred yards out. He had trained the scope of his M-14 rifle on the entrance and beyond, covering Don and Greaver as they began their deadly work.

"You're clear, boss!" James whispered, never taking his eyes away from the optic of his rifle and keying up the mic with his left hand.

"Roger that...Nick, we're moving into the

compound through the front gate." Done replied to all listening on the secure radio channel.

"Copy that. We're moving to the side wall entrance!" Nick responded.

Nick and Kelly slowly moved to the opening. Nick felt on the wall and pushed with his left hand, his rifle in his right hand, holding it by the pistol grip at the high ready position. He pushed on different areas of the wall with his left hand, looking intently with his night vision goggles at the wall. His hand abruptly stopped. He felt a metal latch. The latch had been painted the same color as the wall to blend in. The latch pushed inward, exposing the bottom end protruding outward as he pushed. Nick slowly pulled outward on the bottom portion of the latch, and the opening in the wall became visible as more light filtered through the now-evident doorway. Kelly had moved to the side of the door in the wall as she saw it was opening into the courtyard. As the opening grew larger with Nick's pulling on the latch, Kelly, standing in an isosceles stance, brought her silenced MP-5 machine gun up to her shoulder and tucked her head down tight onto the shoulder stock to look for work as the compound yard exposed itself to her. Standing just ten feet away, a guard, holding an AK-47 with both hands at waist height in front of him, turned to look in the direction of the now slowly opening doorway in the wall. The area inside the wall was lit with night lights on scattered poles and the fascia of some of the buildings causing Kelly to squint her eyes as the display in her night vision goggles got brighter. Kelly stepped one step forward to get a better view of the compound and saw the guard turn to look in their direction. Without hesitation, Kelly squeezed the trigger on the Heckler & Koch, which released one round into the middle of the upper back of the guard, dropping him instantly to the ground as paralysis took control and death quickly followed.

"One guard down. We're inside the wall!" Nick said into his mic.

"Roger that...we're going to hold up near the gate. Let us know if you find Greg."

"Copy, moving!" Nick acknowledged.
Kelly had already grabbed the dead guard under both arms and began to drag his body toward the opening in the wall as Nick picked up both of the guard's legs and helped Kelly move the body through the doorway of the wall to the outside of the compound.

Nick and Kelly moved in the shadows of the building near the wall's opening. They moved in the direction of the muffled sound of music. Both moved slowly and methodically toward the music with their weapons held to their shoulders. Kelly was in the lead with her silenced weapon as they approached the corner of the structure. She pulled her rifle in a little and dropped it down under her armpit to look around the corner. A guard was walking between two structures around the corner. She pulled her head back, re-shouldered her MP-5, held up one finger, and then made the walking symbol with two fingers as Nick looked on. Understanding her sign language, she spotted a walking guard around the corner. Kelly leaned out around the corner to find that the guard had passed, and the alley was clear. Kelly led Nick across the small alleyway to the shadows of the next structure. As they moved, Nick turned every few feet to check their rear and ensure no guard had happened upon them. Kelly's subconscious noticed that the structures and inside of the compound were elaborate, with manicured flower beds and green grass, and the main structure had white stucco outer walls that reached two stories as Nick and Kelly moved down the wall of the second structure a second sound of running water mixed in with the muffled music. Kelly approached the corner, pulled her rifle in again, and looked around the corner to see a running water fountain surrounded by small walkways and flower beds. *This might be the center of the compound*, she thought.

"Don, we're still moving toward the music. Y'all still good out there", Nick said as he keyed up his mic.

"Roger that, we don't hear any music, but we've had a few guards pass through the yard. Ya'll need to hurry the fuck up. Only a matter of time before they realize the front gates down!"

"Good copy," Don replied as Kelly looked back, hearing the conversation in her earpiece.

Nick and Kelly moved past the fountain to the shadow of the wall of one story structure and moved toward now louder music. The muffled sound of the music instantly got louder and then muffled again with the sound of an opening and closing door. Kelly and Nick froze in the shadows as a figure walked across their front, passing the shadowed wall and continuing toward the two-story residence. Kelly noticed that the person was not carrying a noticeable weapon and was an older-looking male. Kelly and Nick watched as the male mumbled under his breath as he walked past and disappeared into the side door of the primary residence. Kelly looked back at Nick as they nodded in agreement that through that door was more than likely their main objective, and in the back of both of their minds, they knew Greg might be dead or incapacitated and not alone! Kelly snapped her head back to her front, shouldered the MP-5, and moved quickly to the left side of the door as Nick moved to the right side.

Nick kept his rifle trained on the door with his right arm and hand while reaching for the doorknob with his left. Nick slowly turned the doorknob. He felt the latch bolt release from the plate, and the door opened inward. Kelly had already flipped her goggles into the upward position on her head. The light became bright and the music louder as the door opened. Greg was seated in the chair toward the back of the room near a jail cell. Greg's head was hanging, looking down, his arms tied behind him and to the chair's backrest. He was bare-chested, the hole in his shoulder now dark red with a spider web of bloodshot blood trickling down from Greg's head onto his Multicam pants-clad legs. A small stream of blood traveled from the base of the chair down the slight decline to the drain in the middle of the floor. Thiago was having his turn with Greg, standing over him with leather gloves on his hands, his right hand drawn back to strike again as Kelly quickly took the entire scene in.

She pulled the trigger once on the MP-5. The 9mm, full metal jacketed round traveled across the room, finding its mark at the left cheek of Thiago's face as he turned his head to see who was entering the room. The bullet traveled through Thiago's cheek into the base of his skull, dropping him instantly to the ground. A crumpled corpse now lay in Greg's blood at the feet of the chair.

Santiago had been sitting on the edge of the desk at the left side of the room when Kelly breached the doorway. As he saw his friend crumple to the floor from the thump sound from Kelly's silenced rifle from the doorway, he reached for his pistol under his shirt, then thought better of the idea and placed both hands above his head. Kelly swung the silenced barrel of the MP-5, pointing it at Santiago's head. As she applied pressure to the trigger, her brain registered that Santigao was giving up and let her finger relax. Kelly and Nick entered the room with her rifle still trained on Santiago. Nick slowly closed the door behind them and turned the knob on a deadbolt to lock it.

"We've got 'em!" Nick exclaimed, a little out of breath into his mic.

"Roger that... he alive?"

"Standby," Nick replied into the mic as he moved to Greg's side.

Greg knelt next to Greg and felt for a pulse on his neck—

"He's alive!" Nick excitedly said aloud, keying up his mic, "He's alive...not in good shape, but alive."

"Roger that, good deal! Can you...", Don paused mid-sentence as two guards walked out of the shadows from the side of the residence in his and Greaver's direction, "We've got company standby."

The guards walked toward the front gate, "Miguel...Miguel! Estas durniendo de nuevo?" one of the guards asked aloud, projecting his voice toward the front gate and asking if they were sleeping on duty.

The beautifully manicured hedges near the front gate secreted Don and Greaver as they knelt at the edge of the hedge. James, who was still in his same position on the road leading into the gate, had heard the conversation and now had his crosshairs on one of the two guards walking up to the gate.

"I've got 'em, boss...give the word", James whispered into the mic.

The two guards walked up the broad driveway

toward the gate. Don looked for another option of taking out the two approaching guards but could not devise a plan that did not involve a lot of noise and him or Greaver coming out unscathed.

"Send it!" Don muttered into his mic.
The 7.62 projectile traveled the short one hundred yards striking the guard before the crack-boom of the rifle echoed through the compound, sending one of the guards backward onto the ground. The second guard was raising his AK-47 in the direction he heard the shot when Don beat him to it and placed two rounds from his rifle into the man. Both guards lay in the middle of the driveway. The echo of the initial gunshots rolled through the compound like claps of thunder.

Chen set up straight in his chair, a look of concern on his face as he looked at Gurillo and Lucas Perez. With guns drawn, two guards burst into the living room and moved to protect Lucas. Chen's bodyguard, who had been dozing off in the corner of the room, sprung up, pulled a T75 pistol from its holster under his suit jacket, and moved across the room to Chen. Guirillo got up and moved near Lucas as they made their way to the hallway leading from the living room to the residence's kitchen.

Senior Lucas Perez was a man that planned things out. Just as he had planned and designed the building in the compound to house a prisoner or two, he had designed and built a small barracks building to house the guards that filtered in an out-on-work rotation to guard him and his family's empire. The barracks were designed to accommodate twenty-five men with bunks in three separate rooms and a shower room with four individual shower stalls and four toilets. Senior Lucas Perez was conscientious that his men needed to enjoy their downtime and had a large living room built in the front of the barracks with multiple televisions, video games, and two pool tables.

The loud reports from the Ground Branch's rifles sent the twelve men sleeping in the barracks into a frenzy, scrambling to put on clothes and grab weapons. They all screamed at each other to move faster, and they spoke back and forth as they dressed. Were they being hit by a rival Cartel, or could this be the Mexican military that someone forgot to pay this month?

Greaver shouldered the M250 and moved toward where the large fountain, circle drive, and several vehicles were parked. Don followed close behind, scanning their sides as they approached the parked cars. They could hear men hollering in Spanish all around the compound.

"What's the plan, boss?" Greaver asked out loud.

"Find those weapons! Nick's got Greg."

"Roger that! What's our ROE?" Greaver asks

about the rules of engagement.

"No ROE, we aren't supposed to be here anyway. Kill 'em all!"

"Good copy, boss." Greaver acknowledged.

The AK-47 rounds flew across the front lawn of the compound and hit the ground and the side of the fountain causing concrete dust and small chunks to jump in the air. Greaver heard the report of the fully automatic AK-47 to their right side. Greaver stood up and over where Don knelt and squeezed the trigger on the M250. The belt began to feed into the side of the receiver from the pouch and spit out projectiles at eight hundred rounds per minute. Greaver held the trigger for only two seconds sending a stream of copper projectiles toward the incoming fire. A second and third guard emerged from the left side of the residence and sporadically fired their weapons toward Greaver and Don.

James heard the melee in the compound, picked up the M-14, and moved to a more formidable position closer to the opening in the gate where he could see more of the interior.

"I'm moving for a better position, boss"

"Roger that, we're about to move. Can't stay here!" Don replied into the mic.

Noise discipline had been an essential part of the operation until now. Kelly and Nick had both been startled at the loud succession of gunshots. Nick had been cutting the zip ties on Greg's arms to the chair back, and Kelly had been staring down the sights of her MP-5 at Santiago's head. The loud snapping of rifle fire caused Kelly to look toward the door giving Santiago the split second he needed to lunge at Kelly. Santiago grabbed the suppressor on the end of the MP-5 and pushed it upward as Kelly's finger pulled the trigger sending several projectiles into the ceiling. They both tumbled to the floor near the desk as Kelly struggled to maintain control of the MP-5. Santiago punched Kelly several times on the left side of her head and jaw, knocking her out and releasing her grip on the rifle. Nick, knife in hand, sprang up from cutting Greg's bindings and slipped in the blood on the floor, clambering and trying to stay afoot.

Still standing near the rear of one of the Land Rovers, Greaver leaned out with the M250 to his right shoulder and pulled the trigger. The belt fed through the receiver, and spent brass hulls expelled out of the right side of the weapon onto the ground and made tink, tink sounds as they bounced off the vehicle's bumper.

"Move!" Greaver yelled in his deep guttural voice.

"Moving!" Don exclaimed as he jumped from his kneeling position and sprinted for the edge of the steps of the residence.

Men scrambled inside the home, some protecting

their bosses and one female guard running to the upstairs master bedroom to protect Julieta Perez. Chen saw the black pelican case where it had been set down by Santiago when he had arrived earlier in the evening. He grabbed the handle of the pelican case and swung the case on top of the table. Chen did not have a problem reading the stamped Chinese wording on the outside and inside of the box—his native tongue. Chen began flipping the switches inside the now open Pelican case. Chen thought *any technology the men assaulting the compound had would fry it and give them an advantage.* It took the weapon thirty seconds to come online and give the green light that it was ready. Chen pushed the large red button on the keypad. The house went dark, along with every other light in the compound and surrounding structures.

Santiago was still straddling Kelly's midsection from where they had struggled on the floor. He quickly reached to pick up the MP-5 that Kelly had let go of when she passed out from the blows to her face. Nick made it to Santiago just as the lights went out.

Greg was in and out of consciousness. He awoke to the room completely dark with the sounds of two men grunting and fighting one another and the sound of sporadic gunfire outside of the building they occupied. Nick had just cut the ties to Greg's arms and hands before leaving him to help Kelly. Greg felt that he could move his left arm and hand, but his right side did not have much mobility, and it occurred to him that the wound in his right shoulder had not improved. Greg leaned over in the darkness and felt down his right side as he attempted to reach down and free his legs from the ties that bound them to the chair. Greg could hear the men grappling near him and the occasional cuss word in English and successively in Spanish. Greg became a little more cognizant as his adrenaline flowed through him, hearing the now louder screams from the fight and not knowing who was winning. The screams became gurgling sounds as the tussling slowed, and the room became silent.

Greg was almost panicking, knowing this was it for him if the right side did not prevail. His right arm dangling, useless to that side of the chair, struggling with his good left arm and hand to break the thick zip tie wrapped around his right leg and the right portion of the chair. A hand grabbed Greg on his leg, straddling him and causing him to rare back in the chair, still dark in the room.

"I got you, brother! It's me, Nick. I got you", Nick said in the darkness, completely out of breath.

"I don't know...walk...where," Greg attempted to speak, but the blows to his head and the combined concussions did not afford Greg a voice.

"Don't try and talk. We're gettin' you outta here. Just hang on! I gotta check on Kelly. Just hang

tight for a minute."
Greg crawled on the floor and felt for Kelly. He first felt the lifeless body of Santiago. Nick had prevailed in the fight for his life and had driven his knife deep into Santiago's chest. Nick was not even sure how he had done it in the darkness. Still, in the fight, Santiago had pinned him to the floor with the receiver of the MP-5 against his throat and, in sheer reaction, had been able to work his knife into Santiago's chest, causing him to initially scream and fall to the side of Nick. Nick had been able to maneuver over Santiago while still driving the seven inches of steel blade deep into his chest, causing Santiago to lose his breath. Santiago's last words had been uttered through the gurgling sounds of his lung gaining air through the sucking chest wound.

Nick found Kelly, reached for a flashlight in his vest, and it would not click on. Nick thought for a second, pulled up his left sleeve to uncover his watch dial, and the bright tritium markers on the MTM had all stopped. *They used it again*, he thought. Kelly began to make noises, and in the darkness, Nick reached for her—

"Hey, hey...you good? We've gotta move. Kelly, come on! Wake up."

"Why's it dark?"

"EMP hit the compound"

"Again?"

"Yes, again! Come on. We gotta get Greg outta here."

In the darkness, Kelly felt for her MP-5 and Santigao's dead body while feeling the cold metal receiver of her weapon. Spitting on the dead body as she gained her composure and her weapon and crawled across the floor to where Nick was trying to free Greg from the last of his restraints.

"Watch that door. I don't know what's going on out there, radios out," Nick told Kelly.

Kelly shifted her attention in the direction of the door, her eyes now adjusting to the darkness and the tiny bit of ambient light coming from the night sky and filtering through the door crack and small windows high up on the walls in the room. Sporadic gunfire was going off all around the outside of the building they were in.

The massive wooden door to the entrance of the residence opened slowly. Everything was dark, and Don could hear the clamoring of feet and things being knocked over in the house. Don took his non-working night vision goggles off his head and put them in his dump pouch hanging off his combat belt's rear. Greaver was behind Don halfway up the entrance steps, kneeling to change out the one-hundred-round belt-fed magazine pouch to his M250, scanning his surroundings while doing so. Greaver knew that he had to change the ammo pouch quickly. He could already hear more Spanish-speaking voices getting louder. Don moved into the residence to a wall that he could see from the starlight shining in from the tall windows throughout the house. Greaver pulled the charging handle back on the machine gun, sending a fresh live round into the chamber and, at the same time, moving to the massive front door. He quickly peaked in, and Don gave him hand signals that implied that he could hear people inside and that he was moving further into the residence. Greaver acknowledged with a like hand signal and temporarily posted at the door, guarding their rear.

The situation had become frustrating for James, who was techy by nature. The illuminated reticle inside his NightForce scope had gone out, his radio was no longer working, and his night vision goggles were worthless. He banged on the side of his radio, attempting to correct whatever had caused it to stop working. James again moved closer to the entrance gate without any type of communication and knowing what was happening inside the compound. James had been involved with enough conflicts to recognize the sound that an AK-47 makes when it spews its lethal language, and he had been around Greaver and his M250 long enough to know the sound of its eight-hundred-round-a-minute rate of fire. He could hear the M250 unleashing its rain of copper around the front of the residence. James crawled to the hedge inside the gate entrance, which Don had previously occupied, and set up his position. James' eyes had adjusted to the low light, and the quality glass inside of the NightForce scope was gathering every bit of the ambiance emitting off of the stars in the night sky, allowing him to see just enough of the black, cross-shaped reticle inside the tube.

James had not agreed with wearing the all-black uniforms that Don had chosen for them for this mission but now thought *Don must have had a premonition.* Their all-black uniforms had now become optimum in the total darkness and had made it easy for him to distinguish between friend and foe as targets presented themselves. The M-14 spit out its lethal medicine as each report dropped a Cartel guard to the ground. Greaver had now run the M250 dry for a second time and was again changing the magazine pouch. The sound of James M-14 was music to his ears, knowing he had covering fire. The Ground Branch Agents had trained so much with one another that they knew each other's every move and every sound, which was extremely important in this type of situation. Comm's out, optics out, hand signals, and good old-fashioned gunplay, or as Greaver liked to call it, *up close and personal*!

In the darkness, Nick helped Greg to his feet. He took Greg's right arm and pulled it across his shoulders while lifting Greg with his left arm under Greg's armpit. Nick kept his right side free from obstruction to access his rifle that was dangling from its tether. Kelly cycled a fresh round into the chamber of the MP-5, making sure it was still functional after the melee on the floor. She shouldered the weapon and moved toward the door, with Nick carrying Greg a few feet behind. Kelly reached for the door and felt for the lock in the dark, turned the bolt, and slowly opened the door. Kelly backed away from the now-open doorway and scanned the outside for any hostile targets. Not seeing any threats, Kelly moved through the doorway and back toward the wall and courtyard she and Nick had followed to get to the building. Nick trailed close behind, turning and checking their rear while holding up Greg and helping him move as fast as possible.

The sound of gunfire was loud and echoing through the compound as the sound bounced off of the buildings and stucco walls of the surrounding fence. Between the sounds of gunfire, they could hear Spanish-speaking voices yelling here and there around the compound. Nick and Greg stayed in the shadows of the wall as Kelly ran across the courtyard toward the fountain erected in its center. Kelly felt the blow to her lower abdomen and the burning sensation as the projectile struck her just below her bullet-resistant vest. The bullet had gone through and through just above her hip bone on her right side. Kelly stumbled and fell near the fountain. Nick had been looking back down the wall in the direction they had come from, making sure someone did not happen upon them or follow them from the building they had been in. He heard the gunshots ring out from across the courtyard and snapped his head back to the courtyard's direction to see the gunman with a shouldered AK-47 firing at Kelly. Nick swung his rifle toward the courtyard, temporarily dropping Greg, who fell to the ground, as Nick held the gun with both hands and pulled the trigger. The gunman across the yard fell out of Nick's sight. A second gunman ran into view near where the first had been. Nick re-positioned his sights on the second man and pulled the trigger, sending him out of sight below the ornate bushes that lined the side of the courtyard. Nicked helped Greg back up, and they both hobbled across the open yard to Kelly, who was attempting to open the IFAK that Don had included as part of their kit.

"Fine, time to get yourself shot!" Nick said, trying to make light of the moment.

"Wasn't intentional, I promise!" she responded.

"Keep an eye out...let me get you fixed up" Nick opened the IFAK and pulled out a package of quik clot gauze. He reached to Kelly's backside and felt for an exit wound which he found, "It went through...hang on, I'm working on you."

"Give me a gun...I can shoot." Greg said as he lay on his side nearby.

"Alright, buddy, here ya go! Watch our rear while I finish up on her." Nick commanded as he pulled the Sig pistol from its holster and handed it to Greg.

Nick packed the gauze into the wound in Kelly's lower abdomen.

"Motherfucker that hurts!" Kelly said, grimacing.

"Sorry, just hang on!"

Nick quickly finished packing the wound from both sides. He pulled out a rolled bandage and wrapped it around her waist, covering the wounds and binding the bandage tightly.

"Alright, can you move…cuz we gotta get outta here," Nick asked.

"Yeah, just help me up."

Nick helped Kelly to her feet. She adjusted her weight and shifted her machine gun to the low-ready position. She felt the tenderness of the wound and felt pain as she shifted her weight to her right side, causing her to move with a limp. Nick pulled Greg back up to his feet and supported him as they began to move. Greg felt slightly better about the situation now that he had a pistol in his hand. He thought, *if I'm gonna go down, I'm gonna go down fighting*!

The trio moved back down the alleyway to where the secret doorway in the wall was located. Kelly limped a few feet ahead of Nick and Greg. She passed up the opening in the wall by several feet, keeping her gun at the low ready with her back to Nick and Greg. Nick pushed in reverse on the latch in the doorway, and it opened as Nick pushed the door with his shoulder while struggling to get Greg through simultaneously. Kelly glanced back and forth between Nick and Greg and back at the expanse of the compound, looking for work. Kelly was wounded but still lethal.

Julieta Perez had gotten as small as she possibly could, standing to the side and close to the one female guard her husband had hired to go everywhere with her. Julieta had thrown a fit when the business had grown so large and dangerous that she had to have a bodyguard go with her everywhere. Julieta thought it more conspicuous to hire a female bodyguard. It made Julieta feel more normal during her outings to town and other places to be escorted by a female bodyguard rather than a male. Julieta had come from humble beginnings but had grasped and held on for dear life the prosperity the wife of a Cartel leader brought.

The female guard punched in the code in the keypad hidden behind a set of large books on a bookshelf in the master suite of the residence. She held a Glock pistol in her left hand as she banged on the keypad with her fist after the third try had not opened the safe room door stealthily hidden in the wall. The sound of gunfire, now inside the residence, was deafening, and Julieta slid down the wall next to her female guard holding both hands over her ears and praying under her breath. Senior Lucas Perez had the safe room built into one of the residence's walls when they purchased the compound several years prior.

He had hired a Swiss security company to fly in and make the room. This company specializes in safe rooms. The room had been constructed of six-inch thick concrete and steel with a copper mesh skin encasing the room. The safe room had been constructed for any emergency, including radiation and EMP attack. The room was powered from the inside by its own set of lithium-ion battery-powered 2000-watt generators. Two PONTIS EMP and radiation-proof surveillance cameras had been purchased along with the rooms construction. One camera was installed outside of the safe room, looking down on its entrance. The second was installed outside the master suite looking down the long hallway toward the main entrance to the residence and the stairwell.

The rival Cartel to the south had recently threatened her husband and his family. The border crossing in Ciudad Juarez was one of the most prominent entry points into the United States, and whoever held that port held a gold mine. Julieta had not known every facet of her husband's business. Certainly, she had no idea that Agents from two Agencies in the United States could or would stage a rescue mission to assault her family's compound.

The female bodyguard wiped the sweat from her brow with the back of her gun hand and attempted again to enter the code into the pad. 132435, she pushed each button, this time slower and more methodically. *Click!* The wall opened to a ten-foot by fifteen-foot room surrounded by concrete and steel. Two monitors were on top of the desk that was set against one of the walls opposite a leather couch and a small dorm room-sized refrigerator well stocked with water.

Julieta sprung up from where she had been crouching on the floor and quickly entered the dark safe room. Her guard backed into the safe room behind her as she watched their backside for any threats to Julieta. The guard pushed the close button on the keypad inside the safe room on the opposite side of the wall from the bookcase. Once the steel door closed them inside, the guard punched in the code again from the inside. This action made the safe room unlockable from the outside, even if someone were to get the code. The light from the keypad was the only light in the room. The guard moved to the desk, reached underneath, and flipped the power switch to one of the two generators to the ON position. The room lit up with light from two LED bulbs plugged into the battery. The guard switched on the DVR system and the two computer monitors, one to monitor each camera. Julieta sat on the couch in a state of shock. The female guard stayed silent because of the seriousness of the situation and stayed focused for the sake of both of their survival.

The starlight showed through the large bay-style windows into the residence. The tiny bit of light cast shadows throughout the house from lamps, chairs, couches, and walls. Don had not moved from his position near the inner wall for what seemed like several minutes, long enough to let his eyes adjust to the darkness. Once he felt that his eyes had adjusted, he backed away from the corner, shouldered his rifle, and inched around the corner, cutting the pie as it was taught and used by special operators. The inside of the house had become somewhat quiet when he had paused for his eyes to adjust. Don and a dark figure across the room emerging from the shadows saw each other simultaneously. Don's training and experience overcame the dark figure by gaining half a second on him, pulling the trigger out of reflex. The first round dropped the figure to one knee, and the second put him on the large living room floor. Don moved forward, keeping the right-hand wall of the living room on one side. That would be one side he would not have to worry about. Cigar smoke and the hint of whiskey still lingered in the room.

Greaver, now knowing that James would be covering the grand entrance to the house, moved to the front door. Greaver, with the M250 shouldered, peeked inside. He could see Don moving along the right side wall of the living room.

"Tsk...tsk", Greaver made the noise to get Don's attention.
Don abruptly stopped, turned, and saw Greaver in the doorway, and knife hand motioned that he was

moving further into the house.

Greaver moved down the left-hand wall and had to pass in front of the large windows. He was scanning the room and noticed something on the floor near one of the couches.

"Tsk...tsk!" Greaver again made a noise that Don knew.

Don snapped his head around to see Greaver pointing at a black Pelican case lying on the floor. Greaver moved to the box as Don stayed in place and covered him. Greaver quickly opened the box, looked over in the starlit room at Don, smiled, and nodded. Greaver closed the case and hid it in the darkness of one of the room's corners. *One down*, he thought! Greaver moved to one of the many entrances into the room and passed by the body of the figure that Don had shot minutes before. The man Don had killed was not Hispanic but Chinese. A pistol lay near the corpse, and Greaver kicked it away from the body toward the opening under a nearby chair. Don moved, heel to toe, down the right side of the room and came upon the glassed-in smoking room. Don could barely make out bottles of expensive alcohol lining the walls and shook his head. That instant of mesmerization almost cost Don his life as bullets began to impact the glass walls of the smoking room and shatter. Don flinched and turned to see the muzzle flashes coming from a doorway to his immediate front. Greaver had been more vigilant and had already begun pulling the slack out of the trigger on the M250. A stream of hot copper from Greaver's machine gun crossed the room and penetrated the wall next to where the muzzle flashes had come from. Don did not fire a shot as he heard something hitting the floor and gurgling sounds coming from the direction of the flashes.

James M-14 rifle fired three times almost in succession. It was a familiar and relieving sound for Don and Greaver, knowing that James was still covering their rear. Greaver and Don heard other gunshots that sounded more muffled and to their front on the outside walls. Both came to the same conclusion. Nick and Kelly were in a gun battle. With comms out, Don hoped they had been able to locate and rescue Greg.

Surrender might be an option. If this is Americans, they will just let me go again. If it's a rival Cartel, they won't kill me. That would be bad for business, Chen thought. Chen hunkered down in a large room just off the main hallway to the massive living room in what appeared to be Senior Lucas Perez's office. Bookshelves lined the walls of fine teak wood, and two high-back leather guest chairs faced a solid mahogany desk with paperwork scattered across its top. He had dragged a pelican case with an EMP weapon in it and a case full of his money into the office after he fired off the EMP. His bodyguard had been posted up outside the office door at the living room entrance when Don had dispatched him. Chen contemplated his options and decided to open the door and give up to whoever was on the other side of the door with hopes of diplomacy.

Greaver was at the corner of the hallway and living room, standing almost directly over Chen's guard's body when he heard the door creaking to his left. In the darkness, Greaver was not taking any chances and squeezing the trigger, sending several rounds from the belt of ammunition into the slowly opening door. Greaver heard the crumpling of a body as it hit the floor, and the door opened wider as the dead body pushed against it.

Don heard the M250 and then the sound of a body hitting the floor. He quickly turned his head toward Greaver—

"Check it!" Don loudly whispered.

Greaver moved slowly to the open doorway of the dark office. The drapes were drawn in the office, not affording much light. Greaver held the M250 tucked under his right arm and gripped it with one hand as he took out a glow stick, cracked it between his fingers, and tossed it into the room. Greaver moved quickly into the room, checking each corner for work. The space was empty. The glow stick had landed on a Persian rug in front of the mahogany desk. Its green light eerily fills the room. Greaver noticed two Pelican cases sitting upright on the desk. Greaver opened each case, sealed them back up, and exited the room holding each case, one in each hand. Greaver moved quickly to the same hiding spot in the corner of the room in the shadows and dropped the two cases.

Don glanced back and saw Greaver crossing the living room in the darkness holding two cases, and he knew exactly what that meant.

Greaver gave a "Tsk, tsk!" sound, signaling Don that he was ready to move. Greaver caught up with Don on the opposite side of the living room against the wall as they moved forward. Greaver swung around every few seconds, checking their rear and watching the hallway Chen had been down. Don moved to the entrance of a long hallway. The hallway was dark and opened up on the opposite end to a dimly lit room with starlight. Don and Greaver were fluid in their movements, covering each other and checking blind spots as they moved. Door to door, they moved down the long hall, one holding the hallway and one checking a room as they moved, alternating at each room. All of the rooms were empty in the hallway. The hallway opened into a large foyer with a stairwell winding up the wall to the second floor. Don moved to the edge of the stairwell to a wall that presented a room just past it with a long dining room table and another door on the opposite wall. Don thought the door might lead to a kitchen after hearing a metal pot falling to the floor and making a clanging sound. Greaver moved to Don and placed his back against Don's back.

"That was a second Chinese male I dropped in the hallway, two cases, one EMP...other was cash," Greaver whispered over his shoulder to Don as he stared up the stairwell and occasionally glanced down the hallway they had just come from, his M250 up to his shoulder at the ready.

"Roger that…good work! Let's clear the rest and get the fuck out!" Don replied, implying they needed to clear the remaining rooms to look for the shoulder mounted EMP weapons. If they found Guirrillo or Senior Perez, it would just be icing on the cake.

James rolled to his left side, pulled out a fresh magazine from its pouch, and stripped the metal magazine from the M-14 that he knew must have been low on round count. Once the new magazine was seated, he pulled the charging handle back slightly to ensure he still had a live round in the chamber. The compound had become silent outside of the house. James could still hear the occasional burst of fire from inside the house, reassuring him that his partners were still alive and fighting. A tiny bit of gun smoke moved across the dim light of the stars shining down on the compound, and the smell of burnt cordite was heavy in the air. The bodies of multiple Cartel guards littered the manicured yard and gardens surrounding the residence inside the compound. James stood up slowly, still scanning for threats. There were none! It had become eerily quiet. The only sound was coming from the trickle of the fountain in the center of the circle drive. James moved up the driveway to the circle drive. He used the back quarter panel of one of the black Land Rovers as cover as he continued to scan the immediate area. He looked over his shoulder and through the rear window into the cargo area of the Land Rover. He squinted in the dim light but could make out two long black cases inside the SUV. James reached down and pulled on the back door handle, which was locked. He looked around, and not seeing anyone, he lifted the heavy M-14 and used the butt of the rifle to break the back glass. The Land Rover came to life, the horn began honking, and the lights were all flashing. James dragged one of the cases out of the SUV onto the ground and opened the case. A shoulder mounted EMP weapon stared back at him. He quickly closed the case and dragged the second case through the broken glass. The honking had become annoying and distracting. James reached through and unlocked the doors. He quickly crawled through to the driver's side, reached under, and pulled the lever for the hood. James opened the hood and disconnected the battery. The vehicle's alarms ceased. James closed the hood and checked his surroundings for threats one more time before running with a case in each hand back out of the gate and into the edge of the trees lining the road leading into the compound.

James dropped each case to the ground and covered them with loose leaves. The sound of cracking limbs and the rustle of bush caused James to shoulder his rifle in the direction of the sounds.

"Blue, blue, blue! It's us!" Nick whispered loudly.

"I almost killed you..what the hell? Put him down here! Ma'am, you look like shit too!" James commented about Kelly as Nick helped Greg to the ground near the black cases.

Kelly was holding her side and grimacing as she tried to sit down on her butt and fell to the ground.

"I'm good...just give me a minute. I gotta catch my breath." Kelly told the group.

"I'm Nick Bradshaw. I heard early over the comms you were around the entrance. I hoped it was you we ran into. Anyone left inside?"

"Not sure about Tangos. I heard my partner's weapon a few minutes ago, so I think they're still inside the compound. I'm going back inside the gate to cover them. You hold out here. Don't let any tangos come up on us from the road! I don't wanna get shot in my ass!" James replied.

"Roger that!" Nick said, nodding in agreement.

James disappeared through the gate in the direction of the circle drive. He peered through the window of the second Land Rover and did not see any other cases. Satisfying him that he had found part of what his team had come for, he backed off from the circle drive to cover both sides of the compound around the outside of the house while his teammates finished hunting.

Senior Perez, Guirrillo, and three bodyguards hid in the butler's pantry concealed through a passageway near the industrial-sized, two-sided, stainless steel refrigerator in the kitchen. One of the guards backed into the butler's pantry as he, covered the group and knocked a metal mixing bowl from one of the marble countertops. The bowl crashed to the ground and sounded like a cymbal being played throughout the first story of the residence. The group had heard the gunfire outside and in the gardens surrounding the residence and thought it better to stay inside. Senior Perez hoped that his entourage of guards had quelled the attack. Before taking refuge in the butler's pantry, Senior Perez had thought of trying to make it up the stairs to the safe room in the master suite but knew that his wife and her bodyguard had already probably sealed themselves shut inside of the room. Besides, if whoever was attacking his compound were after him, he did not want to draw attention to the safe room and his wife, who was inside.

"I'm clearing this room and the kitchen. If I don't make contact, we'll move to the second floor", Don whispered to Greaver, whose back was still against his.

"Copy that, boss, holding!"

Don moved slowly, heel to toe, across the massive dining room. He reached out and pushed against a door that could swing one way or the other from either side. There was no door knob, just a fancy brass plate where the knobs usually go. Don pushed inward on the door and could feel the resistance from the spring hinge. He could see a large kitchen with a twelve-foot-long island in the middle and marble countertops glistened in the light shining through the windows from the stars. In the back of Don's mind, he thought he had to get a place like this one day! An industrial cooking range and refrigerator lined the edge of the kitchen. Don noticed a metal bowl on the tile floor as he peered in from the doorway. *That's what I heard*, he thought. The kitchen was now deathly quiet. The gunfire outside the residence had now subsided, making it eerier. Don looked over his shoulder and saw Greaver still looking toward the second story up the stairwell with his M250 at the ready.

Don moved into the kitchen, easing the spring-loaded door back to its original closed position as quietly as possible. Don again surveyed the room and noticed that the structure around the refrigerator looked more extensive than the way it outwardly appeared. Don thought quickly and remembered going to a couple of fancy parties around Washington, DC, with similar kitchens. While at the party, Don had wondered why the kitchen looked so clean, but plenty of food looked freshly prepared. Curiosity had gotten the best of him, and he asked the next butler, who walked by holding a tray of hors devours.

"So, how do you keep the kitchen so clean and have all this fresh food"

"Sir, it is prepared in the butler's pantry

and then brought out to the guests," the butler answered.

Don had just nodded his head as if he knew what that was, but he was smart enough to figure out that there must be another room attached to the kitchen that guests usually do not see.

Don pulled his M-4 up to his shoulder and moved to the side of the room where the double Viking ranges were built into the marble countertop. Next to the refrigerator, on the left side, were two large double pantry-style doors. Usually, they would have appeared to be a pantry that contained canned goods and sundries, but this type of kitchen lent itself to something else for these types of doors. Not knowing what might be on the other side of the doors, Don squatted down behind his side of the massive island. He stripped his magazine, knowing he had fired multiple rounds from it and not sure what might be left. He pulled a fresh magazine from his mag pouch on the front of his vest and seated it in the magazine well. Don stood back up with his M-4 pointed toward the double pantry doors. He moved up the side of the wall to the rightmost door and reached out with his left hand. Multiple holes began popping through the fir wood doors, splintering small pieces of wood, followed by numerous gunshots from inside the doors. Don quickly drew his hand back, squeezing it to make sure it had not been hit at the same time, backing away from the wall and pointing the M-4 at the wall and edge of the double doors. The numerous bullet holes gave way to a small bit of light showing through each bullet hole that was now in the door casting small circles of light onto the side of the island. Don used his right thumb to flick the switch on the left side of the rifle to fully automatic. The M-4 came to life as Don kept the pressure on the trigger and moved the muzzle from side to side to hopefully spread rounds throughout the room on the other side of the wall. After thirty-one rounds of ammunition spew from the muzzle. The bolt of the rifle locked back on the weapon signifying it had been run dry. Don ducked down behind the back corner of the island and again swapped out magazines. Don could hear movement through the wall and whispering in Spanish.

Greaver had been in enough gunfights inside of structures in a team environment throughout his career to know that he had a job to watch the hallway. The sound of the gunfire would not waiver his training and experience. Early on, his special operations training had taught him that during a building entry, each man had a job to do and to not deviate from that job. No questions asked, and do not go to the sound of gunfire if you have a specific job unless you are commanded to by a team leader. Greaver would hold his position at the stairwell unless commanded otherwise or something exigent happened.

Don had not been interested in taking prisoners. This was not that type of battle or situation. Therefore he did not offer a verbal resolution to the men huddled inside the bullet-riddled room. The one thing he was sure of was that whoever was on the other side of the wall was capable of violence.

"Cuanto te pagan?" How much are they paying you? Came the voice of Senior Perez screaming through the wall. "Lo doblare'" I will double it, he said.

Don did not entertain the proposal, nor did he answer. As much as Don wanted to taunt the Cartel boss, he knew it might jeopardize his plan. Don slowly stood back up, M-4 pointing at the wall and doors. The small amount of movement caused noise that again drew fire from inside the room. Don could see that the gunfire from inside the room was being directed at the double doors of the butler's pantry. Don pointed his rifle lower, this time at the wall in front of him, and swept the wall with thirty more rounds of .556 ammunition. The voice from inside the wall was silent, but Don could hear movement. Again he stripped and replaced his magazine. Don waited a few seconds before again approaching the double doors. He slowly reached out with his left hand, paused for a second, then quickly opened the door. Guirrillo was the only person inside the room that Don recognized. The distinct tattoo on his neck, among other features, gave it away. Guirrillo was alive, barely, gasping for air from the bullet that had deflated his right lung as he had hidden near the floor of the room like the others. Don was not sure how each man had been struck or when but the men had not been able to hide from sixty bullets that had crossed through the room from Don's rifle. The guards lay across the floor between Guirrillo and Perez, their bodies contorted with their pistols lying near them. Don kicked the guns away from the bodies as he crossed the expanse of the small room to where Guirrillo lay, gasping. Guirrillo looked up at his killer, instantly recognizing him as one of the Americans. Unable to speak, his eyes wide in disbelief, Guirillo slowly passed away. Senior Perez had been killed in Don's initial burst of fire and lay face down near Guirrillo. As Guirrilo took his last breaths, Don pulled a Cuban cigar from one of the pouches on his chest carrier and removed it from its plastic tube. He placed the cigar in the center of Guirrillo's bloody chest. Don had done some quick research before the operation and found that the Golfo Norte Cartel's most significant rival to the South was notorious for leaving a specific brand of Cuban cigar on the chest of their adversary. Out of all the high-tech equipment, helicopters, and other gear he had gathered in the short time before this operation, this specific cigar proved to be the most challenging. A friend of a friend was able to locate this particular brand in a Tercedor cigar factory in a suburb of Havannah called Taller Gomez. Cuban cigars are not cheap any way you go, but this specific cigar had cost Don almost four hundred dollars by the time he figured in jet fuel and pay-offs.

Don had not been sure at the time who the other older gentleman was but concluded that he must have been someone of importance to own this compound. In Don's mind, he had been tasked with a mission, not a kill-or-capture mission, but a kill-and-rescue mission.

Despite his training, Greaver was still anxious about what was going on in the other room. The lack of communication was driving him insane. The door Don had disappeared through suddenly opened, causing Greaver to shift a little in that direction until he saw his boss.

"I killed Guirrillo and some other guys in there. I haven't heard any other gunfire in a while. I'll hold here. Go check on James and the others. See where we're at with Greg and the EMPs."

"Copy that, boss, moving."

Greaver disappeared down the hallway into the darkness the way they had come from. Greaver moved cautiously through the house, across the living room, and to the massive front doors. Greaver peered out of the doors into the darkness of the compound. Not knowing if anyone was still alive, Greaver moved down the front steps to the walkway with his M250 at the ready. James, who had been kneeling in the shadows near the circle drive, stood up when he saw it was Greaver.

"Hey, brother!" James blurted out, startling Greaver.

"I almost shot you! We need to move quickly. No idea if anyone's coming to help these guys or if they got a call out before that EMP hit us." Greaver said.

"Good news, I found two of the shoulder mounted weapons...they were in that SUV."

"Good job, We found a suitcase weapon inside and some cash. You seen the other group with Nick?"

"Yep, got 'em. They're holding the road just past the gate. Two of them are wounded pretty bad."

"Copy that. I'm going to give the boss the sitrep. Go help Nick and them, and We'll be right back."

"Copy," James acknowledged as he turned to jog back toward the gate.

Don intently watched the stairwell leading to the second story of the Cartel mansion. He had not heard any movement in the house since Greaver left to reconnoiter the outside. Don heard a noise coming from the end of the hallway, followed by—

"Blue, blue, blue!" Greaver said down the hallway before sticking his head out to check the hallway to see if Don was still in position.

Greaver moved at a faster pace now, more comfortable that the threats had all been neutralized.

"I think we got it all, boss," Greaver said, out of breath, "James found two shoulder-mounted weapons, and we have the suitcase weapon and cash. Greg and the female Agent are hit pretty bad."

"Roger that, I haven't heard anything in the house, no movement. We gotta figure out how we're gonna get outta here."

"One of those Rovers outside has a light on the dash blinking."

"What the hell, like it still works"

"Yep, one definitely works. James set the alarm off on one of them. I didn't check the other one. I just noticed the light when I passed it."

"I thought I heard a fucking car alarm going off! Copy that. Let's get movin'"

Don and Greaver moved quickly back through the living room. Greaver paused in the shadows to pick up the two pelican cases he had placed there. Don had already scrambled out of the front door and down the front steps to where the Land Rovers were parked. Sure enough, Don could see a small red light blinking on the dashboard of the Land Rover that James had not busted the windows out of. Greaver followed shortly after placing the Pelican cases on the ground next to the SUV.

"Go back in and check the pockets. We need keys. These things are almost impossible to hotwire."

"Yes sir," Greaver turned and trotted back into the house.

A few minutes later, Greaver returned, jingling two sets of Land Rover keys.

"Found 'em on a couple of the guys you capped in the kitchen!" he said, smiling as if he had found a million bucks.

Greaver began pressing the unlock button on both remotes, and both Land Rovers came to life, flashing the front lights and making a clicking sound of the doors unlocking. Don grabbed both cases and threw them into the back cargo area.

"I'm driving. You cover us. Just in case," Don told Greaver, who was already loading up in the front passenger seat.

The Land Rover spun gravel as Don accelerated through the circle drive and down the driveway toward the partially open gate. James was moving toward the entrance from the outside, cautiously approaching the dark SUV that was attempting to exit the compound. Don rolled the driver's side window down, seeing that James was unsure, and yelled, "Blue, blue, blue." James slung his rifle on his shoulder and pushed the gate to its fully open position as the Land Rover sped through and skidded in the gravel as it came to an abrupt stop twenty yards outside the gate.

Don looked out the driver's side window and saw Nick, Kelly, and Greg. Nick was already helping Greg to his feet when Don ran the short distance from the SUV to help Kelly, who was struggling to get up from the ground.

"You look like shit," Don told Kelly.

"Why does everyone keep saying that!" Kelly responded.

"Come on, I gotcha," Don said as he put his arm around Kelly's shoulder and helped her limp to the

SUV.

Greaver was partially standing outside of the front passenger side of the SUV with one leg planted on the front passenger floorboard and the other planted outside on the ground holding his M250, scanning the darkness for threats. James ran and grabbed the weapons cases he had stashed in the woods and slung them up into the cargo area of the SUV. All six Agents were onboard the Land Rover speeding down the road and away from the carnage that was getting smaller and smaller in the rearview mirror.

The house had grown quiet. The gunfire had stopped, and the shouting had ceased. Julieta Perez was still cowering on the leather couch in the safe room, wringing her hands and mumbling under her breath. Tears had welled up in her eyes. Her guard was staring at the computer monitors. She had not seen anyone on the surveillance cameras and thought maybe her boss and the other guards she worked with had repelled the intruders. The knot in her stomach told her otherwise. The female guard stood from the desk and pulled her pistol from its holster. She walked to the steel door and punched in the code to open it. As the door slowly opened on its mechanical mechanism, the guard raised her pistol to address any potential threats that might have still been lurking in the house. It took her eyes a few seconds to adjust to the house's darkness. Once outside the safe room door, she turned and again keyed in the code to close the door behind her. After all, her primary job was to protect Julieta, and she was the highest-paid of the guards. Senior Perez had sought her out and had studied her impeccable pedigree of personal protection.

The guard moved slowly through the second story of the residence. She was looking side to side into each room as she passed. The dim light cast shadows on each room's open door to the hallway floor. The second floor was pristine. Like nothing had happened except for the power outage. The guard eased down the flight of stairs from the second floor to the first. Her weapon was still up and at the ready. The first floor was as quiet as the second. The only difference she noticed was the air in the rooms. It was different. A familiar smell. Burnt cordite.

The guard pushed open the door to the kitchen from the dining room, and the reality of what happened downstairs and to the remaining compound was evident. From the doorway, she could see the butler pantry doors open next to the refrigerator. The doors and the wall adjoining it were riddled with holes. Spent cartridge brass littered the floor and on top of the island. The guard walked slowly through the kitchen opposite the butler's pantry so that she could have a good, tactical angle on the room. Small bits of starlight were still shining through the room's high windows, casting light down onto the lifeless bodies. Steam is still rising from the corpses. She lowered her pistol as she approached and placed her left hand up to her mouth in shock. The shock turned to anger as she recognized the semblance of the Cuban cigar on her boss's business partner's chest.

It was now almost 04:00 in the morning, and the Blackhawk was making its second pass over the pre-designated pickup LZ that Don had given the pilots the coordinates to just before dropping them in the area of operation earlier in the night. They had made the first pass at the designated pickup time of 03:30. Don had figured that would give them plenty of time to complete the operation. The CIA Air Branch pilots had been around a block or two when it came to dealing with special operators. The pilots knew that time was fluid in their world. A precise time sometimes is relevant. Relevant to the situation at hand.

The Blackhawk banked to its port side and could now see the infrared strobe blinking through his night vision goggles. The helicopter settled down to the desert floor, fifty yards from the black Land Rover. The crew chief armed himself with his M-4 rifle and jumped to the ground to cover his passengers. Don was the first to greet the crew chief, screaming at each other over the rotor noise—

"Thanks for waiting on us!"
"No problem, sir...nice ride!"

"Borrowed it. The owner won't be needing it back!"

"Roger that, sir!"

"We've got two wounded, both are walkie-talkies, but we need care pretty quick."

"Roger that, I'll relay," the crew chief said as he pushed his helmet mic closer to his mouth to relay the information to the pilots since Don was not wired in yet.

The crew chief helped Nick load Greg and Kelly, who both made painful faces and grimaced as they were heaved up into the helicopter. Greaver and James hauled the Pelican cases from the back of the Land Rovers and tossed them up to the Don, who had climbed in to help stow their gear.

The Blackhawk helicopter lifted from the ground and began its clandestine journey north. The green light of the interior cabin of the aircraft was the first real light they had all been in since hours before. Don and Nick were seated across from each other, and both had donned a set of earphones and microphones wired into the helicopter's internal communication system. Don looked across at Nick and studied him briefly before conversing with him—

"What the hell happened to you? Sure you not hit?" Don said, referring to the extreme amount of blood on Nick's fatigues, jacket, and face.

Nick looked down at himself for the first time since the battle and realized how bad he looked—

"Not mine! Some of it's Greg and Kelly's, but

most of it's that bastard who was torturing Greg. Greg said he was the one that attacked our security column in El Paso."

"Either way, you look like shit. Tell me the story later." Don said with a smile on his face.

Nick gave a thumbs-up to Don. He glanced to the helicopter deck where Kelly and Greg lay as the crew chief was treating them with help from James. Kelly had seen Nick give Don a thumbs up and gave one herself to Nick. Nick smiled.

"Is that the watch Thompson gave you?" Don asked, staring at Nick's arm and referring to the MTM watch that the FBI El Paso SAC had given Nick.

Nick looked down at the non-working watch on his left wrist and laughed—

"Yeah…he's gonna be pissed!"

CHAPTER 13

The Home Front

The following day, near mid-morning, the Secretary of Defense John Baker was summoned to the oval office at the White House. Baker slumbered past the Secret Service Agents in the hallway and was let into the oval office by the President's assistant.

"Oh, come in, John. Good to see you this morning. Sorry to call you over so early, but we have a situation, or maybe not. That's why you're here." The President stood up from behind the resolute desk and walked around to sit in one of the high-backed leather chairs facing the long couch that sat directly in front of the painting of George Washington. The President motioned for John to sit on the couch.

"It's ok, sir. It was a nice drive in this morning. Weather's nice for a change."

"I'm not going to mince words, John. Earlier this morning, I received a phone call from President Vazquez of Mexico, who expressed concern for the sovereignty of his Republic. Now I know I started this thing. This incursion into a foreign country to do what I thought was best, and I take full responsibility for what happened. Still,

I made it clear that we would not send any more operators south of our border as a rescue mission or anything resembling it."

John sat on the couch, legs crossed, listening. The President continued—

"I received more information from sources this morning telling me that our kidnapped DEA Agent is now back stateside. How did that happen? I'm happy he's home and safe, but for god's sake, John, I thought I made myself clear!

John, who had been taking what he considered a tongue lashing, attempted to explain—

"Sir...." John said, but the President abruptly cut him off.

"Now, I don't know how this worked out, but President Vazquez's main reason for calling this morning was to ask for our help taming the Cartels. He told me that two nights ago, a Cartel from the south of Mexico attacked a compound in central Mexico and killed not only that Cartel boss but a visiting one as well."

"That's not too shocking, sir. That happens all of the time down there. I don't understand."

"Let me finish, and you will...he went on to say that among the dead at the Cartel compound were two Chinese nationals and, if I had to guess, probably the same group we brought back from our operation and cut loose."

"Wow, sir! I ah, I get it, ok. Well, you know the saying, you live by the sword, you die by the sword. So they want our help," John said, as a smile came across his face, his first semblance of satisfaction of knowing what had really happened.

It had gotten down to twenty-six degrees overnight in parts of Virginia as the cold front moved across the northwestern portion of the United States. A light dusting of snow lay across everything and had made the drive to work in the small town of Fredericksburg slippery. The old building had been built in the late 1800s but had been remodeled to acquaint its occupants with the conveniences of the modern world. The building had been constructed along one of the many cobblestone streets in downtown Fredericksburg and gave the town the feel of being back in a simpler time, especially on a cold day like today. The mushy snow squeaked under his leather dress shoes as he walked up the five stairs to the front door of the building.

Mitsy Bradshaw had just poured her second cup of decaf coffee and sat back down at her desk, holding her belly so as not to strike it on the desk while she slid into her office chair.

"Mitsy, you have someone here to see you." The secretary said.

"Ok, I'm not expecting anyone. Did someone schedule a…"

Nick walked to the edge of Mitsy's doorway into her office, holding a bouquet of flowers.

EPILOGUE

The pink blooms on the cherry blossom trees signified the onset of spring. They were blooming all over Washington DC, making the already perfectly groomed government landscape that much more beautiful. Some of the cherry blossom trees lined the streets and alleyways, and others were scattered through parks, greenspaces, and memorials. One such memorial had pathways that formed a circle with a stone wall that formed the outer edge of each pathway.

The statue of the dark bronze-patinated lioness looked ready to pounce across the path. Its young, also sculptures of dark brown patina, were frozen in mid-play across the pathway from their mother. She guarded not only her litter but also the men and women whose names were etched into the stone wall she sat upon.

Jim Cado strolled up to the entrance of the law enforcement memorial pathway. His eyes had already begun to fill with tears. He had not been sure of how he would feel at this moment, but he knew it was something he had to do. He walked past the lioness and placed his right hand on her cheek. Her bronze flesh was cold, and he patted her twice as he continued to walk down the pathway as if to say, *thank you for watching over my brothers and sisters.*

Jim walked to the wall and to the section where the appendix had shown the last name of Keller. Jim carried a pencil and a small piece of paper provided by the memorial. He stopped at a section and began to scroll the wall with his right index finger, name by name. His finger stopped and began to tremble. SPECIAL AGENT JOSEPH KELLER was the name his finger had stopped on. Jim held the piece of paper over the name with his left hand and began etching over the characters with the side of the pencil lead. He finished the etching and held it up. Tears were now rolling down Jim's cheeks. He stepped back, gave the name on the wall one last look, and muttered under his breath—

"Thank you for saving us that day on the river. Nec Timeo Nec Sperno, brother."

Jim composed himself, turned, and walked back the way he had entered the memorial pathway. He exited the memorial and turned left on the sidewalk next to F Street NW. Jim walked a short distance where he passed a metal park bench with a bearded black male seated on it, one leg crossed and one arm stretched out across the length of the bench's backrest.

"Beautiful day, don't you think?" the black male asked as Jim walked by.

"Yes sir, it is," Jim said, displaying a fake smile and nodding at the unknown gentlemen seated on the bench as he continued to walk past him on the sidewalk.

"You know... he screamed and cried in his last moments"

"Excuse me!" Jim stopped abruptly and turned toward the man on the bench with a puzzled look.

"The man that sent the men that killed your friend. The others died pretty quickly, but not him, no. He screamed a little." The man had taken his arm from the backrest and unfolded his leg. He now sat leaning forward and looking up at Jim.
Jim was taken aback and not sure what to say or do.

"I read your file, Jim. That is after Nick Bradshaw told me about you. My outfit could use a man like you if you're interested. The name's Don. Don Powers."

ABOUT THE AUTHOR

Jason Garbo

In his edge of your seat first novel, Jason Garbo dazzles the readers mind with descriptive landscapes and tactical prowess. He takes the reader from Quantico, VA to Washington DC...Texas...Mexico and the depths of the FBI...the CIA and the DEA SRT.

Tha Author lives in Louisiana with his wife and children. Garbo served in the special operations community for over ten years and is currently employed in the public sector.

Made in United States
Troutdale, OR
06/11/2023

10553571R10181